SHIELDING YOU

BAYTOWN BOYS

MARYANN JORDAN

Cover Design by: Graphics by Stacy

Cover and model photography: Eric McKinney

ISBN ebook: 978-1-947214-66-8

ISBN print: 978-1-947214-67-5

❀ Created with Vellum

Author's Note

Please remember that this is a work of fiction. I have lived in numerous states as well as overseas, but for the last twenty years have called Virginia my home. I often choose to use fictional city names with some geographical accuracies.

These fictionally named cities allow me to use my creativity and not feel constricted by attempting to accurately portray the areas.

It is my hope that my readers will allow me this creative license and understand my fictional world.

I also do quite a bit of research on my books and try to write on subjects with accuracy. There will always be points where creative license will be used in order to create scenes or plots.

FOUR YEARS AGO

Hannah Freeman stared at her reflection in the bathroom mirror, her hands gliding down the front of her uniform. A tingle of pride zipped through her at the sight as it had for the past month. Navy pants. Navy short-sleeved polo. Over her left breast was embroidered Easton Police Department and underneath that was her title: Chief of Police.

Chief. She made bug eyes at her reflection and grinned, not caring if the silly expression didn't match the dignity of the uniform.

When she had applied for the police chief position, her chances were a complete tossup in her mind. *Young. Female. A tiny Southern town.* Stunned when she received a phone call from the mayor a week later, she was even more shocked when they wanted to interview her almost immediately. Within a month, her exemplary military and police credentials had the town offering her the position despite her youth and sex. Only a few had openly expressed doubt that a female would be able to handle the pressure of being police chief. And she was determined to prove them wrong.

Now, a month later, she filled her days getting used to new duties, the townspeople, and her staff of one receptionist, Pearl, who doubled as the dispatcher for calls that did not go through 9-1-1, Mason, a police sergeant, and three officers. But today was special—it was her chance to meet the other area chiefs and sheriffs at the monthly law enforcement leaders' meeting.

The Eastern Shore of Virginia consisted of only two counties, physically separated from the rest of the state, joined at the southern tip to Virginia Beach by a seventeen-mile bridge that crossed over the Chesapeake Bay. North was Maryland. Besides the sheriffs of the two counties, there were only four towns that were large enough to have an individual police force. Legal jurisdictions dictated their areas of operations, but it appeared they assisted each other as much as possible. Hence, one of the reasons the leaders of local law enforcement met monthly to discuss concerns that they shared.

Nerves slithered through her, but she tamped the negative emotion down with the knowledge that she was not the only new hire. Mitch Evans had just taken over as Police Chief of Baytown, and Dylan Hunt had been hired as Police Chief of Seaside six months ago.

Driving into Baytown, she called Pearl to remind her that she would be at the meeting and not back into the office until after lunch. She had not had a chance to visit Baytown but knew they had the only public beach in the county and summer vacationers would fill the rental houses. Main Street was quaint with little shops and she decided to visit soon when she was not on duty.

Now, driving to the Baytown Police Station, she was struck with how much larger Baytown was than Easton. All the towns on the Eastern Shore were small, but Baytown had over a thousand residents, whereas Easton only had about three hundred. She parked near the front of the two-story brick building and smoothed her hands over her uniform again before pulling on the glass door leading into the station reception area.

"'Morning!"

The greeting rang out from the elderly receptionist sitting behind the counter. Her curly, blue-tinted grey hair bounced as she waved.

"Oh... good morning. I'm—"

"Know who you are, Hannah Freeman. You have the distinction of being the only female police chief out here," the woman announced, her curls still shaking. "Kudos to Easton for finally hiring a woman! I'm Mildred Score, by the way."

A female officer wearing a Baytown uniform walked from the back hall and smiled toward Hannah. "Hello, Chief Freeman. I'm Ginny Spencer. It's nice to meet you."

Shaking Ginny's hand, she accepted the warm greeting, glad to meet another female officer. "Hi. Call me Hannah."

"I understand you were MP... Army?"

"Yes, I was."

"Same for me. I know you've got to head into the LEL meeting, but I'd love to grab coffee or drinks sometime when we have a chance," Ginny invited. "There's not a lot of us female officers around."

"That'd be great." She cocked her head to the side and asked, "By the way... LEL?"

Mildred walked up and said, "That's the shortened version of Law Enforcement Leaders. Otherwise, it's too much of a mouthful to say! Come on back."

Waving goodbye as Ginny left the building, she followed Mildred's bouncing curls toward the staff workroom.

"The LEL meeting is in here. Coffee's on the counter. Make yourself at home." With that, the efficient Mildred offered a nod before heading back to the front.

Walking in, she was surprised her feet did not stumble at the sight of the four men already in the room. She was no stranger to attractive men, but the four in front of her exuded masculinity and military bearing as well as open friendliness, ramping up their handsomeness.

Coming to her senses, she squared her shoulders and stepped forward, her hand extended in greeting. Mitch Evans, tall, with a lean, muscular body, welcomed her to their group and Baytown. Colt Hudson, Sheriff of North Heron County, was huge. Tall, muscular, with thick dark hair and an intense gaze, he smiled widely as they were introduced. Next came Liam Sullivan, Sheriff of Acawmacke County, and Wyatt Newman, the Police Chief of Manteague, equally as handsome. She wondered if it was against regulations for a law enforcement leader on the Eastern Shore to be balding, pot-bellied, and cursed with bad teeth.

"Grab some coffee, Hannah," Mitch invited, waving his hand toward the counter. "We're just waiting on Dylan."

Before she had a chance to move to the other side of the room, she turned at the sound of someone rapidly approaching. She blinked as his hands darted out to land on her shoulders in an effort to keep their bodies from crashing together. As she stared up into his face, a thought flashed through her mind... *You can crash into me anytime.* Just as handsome as the other men in the room, this one had a boyish, lopsided grin and hazel-green eyes. Tall, with a runner's muscular body, her gaze darted from his brown hair swept to the side, all the way down to his boots. His uniform was similar to hers except he sported khaki pants and a navy shirt with Seaside Police Department emblazoned over his heart. And, like hers, Chief of Police declared his position.

By the time her gaze dragged back to his face, his grin quirked up even more on one side and his eyes actually twinkled. While the other handsome men had an air of confident professionalism, this man oozed an air of lighthearted enjoyment of life.

"You must be Hannah. It's nice to meet you. I'm Dylan. Dylan Hunt."

She reached her hand out, and as his fingers closed over hers, electricity zapped about the room, circling around the two of them, blocking out everyone else. She jerked, forcing her lungs to fill with air, certain she must look like a fool. Heat crept over her, and she prayed her face was not flaming red. Shocked at the instant connection, she glanced up at Dylan, surprised to see the same wide-eyed, shocked expression on his face. He stared at their hands before he lifted his gaze to hers. If it hadn't been for the other men in the room, she wasn't sure she would have remembered to pull her hand back.

As they sat down around the table, she noticed Dylan moved quickly and sat next to her. Mitch began the meeting, and she worked to steady her breathing, quickly falling into the rhythm of her job. Pride and competency filled her, and she hoped no one had observed her momentary lapse of professionalism.

Dylan Hunt had kept his eye on the speed limit as he drove into Baytown, not wanting to be pulled over even though he was in a Seaside Police SUV. Baytown's speed limit was only 25 mph and he knew town visitors would be in the area. Glancing at the clock on the dashboard, he hoped everyone was still greeting each other over coffee and not aware that he was late. Yesterday had been his first day off since taking over his new position, and last night he'd celebrated a little too much.

Finally, jerking into a parking spot at the Baytown Municipal Building where the police station occupied one side, he rushed into the reception area with a wave and a wink toward the elderly dispatcher.

"Hello, Chief Hunt! They're all back there waiting for you." She sent him down the hall to the department workroom. Rounding the corner, he darted into the room, almost plowing over the woman standing directly in front of him. She turned, her eyes wide, and his booted feet skidded on the waxed tile floor. His hands snapped out to grab her shoulders to slow his forward progression and keep from slamming into her.

He knew the town of Easton had hired a new female chief but hadn't met her yet. Shocked, he never expected to come face-to-face with such a beauty. Her dark hair was pulled back into a military regulation bun, and he remembered hearing that she'd been in the Army. Her makeup was subtle, certainly not like the women he usually met at bars, but with her beauty, she didn't need much to play up her perfect features. Blue eyes. Porcelain skin. Plump lips.

As his gaze skimmed the rest of her petite frame, it was evident she had curves hidden under her uniform. He grinned widely when he realized her gaze was drifting over him as well. But when her eyes lifted to his face, his breath caught in his throat. The clear blue orbs held him captive as though she could see straight into his soul. He couldn't tear his gaze away, but neither could he think of a quick-witted response. Her deep perusal was not something he was used to. Most women were more interested in seeing him shirtless and flexing his muscles.

Afraid that she would find him lacking, he threw his hand out, rushing to introduce himself. Her breath hitched when their fingers touched. Suddenly, ensnared in a web of electricity around them, he was uncertain what was happening.

He had never had such a reaction to a woman. *Flirt?*

Absolutely. Quick fuck? When it was right, yes. Long talks, walks, dates? Hell, no. But right now, with her hand still in his, he wanted to know more about her and wanted to be a man good enough to have that privilege.

The scraping of a chair jolted him out of his trance, and she jerked her hand back, a blush rising over her delicate cheeks. Offering a quick nod, she turned and moved to the table. He had just enough time to pull out the chair and settle into the seat beside her.

"I know introductions have been made, but with some new folks here, Dylan, why don't you tell us about yourself?" Colt suggested.

"Not much to tell. Born and raised just outside of Seaside. I was a few years behind Mitch and also went to Baytown High School. My gramps was a fisherman, so was my dad. My older brother joined the family business, but I'm afraid I was the black sheep of the family."

Not shy, he never minded talking about himself, but as Hannah's eyes stayed riveted on him, he was suddenly self-conscious. With a self-deprecating chuckle erupting, he continued, "I joined the Navy right out of high school, knowing that I loved the sea but didn't want to be a fisherman. While in, I earned an Associates in Criminal Justice and worked with the police. When I got out, I came back to Seaside hoping to work for the Sheriff's department, but the Police Chief position became available and no one else put in for the job." He shook his head. "I threw my application out to the town council and was shocked as shit when they accepted me."

"But black sheep?" she asked, her head tilted to the side as she held his gaze.

The pose was adorable, and her voice was soft. He blinked, attempting to focus on his story again. "Oh, yeah. Well, my gramps has been pissed at me since I joined the Navy. He thinks I betrayed the family business. 'Fraid that hasn't changed since I came back to be in law enforcement." He shrugged, adding, "He says I'm being uppity." Almost afraid to look to the side, he accepted the acknowledging laughter from the others.

Hannah's soft voice cut through the noise. "Don't worry about what anyone else says... stay true to you."

His gaze swung to the side, seeing the smile on her face directed toward him. He blinked again, and the idea of spending time alone with her just to hear her soothing voice slammed into him.

"Mitch? What about you?" Liam said, interrupting Dylan's musing.

"I'm not sure there's much of a surprise about me. I was born and raised here in Baytown. My grandfather used to be the Police Chief and my father was an officer. When my grandfather retired, my father took over as Police Chief. During that time, I did a stint in the Army with Military Police and then worked as an investigator for the FBI. My dad had a heart attack several months ago, and the Mayor contacted me to see if I wanted to take over the position. Honestly? I was tired of the bureaucracy and ready for a change. I almost considered working for a security company, Saints Protection, having befriended the owner." Shrugging, he said, "But the call of the Bay was hard to ignore."

The others looked toward Hannah, and she smiled. "I suppose my story is much like Mitch's. Army MP after I earned a degree in Criminal Justice. My father worked for the FBI and my brother is a detective for the Hope City Police Department. Everyone in my family assumed that I would go for a position with the FBI, and one was offered to me. It's just not what I wanted."

"You turned down the FBI to work at Easton?" Dylan asked, surprise running through him.

She laughed, and the sound was so pure it was hard for him to focus on her explanation.

"I'm not sure my family has forgiven me. That makes me the black sheep of *my* family. But yes, the Bureau was not what I wanted. I was thrilled with the idea of working in a place where I could get to know everyone. To truly feel like I'm making a difference."

He knew she'd just put them in the same category with disappointing their families, but her pedigree was law enforcement elite, and he was just... good ol' boy Dylan. He was happy with who he was and what he was doing but couldn't imagine turning down a job with the FBI.

After the rest of the introductions, the meeting began. Focusing his attention on the agenda, Dylan loved the shared information and the camaraderie built during the hour. He had experienced that type of professional relationship when serving in the military but wasn't sure if he would find it in his new job.

Even though he took his responsibilities seriously, the delicate scent of Hannah's shampoo wafted by, continually pulling his thoughts away from the subjects at hand.

When they finally broke for lunch, Mitch suggested Finn's Pub, a short walk down Main Street. The sidewalk forced them to naturally walk in pairs. Mitch and Colt took the lead, falling into a discussion about the possibility of bringing an American Legion chapter to the area. Wyatt and Liam walked behind them, discussing some of the concerns in their county. Dylan made certain to align himself with Hannah, pleased that they were walking together. "So, how are you settling in?"

"Very well, I think. I'm staying at an inn that gave me a good rate. I really don't want to move until I find a place to buy, but so far, I haven't even had time to look." Smiling up at him, she asked, "And you? But then, you said you were from this area."

"Yeah, I know this county very well. Of course, being the police chief makes it all so different."

"I'm sure you'll do fine." She slowed her steps as they approached the pub, allowing a group to come out of the old brick building.

He wished he could reach down and touch her hand again just to see if the electricity that had passed between them earlier was real or imagined. He had been with more than his fair share of women, but that reaction had never occurred.

Once inside the pub, he maneuvered to slide in next to her as they were shown to a large booth. Not wanting to crowd her, their hands nonetheless met when they both reached for the menus lying in the middle of the table. And sure enough, he felt the jolt once again. A quick look to the side at her wide-eyed expression let him know that she felt it, too.

He settled back against the wooden booth, a grin on his face. Good food, new friends, and a professional camaraderie that would benefit them all. On top of that, the chance to get to know the beautiful Hannah.

When the meal was over, he said his goodbyes to the men first before turning to her. "Let me give you my personal phone number. Our towns are close together, but in case you need anything, you can get hold of me quickly."

She held his gaze for just a moment, then her lips curved upward slightly. "Sounds good. I'll share mine, too."

That evening, his fingers hovered over the keypad on his phone, desperate to call her. But he decided to wait, just for a few days, to see if the desire waned. It didn't. And lucky for him, when he did call to ask her out, she accepted.

TWO MONTHS LATER

Hannah lay on her back in the middle of the bed, staring at the ceiling fan as it slowly turned. She processed her day, thought about what she needed to do tomorrow, and made a mental checklist of errands to run on the weekend. Anything to pass the time while waiting on the call. *I'm as bad as a teenager waiting for the phone to ring.*

Hannah was sure that life couldn't get any better. Three months as the Chief of Police. Two of those months dating Dylan, although in secret. She hated sneaking around, but with both of them working as police chiefs, she insisted they needed to be cautious. Small towns were full of eyes and gossip, something she hoped to avoid.

When her phone finally vibrated, she grabbed it, grinning as soon as she saw the caller ID.

"Hey, handsome," she answered.

"God, hearing your voice is the best part of my day," Dylan said. "I miss you."

"We just saw each other yesterday."

"Waving while passing each other on the way to the jail is hardly seeing each other."

She chuckled but could hear the longing in his voice. "Yeah, I know."

He had been ready to shout it out the first time they went on a date, but she'd convinced him they needed to go slow. And that included intimacy. They'd kissed... *and damn, that man can kiss!* When no one was around, their lips were locked, noses bumping, tongues tangling, nips and licks with bodies pressed tightly together.

"There's a concert in Virginia Beach in a few weeks. How about we meet somewhere and go together?"

She laughed. "One of your country bands?"

"No," he retorted. "Actually, it's the Virginia Symphony Orchestra. I know how much you like classical music."

She sucked in a quick breath. "You'd do that? You'd go to a symphony with me?"

"Hannah, I've never said this to anyone before... but I'd do anything for you," he replied.

She blinked as tears stung her eyes. "I... wow..."

"I know some people would say this was fast, but I know what I feel. And what I feel... I've never felt before. I love learning everything about you."

"Yeah? What have you learned?"

He chuckled. "You hate scary movies, which makes no sense."

"Lots of people hate scary movies!" she protested.

"Yeah, but you're a police chief. Hell, you were in the Army!"

"Humph," she groused. "Well, we both like old comedies on TV."

He sighed heavily. "God, I'd love to be with you right now. Piled up on the bed watching TV."

She was still thinking about that image and how much she would like it when he added, "But then if I was there on your bed, we wouldn't be watching TV!"

Now, she had a completely different image in her mind... a naked Dylan and how much she wanted that to be a reality. "God, yes," she breathed.

"Jesus, I need a cold shower."

Belting out a laugh, she said, "Go on, and I'll see you tomorrow. Plan on a picnic."

"A sunset picnic with you? I can't wait, Hannah. Just knowing I'll see you at the end of the day will make everything perfect."

Disconnecting, she continued to lay on the bed, her heart soaring and a smile firmly in place on her lips. She'd made it through college with a few dates and only one boyfriend, but when he discovered she wanted to go into the military, the relationship ended. Her years in the Army resulted in a few nights of shared pleasure with like-minded men, but no dating. She had begun to wonder if she was destined to be alone. *Too independent... too career-minded... too able to take care of myself.* Rolling over, she stared at the moonlight through the curtains and smiled.

The next evening, the sun was dropping low in the sky, but the couple lying on the blanket draped over the sandy beach had no concept of time. Their legs were tangled together, arms pulling them tightly, breasts against chest, hips grinding together. And their lips were sealed together in long kisses.

Dylan's tongue tangled with hers, sweeping through her mouth, firing synapses throughout Hannah's body. Her breasts felt heavy. Her nipples tingled. And with his erection pressing against her core, the desire for friction made the layers of clothes between them nothing more than an irritant.

As they lay facing each other, her head rested on one of his biceps, and his hand pressed against her back, holding her close. With his other hand, he cupped her jaw, sweeping his thumb over her cheek, and moved his lips over hers. Like everything about Dylan, even his lips were strong.

Her free arm had bent at his back, her fingers dragging through his short hair. Even though there was no space between their bodies, she still felt the need to bring him closer, so her hand slid down the muscles of his back, her fingers spread wide to tighten over his ass.

He groaned, the vibrations rising from his chest through their kiss to where she swallowed the sound, wanting to claim it as much as every part of his body.

His hand slowly moved from her cheek over her shoulder, and shifting back ever so slightly, moved between their bodies so that he could mold her breast, his thumb now teasing her nipple. He slid his thigh between her legs, and she ground her hips against the material of his shorts, not caring that at the age of twenty-seven she was dry-humping like a teenager.

His hand continued on a downward path, squeezing her ass, then his fingers slipped underneath the loose material of her shorts, finding the swollen bud that ached for attention. With his tongue still thrusting into her mouth, he slipped a finger into her core. Soon she cried out as her orgasm crashed over her, this time allowing him to continue kissing through her moan.

His fingers left her body and he separated from her lips long enough to suck her juices from their tips. He barely had time to slide his fingers out before she latched onto his mouth again, this time tasting her own essence mixed with his undeniable flavor.

After another moment, he placed his hand on her shoulder and gently pushed her backward, a mewl of discontent erupting from her.

"What's wrong?"

He sat up, dragging in a deep breath, a lopsided grin on his face. "Nothing's wrong, babe. Not a damn thing."

"Let me take care of you," she said, her hand reaching for his belt, surprised when his hand latched onto hers, stilling her movements.

"No," he groaned.

"No?" She swung her gaze over the beach, but there was no one around.

"I want it... you've got to believe that I want it... this... you."

His face appeared ravaged. She pushed up to a seated position on the blanket as well. Licking her kiss-swollen lips, she breathed deeply, leaning forward to place her hand on his thigh, not wanting to lose the physical connection.

"What I feel for you is real... more than anything I've ever felt," he continued.

She said nothing, giving him time to gather his thoughts.

"It's true that I've earned a one-and-done reputation, but it's not as bad as it sounds. And it's overblown. I've never led a woman on... they know the score. Plus, until I felt a spark, I never saw the reason to take the time and energy to date someone."

"And do you feel it now?"

His grin widened as he cupped her face, kissing her lightly. "Oh, yeah, babe. It's a spark that just keeps flaming stronger."

Dylan was no fling and considering how much she cared for him, she was ready. And if the bulge in his shorts was any indication, he was ready, too. Their eyes met and she asked, "What do you need, honey?"

"You," he chuckled, scrubbing his hand over his face before wrapping his fingers around hers still resting on his leg. "But, Hannah, I want to do this right. This is different for me. This isn't sex, but something so much more. You're so much more."

She licked her lips again, unable to keep her smile from widening. "I feel it, too."

He kissed her moist lips, nibbling the corners. "I want to take you out on a date... a real date." A little gasp slipped from her, but he continued. "It can look like just two friends to everyone else, but I want to take you to dinner."

She waited to see if panic would set in at the idea of him taking her to dinner, but all she felt was excitement. "Okay," she whispered, her lips curving once again.

Eyes wide, he grinned. "Okay?"

"Yeah… okay."

Two days later, she hustled into her room at the inn and jerked off her uniform polo and pants on her way into the bathroom. She was tired of living in one room but didn't want to sign a year's lease or purchase a home until she was sure it was right for her.

Showered, she dressed quickly, keeping one eye on the clock. She was meeting Dylan at The Wharf Restaurant. Grinning, she had a surprise for him. *Tonight, we sleep together… tomorrow, we let the world know we're a couple.*

Thirty minutes later, she walked into the restaurant, her gaze immediately zooming in on him. He stalked toward her as though his eyes had been pinned on the door waiting for her to enter. As they reached out and clasped hands, she fought the urge to lean in and kiss him. Just like the first time, she felt tingles travel from his hand up her arm, zinging straight to her heart, and by the look on his face, he still felt it, too.

They followed the hostess to a table near the windows overlooking the water. His fingers grazed her shoulder as he held her chair before taking his own.

After giving their drink orders, he held her gaze and smiled. "You still feel it, don't you?"

"Every single time."

"Me too. That's part of what I was talking about on the beach. I've never felt that before. Never."

Soon their meal came, and like each time they were together, the conversation flowed while the undercurrents of desire pulled them closer. As they finished eating, she fiddled with her napkin, nervous but ready to let him know what she wanted. "Do you remember what we talked about the other night?" Seeing his head tilted slightly in question, she amended, "About us taking things to the next level?"

His hazel-green eyes flared as his smile widened. "Oh, yeah. But, Hannah… no pressure. I don't want you to feel rushed. I don't want you to feel anything with me except comfortable."

Her heart warmed at his words, and she battled the desire to reach across the table and take his hand. Hell, what she was really battling was the desire to leap across the table and land in his lap. Pressing down those thoughts, she focused on her next words. "I'm ready. I'm ready for us to be a real couple… in every sense of the world. I just can't figure out where. I suppose we can go parking in your truck, but that seems so adolescent. And I only have a room at the inn—"

"What about my cabin?"

"Your cabin?"

He shook his head and said, "Nobody's around. It's on a large plot of land that was deeded to me by my gramps, and I'm going to build a house on it. But for now, there's a small cabin where I'm staying." He grimaced before adding, "It's simple. You deserve something fancy, but it's all I have right now."

Her lips curved at the idea and her breath left her lungs in a rush, her body wound tautly. "I just want you, Dylan. I think your cabin sounds perfect."

He threw money onto the table, and she glanced down, seeing that he had left more than enough for their meal and a hefty tip. Lifting an eyebrow, she grinned. "In a hurry?"

"Oh, girl, you have no idea."

They left the restaurant side by side, their fingers touching. He leaned over and whispered, "You can follow me in your car—"

"Dylan?"

With eyes only for each other, they both startled when his name was called. Swinging their heads around, they spied a woman standing nearby. She was blonde, dressed in a baggy green T-shirt and jeans, and it did not miss Hannah's awareness that she was also very pretty. She glanced toward Dylan, recognition evident on his face along with a lowered brow.

"Melissa? What are you doing here?"

Melissa's gaze bounced between Dylan's and Hannah's before settling on his. "I needed to talk to you. I'm sorry for interrupting, but it's important."

"You *are* interrupting," he said, his voice hard.

The air swirling between them was thick, and Hannah took a step back, her heart pounding and her dinner sitting like a rock in her stomach. She halted when Dylan swung his gaze toward her. "She's an old... um... acquaintance. That's all." Before she had a chance to reply, he turned toward Melissa and said, "As I indicated, this is not a good time."

"It *is* important, Dylan, or else I wouldn't be here. We didn't share phone numbers when I was passing through a couple of months ago, but I asked around town and then saw your police vehicle in the parking lot."

Air left Hannah's lungs in a whoosh, and she wasn't sure she could drag in enough oxygen to keep from dropping to the ground. Her dinner threatened to come back up, and she fought the rising nausea. *Oh, God... why is this woman here?* She was an interloper in the middle of a personal conversation that she didn't want to witness and yet wanted to scream at the interruption. She took another step back, but this time his hand snapped out and wrapped around her fingers.

"Hannah, stay, please. You and I have plans, and now that Melissa has said hello, I'm sure she's ready to leave—"

"Dylan, I'm pregnant."

Dylan stood, his heart in his throat pounding a rhythm that made it hard to breathe. *Pregnant? Pregnant! Mine? No fuckin' way.*

"Aren't you going to say anything?" Melissa asked, her eyes darting back to Hannah before moving to his again.

"I... I don't know..." he stammered. He glanced to the side, the wide-eyed expression of anguish on Hannah's face cutting straight through him.

"Look, I know what you're going to ask. Is it yours? The answer is yes. I wasn't with anyone else when you and I hooked up, and I haven't been with anyone else since then."

At those words, Hannah's eyes widened even more,

and he jerked his gaze back toward Melissa. "We hooked up months ago—"

"Yes, and I'm ten weeks along."

"I used protection—"

"Yes, and it obviously didn't work."

His chest heaved as he exhaled, and he continued to stare toward the last one-night stand he'd had before going out with Hannah. "I don't know what to say," and it was the truth. He had no idea what to say as the nightmare unfolded before him.

"I'll… um… I'll just go… and leave you two to… um… talk." Hannah's quivering voice cut through the awkward silence, the stammering words filled with agony.

"No," he blurted, turning to face her. Afraid if she left he'd lose any chance with her, his mind still not accepting Melissa's declaration.

Hannah sucked in a ragged breath, and her tear-filled gaze lifted to his. Regret, disappointment, sadness, and God knows what else landed on him, and he wondered how he didn't drop to his knees at the impact. She reached out, and for the first time in public, placed her hand on his arm, and he felt the familiar burn through his sleeves. "I have to go, Dylan. I can't stay and hear… watch you… her… I have to go." She blinked and his gaze snagged on the tears sliding down her cheeks. His heart squeezed as her hand left his arm and a deep coldness settled over him. Hannah's gaze swept to Melissa before moving back to him, her last word barely choked out. "Goodbye, Dylan."

He stood, his feet rooted to the gravel parking lot,

and watched her hustle to her vehicle as she swiped at her tears. *She was supposed to be following me home. She was supposed to be with me. This was supposed to be...*

"I'm sorry, Dylan," Melissa said, and he swung his gaze back to her, dragging his hand through his hair. "I know this is a lot to take in, but you deserve to know. We have decisions that need to be made and—"

"Decisions?"

"Yes," she huffed, her voice rising.

He faced her fully, hands on his hips. "Look, you've just dumped this on me, so cut me some slack. You've had time to think about this, and I haven't. You tell me that you're pregnant, but I have no proof. You tell me that the baby is mine, but I have no proof of that either. You show up here when I was obviously with someone else and blurt everything out instead of trying to talk to me privately. So pardon me if I'm not exactly jumping for joy."

Her lips pinched together, she inhaled deeply through her nose, then let it out slowly. "You're right. I've been to the doctor and have no problem showing you proof that I'm pregnant. I'm ten weeks along and you were the only man I was with. It's not like I'm asking you to fall in love with me or marry me after one night—"

"Thank fuck for that," he groused, still in disbelief at the change of circumstances.

Ignoring his outburst, she plowed ahead. "But I've decided to keep the baby, and we'll need to come to some financial arrangement. I'd like you to be involved in our baby's life. One way or another, we need to talk."

As his world continued to tilt on its axis, he was barely aware she had stepped forward until she placed her hand on his arm. Unlike Hannah's touch, he felt nothing but her cold, grasping fingers. He looked past her shoulder, but Hannah's red taillights had long since disappeared, and his heart ached.

3

As soon as Hannah turned onto the main road of Seaside, she wished she'd taken one of the side streets to get to the police station. Going this way meant she would pass right by The Wharf Restaurant's parking lot. It had been a month, but the memories of that night plagued her every second of each day. It was the last thing she thought of before finally falling into a fitful sleep and the first thing that hit her when her eyes blearily opened each morning.

She tried telling herself that it didn't matter, that she and Dylan were so new that her heart couldn't possibly have been involved. But that was a lie. They may have only dated for two months, but in that time, she'd fallen in love.

She had managed to avoid seeing him for the last month, not always an easy feat. Throwing herself into her work, she filled her days getting to know everyone in Easton as well as assisting Colt with some of the duties at the county jail. Desperate to not see Dylan and

Melissa together, she never ate out and grocery shopped late at night.

She pulled extra shifts and attended every town meeting, even those where her presence wasn't required. The mayor and town council were thrilled with her dedication, and while speared with guilt that her reasons were selfish, she reaped the benefit when the small local newspaper ran an article on her, singing her praises. As soon as it hit the mailboxes of the residents, her standing in the community rose from *let's see how the woman chief does* to one where she was greeted fondly every time she was seen.

And the law enforcement leaders' meeting had been postponed from last week, giving her another week's reprieve before she had to be in Dylan's presence.

Of course, it both helped and hurt that no one knew they'd been dating. It helped that no one cast sympathetic gazes her way. But it also hurt when no one hid anything. She had to smile when she heard Pearl and one of her officers talking about seeing Dylan and a pretty blonde together. She pretended disinterest when hearing him referred to as a player. After a while, the pain lessened, and she began to see that perhaps their breakup was for the best.

A real estate agent finally found a small cottage that was exactly what Hannah had envisioned, and she was ready to close the deal. That was the only thought that brought a smile to her face... knowing that in another week, she would be a homeowner.

"I've got this," she said out loud to no one but herself, glancing into her rearview mirror. "In fact, this is good.

I should be my own woman, build up my own department, and find my own way. I've got a house to fix up and a career to focus on. To become involved with someone so soon after moving here and getting a job was a dumb mistake."

She'd been talking to herself a lot in the past month. It didn't keep her from being lonely, but she'd never minded her own company. Now, pulling into the parking lot of the Seaside Police Station, she looked around to see what other vehicles were evident. Having convinced herself that she was better off without Dylan, she still didn't want to go in and be alone with him. She was grateful to spot Colt's, Liam's, and Mitch's vehicles.

Squaring her shoulders and lifting her chin, she threw open the door and marched into the building. The overall effect would have been more impressive if her feet had not stumbled to a halt as soon as she saw him. Dylan's hair was a little longer, still brushed to the side as though his fingers had taken the place of his comb. His hazel-green eyes immediately shot to hers, but instead of his signature quirk, his expression held sadness. Plastering a smile on her face, she walked forward and forced her gaze to shift from him over to the others.

"Hey, Hannah," the greetings rang out.

"Good morning, everyone." She moved to the counter to pour a cup of coffee, seeing where someone had set a cluster of mugs. Her hands shook slightly as she fixed her beverage, and she hoped no one was watching. *Come on, Wyatt. Get here so we can get down to business.*

"I couldn't believe it when I spied you with that blonde on three separate occasions," Colt said. "I didn't know you dated anyone more than once."

Knowing he was talking to Dylan, her back stiffened as she waited to see what his response would be.

"Yeah, well, she's an old... um... friend."

Laughing, Mitch jumped in. "I didn't know you had any *friends* like her."

Her cheeks heated, and she was glad her back was still to the others. Considering their opinion about the women he slept with and how close she'd been to taking their relationship to that level, she inwardly cringed.

It was hard to steady her breathing, and she blew out a sigh of relief when Wyatt hustled in, throwing out greetings. He headed straight to the counter and flashed her a big smile as he fixed his coffee. Forcing her lips to curve upward, she carried her mug to the table, glad the conversation had moved off Dylan. *And Melissa. And how soon before they all know he's going to be a father?*

Sitting down, she was unable to keep her gaze from drifting over to where Dylan sat across from her. He was staring, and she could have sworn his eyes were trying to convey a message, but she had no idea what it was.

By the time the last item on the agenda was checked off and they'd discussed current cases that impacted each other, Mitch received a call that would keep him from going to lunch. Right after, Colt's radio went off and he needed to leave as well.

"I'll head out, too," she said. "We can all grab lunch next time."

"Hannah, can you stay a few minutes?" Dylan asked, drawing her surprised gaze to him. "I have a couple of items to go over with you."

Unable to think of a reason to decline, she smiled her goodbyes to the others as they left the room. Now, alone with Dylan, she once again tried to force a smile.

His eyes held the same sadness she'd seen earlier. He swallowed deeply several times, his unease was palpable. *He's going to be a father... but it wasn't the life plan he wanted.* For a month, she'd thought of her own pain, but standing in front of her was a man hurting as well. *Jesus, what a mess.* Her mind roamed to what kind of father he'd be, and for an instant, her thoughts wandered down the path of imaging the two of them being together, expecting a child.

He lifted his hand and swept his fingers through his hair. "I've tried to call... I... um, I guess I just wanted... hell, I don't know."

He sounded so despondent, she fought the urge to reach out and touch him. Clearing her throat, she remained in place. "I thought it was best not to talk, Dylan. You have a lot going on, and to be honest, I felt you needed to focus on Melissa and the baby."

He winced at her words but nodded slowly. Letting out a long sigh, he added, "This is not the way I wanted things to go. I wanted to be with you—"

The look of anguish on his face penetrated her shell. In front of her was not just a man who was dealing with the consequences of his actions but having to reconcile that those actions had changed the course of his whole life. She sucked in a breath that hitched, wanting to offer words of comfort, but held back. It wasn't her place; he wasn't hers.

"Dylan, I'm not upset *with* you, I'm upset *for* you... for *us*." As the words left her lips, his eyes searched hers as though trying to determine her meaning. Sighing, she felt some of the tension leave her shoulders. "You didn't cheat on me. You were with Melissa before you were ever with me. I wanted more, but it's just that life has now chosen a different path for us. We'll be professional colleagues, and I can truthfully say I wish you the best."

He opened his mouth to say more, then closed it, sighing again. His gaze stayed on hers, and she forced herself to not look away. Finally, he sighed and nodded.

She finally reached out and patted his arm, feeling the same electricity as always. "Be well." With that, she turned and walked back out into the sunshine, her heart still heavy and yet now filled with a sense of relief. She was sorry that Dylan's life had taken a turn he hadn't planned on, but she was determined to take charge of her own life and career.

───

With his hands still gripping the steering wheel even though the engine had been turned off, Dylan sat in his truck, parked to the side of the clinic. *Stuck*. If he had to choose one word to describe his life, it would be stuck. Stuck in a situation he did not want to be in. Stuck having to deal with a woman he did not trust. Stuck trying to force feelings that were not coming naturally.

And stuck having to avoid the one person he wanted to be with.

He lifted his eyes and glanced into the rearview mirror, not surprised at the reflection that stared back. He'd watched his reflection change over the past two months, and the change had not been good. His hair had grown longer until Barbara, his receptionist and dispatcher, finally cracked a joke about it, and he'd managed to make a quick trip to the barber. His uniform had been wrinkled several days in a row when he hadn't remembered to take his pants and shirts to the cleaners, and more than a few whiskers had been missed on days when he just didn't care enough to shave carefully.

Every waking moment had been spent thinking about Melissa and the baby. And, of course, regrets about Hannah. He tried to pull up feelings of excitement about the baby, but it was hard. Actually, it wasn't the baby as much as the mother. A one-night stand with a woman he'd just met in a bar. He was surprised he'd remembered her name.

He had never spent much time thinking about babies. He'd figured that one day he'd find a woman he wanted to spend his life with and would fall into the natural rhythm of dating, marriage, and children. Hannah came to mind, slicing through his thoughts as well as piercing his heart. In the couple of months that they'd dated, he'd felt more for her than he'd ever felt for any other woman. He had never been in love before but had no doubt he'd fallen for Hannah. And then that was blown to hell.

The few times he'd seen her she'd put on a good face, and he didn't think any of their friends or colleagues knew she was hurting. But he looked into her eyes and saw pain, and it gutted him that he was the cause. He had no idea what she saw when she looked at him but was sure he wasn't able to hide his sorrow.

Marriage to Melissa was out of the question. He was not going to pledge his life to a woman that he still didn't trust two months after finding out she was pregnant. But the baby would know his father. The baby would be financially cared for, and he would split custody with Melissa. While he might not feel anything toward her, he would not abandon his child. *My child... but is it?*

Melissa had been avoiding the issue of her exact due date, creating more doubt in his mind, but he'd insisted on a paternity test. She wasn't happy about it, but when he wouldn't budge on offering financial assistance without proof the child was his, she'd given in.

A movement toward the front door of the clinic caught his eye, and he watched as Melissa glanced around the parking lot before walking in. She was already in maternity clothing and he wondered why there was no baby bump showing. He waited to see if paternal feelings of love kicked in, and when they didn't, wondered if something was wrong with him. While it might make him a bastard, he needed proof that the baby was his. If it was, he would alter his life and lifestyle to make sure his baby was taken care of and loved. *I just need to be sure.*

Forcing his fingers to unwrap from around the

steering wheel, he climbed from his truck and followed her into the clinic. She had checked in and was moving to a seat, her head snapping around toward him, a tight smile on her face.

He had always possessed a keen bullshit meter. That particular trait came in handy with his chosen career in law enforcement. And he could swear that something was hidden behind her smile. Today, he was going to find out if his instincts were right.

Dylan sat in his vehicle again, this time staring out the windshield at the little bungalow. Checking the address again, he swallowed deeply, a mixture of emotions rushing through his mind. He hadn't seen Hannah since the Chiefs' meeting several weeks ago and could only pray she'd talk to him... or at least listen to him.

Wiping his hands on his jeans, he climbed down from behind the wheel and began walking up the pine-needle path toward the front porch.

The front door opened before he reached the steps, and Hannah peered through the screen door, surprise written on her face. Wearing yoga pants and a green t-shirt, she looked comfortable in bare feet. Her hair was down, the way he'd always liked it, flowing about her shoulders. Her face was just as breathtakingly beautiful as he remembered.

Opening the screen door, she came out onto the porch, her hand easing the door shut behind her. Brow furrowed, her eyes roamed over him. "Dylan? Are you okay?"

Suddenly unsure, he shoved his hands into his pockets. "Uh, yeah. I... I had some news and wanted to... well, you were the first person I wanted to tell... uh... if you've got time..."

She stared for a long, silent moment, her gaze assessing him, and he prepared to beg if necessary. Finally, she inclined her head toward one of the rockers on the front porch, and while it wasn't the same as her inviting him inside, he was grateful for the chance she was giving him. They settled into the chairs, and she planted one foot onto the seat, wrapping her arms around her bent knee. Slowly rocking, she gave him her attention. Now that he was there, all the words he wanted to say seemed jumbled.

"I can tell there's a lot on your mind," she prodded.

Her soft voice soothed over him, and he'd missed hearing it, letting it seep deep inside. He nodded, then leaned forward and propped his forearms onto his knees, clasping his hands together. "I'm not sure where to start."

"Wherever it feels right."

"I feel like I should start at the beginning, but honestly, I guess I'll jump into the middle." He turned his head and held her gaze, wanting to see her expression. "Melissa's baby isn't mine."

Her eyes widened and she gasped, and he remembered the last time he'd heard that sound. It was standing in the restaurant parking lot, hearing Melissa declare that she was pregnant with his child. Wishing he could erase that event, he hurried to explain. "I was suspicious right from the beginning. I had used a condom... I always use a condom. And hadn't noticed a problem with it, but I know they're not infallible." She remained quiet, and he hoped that was a good sign.

"Anyway, I know it probably doesn't matter, but I feel like I need to explain." He stared into her beautiful face and said, "I was never a great student, but I was a decent athlete in high school. That was all it took to impress girls when I was a teenager, and I'll admit that I let it go to my head. Four years in the military, and I wasn't much more discerning as an adult. Honest to God, I was never a player. I never met anyone that I was interested in having a relationship with, but I never played a woman. I also never slept around nearly as much as most people assume, but I never disavowed them of the notion. Guess I thought it made me sound like a big deal, which is fuckin' stupid."

The rocking chairs had been slightly angled toward each other, but now he scooted around so that he was facing her. "Until I met you, Hannah, I never met any woman that I wanted to spend time with. You were different. You were everything."

Her lips curved slightly, but her eyes gave nothing away. He had no idea what she was thinking. Finally, she prodded, "What happened with the baby?"

He scrubbed his hand over his face, fatigue weighing on him. "I wish I could say I was excited at the prospect of fatherhood, but considering she was a one night stand with someone I met at a bar who was only passing through town, meaning I wouldn't have to see her again... well, the idea of being connected to her even though a child was not what I wanted. And, like I said, I was suspicious."

"Suspicious?"

"Look, I don't know a lot about pregnancies, but she said she was already ten weeks along. Which, of course, made it exactly at the time I'd been with her. I asked her when she realized she was pregnant, and she was evasive. Said her periods were irregular, and she hadn't noticed she was late. Then, she said it took her a while to find me. Hell, she knew I was from this town, and Seaside isn't exactly a metropolis."

He battled back the anger that he always felt when he thought about Melissa, not wanting that emotion to erupt. Sucking in a deep breath, he let it out slowly, forcing his heartbeat to steady. "She immediately said that she wanted financial assistance and wanted me to be involved. When I asked about a paternity test, she became defensive. The past seven weeks have been pretty horrible. I hadn't even told my family yet, but I knew that was coming. She was pushing for it, but I was insisting on the test first."

"What happened?"

"We finally went to have the blood draw to determine paternity and discovered that instead of being seventeen weeks pregnant, she was only twelve."

At this, Hannah gasped again, her eyes jerking open even wider. "Twelve? But... but... how..."

Nodding slowly, he said, "Exactly." Seeing Hannah's expression still exhibiting confusion, he pushed further. "So, when she told me she was ten weeks pregnant, she did so because that's when I had been with her. She was only about five weeks along. Hannah, I wasn't the father."

The air rushed audibly from her lungs. "Oh, my God! I can't believe she lied! Why would she do that? I mean, obviously to trap you, but... how... oh, my God!"

His heart leaped at the sound of Hannah's concern about Melissa's duplicity. "She got pregnant, but the father didn't want to be involved, so she figured I was an easy target. I guess she thought because I was a police officer I would do my duty and take care of everything."

"Dylan, I am so, so sorry. I'm stunned, shocked, angry for you." She shook her head and added, "But I'm so glad that you found out the truth."

"Me, too. I told Melissa that I'd help her find resources for financial assistance, but she said that she was going to head back to her hometown and let her parents know what was happening. I haven't heard from her since she left several days ago, and I don't expect I will."

They sat in silence for a moment, and he had no idea what Hannah's thoughts were but wanted to offer her a chance to let the new information sink in.

A breeze blew through the trees nearby, sending the windchimes hanging from her porch into an erratic, tinkling rhythm. Crickets chirped in the background, and for the first time, he looked around. Her house was small but down a long lane, set apart. It gave her privacy, something he could understand considering he wanted to build his house on his land away from others.

Turning his attention back toward her, he said, "A lot has happened in the past couple of months, and I can't begin to apologize enough for what happened to us. I wish I could turn back the hands of time and go back to our dinner at The Wharf before everything went to hell."

A sad specter moved through her eyes, and her lips curved only the slightest bit at the edges. "I have no idea why things happened the way they did, Dylan, but I've spent the last couple of months realizing that perhaps I jumped in too quickly with you."

He opened his mouth to protest, but she reached out and placed her hand on his arm, stilling his words.

"I had just moved into town. I didn't know anyone and with the stress of a new job and position, it was exciting to start a new relationship. But I've spent the last couple of months focusing on *me*. My career. My staff. My department." She waved her hand around and added, "My home."

He swallowed deeply. While he knew it was a fantasy to think she'd jump into his arms at the news that the baby wasn't his, he'd still held onto a now-crumbling hope. "Are you saying that I've missed my chance?" His heartbeat pounded so loud, he was sure she was able to hear it as well.

"I think... for now, we're best as colleagues. We jumped into dating without even being friends first. Right now, Dylan, that's all I can offer. I hate that Melissa's lies hurt you, but her actions put the brakes on us, which might not have been a bad thing."

The numbness that he'd grown used to over the past

couple of months split open his chest, allowing pain to seep in. He wanted to argue. Prove her wrong. Demand that she give him a second chance. But as the evening sun dipped into the sky and the crickets continued their singing, he leaned back, allowing new thoughts to settle.

Hannah was right. While they hadn't rushed into sex, they'd rushed into a relationship. From there, his life had gone into a tailspin with everything that happened with Melissa. His department leadership had suffered. His effectiveness as police chief had suffered. Plagued with self-doubt, he wondered what kind of man he was and what kind of man he wanted to be.

He looked up and saw her gaze pinned on him, concern pouring from her. He attempted a smile but knew the quirk fell short. "Okay, Hannah, I want you in my life, so I'll take you however I can get you."

With his hands planted on the arms of the rocker, he pushed himself to a stand, and she took to her feet also. He leaned over and kissed her forehead, memorizing the feel of her soft skin against his lips. His voice cracked as he stared at her beauty. "But please, have mercy. When we see each other, know it's killing me, so please... have mercy."

Tears pooled in her eyes and he turned away in haste, not wanting to see the expression on her face. Jogging to his vehicle, he climbed in and headed back to his cabin near the shore.

4

PRESENT DAY

Another wedding. *How many does this make?*

Hannah had lost count of the number of friends' and colleagues' weddings she had attended in the past several years. Not unusual for someone in their early thirties, and she certainly never begrudged any of her friends finding love. Weddings always seemed to make everyone so happy... at least others who were coupled together or singles excited to have a chance to dress up for a date that included good friends, food, and alcohol. But for true singles, weddings served as a stark reminder that others enjoyed what they hadn't found yet. *Or rather, maybe found but gave up.*

As she turned onto the drive toward her destination, she sighed heavily. Stately trees lined the sides, long ago planted by the previous owners who wanted to show-case their home to perfection. Coming to the end of the lane, she spied the huge house in the distance. Cars and trucks now covered the drive and grassy area off to the side.

Guests alighted from their vehicles, laughing and talking as they walked toward the back of the property. Colt Hudson had inherited the stately two-story brick home from his grandparents. It had existed virtually empty with only the lonely bachelor living inside for years and now was filled with life and love. Today, Colt was marrying Carrie, gaining a son in the process.

Hannah sat for a few minutes after turning off the engine, trying to tamp down the multitude of emotions that clawed at her. Colt and Carrie deserved their happiness. Hell, they'd found their soulmate in each other. *Hmph... soulmate. What the hell does that even mean?* She shook her head in derision. *God, when did I become such a cynic?* She knew true love existed. It may have been fleeting, but she'd felt it before.

She looked down at her dress, smoothing her hands over the silky material, hoping it had not wrinkled too much in the short drive from her house. While some of the women were dressed in bright colors, Hannah had chosen pale blue silk. Glancing down at the front, she congratulated herself on finding a style of dress that was both feminine and modest. The square neckline only hinted at cleavage, but the back dipped much lower. High waisted, it flared over her hips, swaying slightly as she walked.

She had inherited her dark hair and blue eyes from her father and her curvy figure from her mother. Her father was tall and lanky. Her mother was shorter with an hourglass figure. Hannah preferred men to look at her eyes and not her boobs while conversing but hoped her appearance wasn't dowdy next to her friends who were more gaily attired.

Shaking off those thoughts, she threw open her door and stood for a moment, once more running her hands over her skirt, twisting around to look toward the back to make sure the dress was not wrinkled. Having already sent a wedding gift, she had nothing to carry other than her purse, and she lifted the small strap over her shoulder. She walked toward the side of the house, wishing that someone else would come along so that she didn't have to find a seat by herself.

"Hannah!"

The sound behind her halted her progress, and as she turned around, she smiled at the approaching couple. "Hello!"

"Your dress is gorgeous," Lia MacFarlane gushed, offering a hug.

Seeing Lia's protruding stomach, she shook her head. "You've gotten bigger since I saw you last! When are you due?"

"She pops in November," her husband responded, a wide grin on his face. Aiden wrapped his arm around Lia. "Her and God knows how many more!"

She laughed at his reference to the number of their friends who were expecting babies.

"Come on, I need to find a seat," Lia said, and the trio walked toward the rows of chairs in the backyard.

Hannah continued to greet more friends and acquaintances, relieved the tension left her shoulders as she slid into an empty seat. Looking upward at the blue sky dotted with a few clouds, she had to admit the day was perfect. She also had to admit that no one deserved a perfect day more than Colt and Carrie.

The gathering quieted as the music began. Sitting at the end of a row, she had a perfect view of Carrie as she left the house and approached the makeshift aisle between the chairs set up in the backyard. Hannah's smile was sincere, even if a small jolt of envy stabbed her heart. *One day for me... maybe.*

Carrie's wedding dress was a simple design of silk and lace, hitting mid-calf in the front and trailing almost to the ground in the back. Walking down the aisle, she was accompanied on one side by her former neighbor and unofficial adopted father figure, George, and on the other side by her son, Jack. Hannah's gaze continued to follow the trio down the aisle before she swung her head around to watch Colt as he waited for them to approach. The look on his face was one of awe and something so undefinable yet pure. The thought that one day she'd love to see a man look at her that way moved through her mind and a little sigh escaped.

As the minister began to speak, she glanced around at the others gathered. She hoped the criminals and miscreants on the Eastern Shore were quiet that day considering the large number of law enforcement that was present at the wedding. She recognized everyone from either their departments or as members of the American Legion.

Mitch and Tori Evans. Grant and Jillian Wilder. Gareth and Katelyn Harrison. Brogan and Ginny MacFarlane. Lance and Jade Greene. Zac and Maddie Hamilton. Hunter and Belle Simmons. Aiden and Lia

MacFarlane. Callan and Sophia Ward. Jason and Rose Boswell. Scott and Lizzie. *Couples.* All couples. In fact, as she looked around, most of the single friends were there as part of families or with dates. It had never dawned on her to bring a date. *And just who would I ask?* Disguising a snort as a cough, she looked down. One person came instantly to mind, but they were colleagues... friends. Nothing more.

Carrie and Colt spoke their vows, drawing her attention back toward the front. Her lips curved slightly at the sight of big Colt holding Carrie's smaller hands and Jack staring up at his mom and new dad, excitement radiating from him as he bounced slightly on his toes.

A tingling sensation slid over her, and she allowed her gaze to drift to the side, snagging on a pair of hazel-green eyes that were staring at her. *Dylan.* The man she'd just been thinking about. Blinking, she stared back and her breath caught in her throat as her attention zeroed in on the quirk of his lips turned upward in his familiar lopsided grin. As always, she smiled in return.

They had settled into an easy camaraderie over the past years but had never dated again. Both focused on their respective towns and the never-ending aspects of their demanding jobs. She knew his grandfather had become ill, and he often helped his brother with the family fishing boats. She occasionally saw him out with a woman and would have to tamp down the little ache that still settled deep inside.

Suddenly, the crowd was cheering, and she jerked her attention toward the front to see Colt and Carrie locked into a deep embrace. Looking to the side again, she could see Dylan's focus was now back on the newly-married couple. Something else caught her attention.

He was alone.

The chairs had been moved to the side, now circling tables covered in white linens. Carrie worked as a waitress at The Diner, and the owners, Joe and Mavis, had provided the food. Dylan had made his way through the buffet line and was eyeing the desserts provided by women from the American Legion Auxiliary. The Auxiliary was comprised of family and friends of current and former military service members. Plus, since they were all friends, they loved getting together whenever possible, and a wedding was the perfect excuse to bring out the cakes and pies. Now, pushing back from the table, his gaze wandered over the group of friends, most coupled and on the dance floor.

Like so many times before, his gaze naturally wandered over a crowd, searching for Hannah. He might not be with her, but that didn't keep him from wanting to know where she was... how she was. After their eyes had locked on each other during the ceremony and he'd felt her smile shoot straight to his heart, he'd only seen snatches of her. Chatting with friends. Leaning over the buffet table. Accepting a glass of champagne.

Pushing back from the table, he wandered around the edge of the dance floor, catching sight of her on the far side. Standing alone, she held a glass of champagne, her body barely swaying to the music, the silky blue material swinging gently around her thighs.

Four years. That was how long he'd known her. Four years. That was how long he'd been interested. They had settled into an awkward relationship after the Melissa debacle, only seeing each other in professional situations. When Mitch finally brought an American Legion chapter to Baytown, he'd finally got to see a little more of her since they were both involved with the meetings and the multitude of activities. Over time, a casual friendship formed. *But more?* She'd never indicated that she wanted more.

"Why don't you go ask her to dance?"

He startled as he looked down to see Katelyn Harrison standing next to him, her assessing gaze pinned on him. Snorting, he quipped, "Who?"

She rolled her eyes, then grinned when her husband, Gareth, slid his arm about her waist. Looking over, she said, "I was just wondering why Dylan doesn't go ask Hannah to dance. After all, he didn't bring a date."

Gareth laughed then turned toward Dylan. "You'll have to forgive her. Katelyn's turning into the area's matchmaker."

He shook his head, not sure that Katelyn wanted to take him on as matchmaking potential. No one knew that he and Hannah had ever dated. That was still a secret they both kept. For the past years, during the times they'd been in the same place at the same time, he'd cringed as their friends often laughed with the tales of his wild youth or his reputation for being a laid back, never-commit-to-one-woman man. While those stories were much more exaggerated than real, he knew Hannah had already experienced his past being shoved into her face. He had hoped they could begin anew, but they'd stayed firmly in the friend and colleague zone only. If nothing else other than for her self-preservation, he could hardly blame Hannah after what Melissa's lies had put them through. "Why would she want to dance with me? Anyway, y'all are always the ones pushing my bad reputation out there."

Katelyn protested. "You may have been a wild one when you were younger, but you're certainly not like that now. I don't think I've seen you with anyone in months."

Not wanting to belabor the point, he joked, "Guess I needed a rest. It was exhausting to be so popular." They laughed at his quip, and he flicked his wrist in a goodbye gesture, then walked around the perimeter of the gathering, feeling the need to keep his eyes on Hannah.

In the years he'd known her, he'd seen her in uniform, in jeans, in shorts, and even dressed up at some of their friends' weddings. But right now, standing in the pale blue dress that showcased her figure while remaining modest, her dark hair clipped back from her face and flowing down her back and makeup that accentuated her eyes, he could not remember her being more beautiful. The invisible pull that had never ceased caused his feet to move of their own volition as he made his way closer to her.

He watched as she set her now-empty champagne

flute on the table, her eyes holding a far-off expression. Sucking in a fortifying breath, he stepped directly in front of her. Her head tilted to the side and her chin jutted out slightly as her eyes held his, and his breath caught in his throat.

"Dance with me." Before losing his nerve, he trailed his fingers along her arm, finally taking her hand, and led her over to where others were dancing, glad that she didn't protest. She remained quiet, her body stiff, but he placed his hand on her waist while clutching the fingers of her other hand close to his chest. The electricity shot between them, burning as bright as always. Warmth moved throughout him, and as he slowly swayed her back and forth to the music, her body relaxed.

She glanced around from side to side before her gaze moved back to him. "No one else to dance with?"

"I'm dancing with the partner I want to have in my arms."

The look on her face was one he couldn't define, and he felt sure that his expression probably mirrored hers. Part pleasure mixed with uncertainty.

As the song continued, they moved around the dance floor, the slight pressure from his fingertips pulling her forward, erasing the space between them. The crowd seemed to fall away, and for a moment, they were the only two people under the blue sky and sunshine.

"I was surprised to see you here alone."

Her voice was soft and melodious, drawing him in as it had since the first time he was introduced to her. That and her drop-dead gorgeous looks, which she seemed to be completely unaware of.

"Didn't have anyone I cared about bringing." He couldn't take his eyes off hers until her tongue darted out to moisten her bottom lip, ensnaring his attention.

"Hmm, coming alone means you can scope out the single action." Her lips now tipped upward, and he battled the desire to kiss her, having no doubt her taste would be as sweet as he remembered.

"You wound me, Hannah," he protested, unable to keep from smiling.

"No, I just know you."

"Yes… yes, you do."

She sucked in her lips, her gaze never leaving his. "I'll bet that you had a date for this wedding, and she had to cancel at the last minute."

Shaking his head, he huffed with exasperation. "Nope. I'm telling you the truth. I'm tired of meaningless. I'm tired of pretending. I'm tired of wishing that you and I could become something more than what we are. I came alone because I had no one else I wanted to be with other than the person I'm dancing with right now." His heart pounded as she smiled, her top teeth landing on her bottom lip.

A light blush tinged her cheeks. His fingers tightened on hers and—

"Hey, Dylan."

The female voice coming from the side caused him to startle as both he and Hannah jumped slightly, their heads swinging toward the speaker. One of the young women who'd been serving champagne was smiling up at him, her eyes bright. Her gaze was pinned entirely on him, completely ignoring the fact that he had his arm around another woman.

"I hate to interrupt, but I'm getting ready to leave. I just wanted to make sure you had this."

A white paper napkin was in her hand, and he reached for it automatically, wondering why she thought he needed it. Looking down at the napkin, he spied a phone number clearly written in ink with little flowers scribbled around. Remembering the conversation he'd had with her, he opened his mouth to respond, but she giggled, waved her fingers, and turned to hurry away.

Hannah stepped back, a pained expression slashing over her face dulling the sparkle he'd seen in her eyes.

"Shit," he groused, reaching out toward her, desperate to explain. "This isn't what you think—"

"I don't think anything, Dylan," she said, her voice still soft. Her lips trembled but curved ever so slightly, the smile now appearing forced. "Thank you for the dance." Taking another step back, she turned quickly and moved through the crowd, leaving him standing alone. Instead of running after her, he stood for a long moment, not believing the shit timing.

A clap on his shoulder drew his attention away from where Hannah had disappeared, seeing Hunter and Belle Simmons standing next to him. Hunter was an imposing figure, large, tatted, with long hair. He was also a detective for North Heron and fellow Legionnaire. Belle was a local girl, a sweet, quiet beauty with long dark hair, and the perfect mate for Hunter. She was the head nurse at the local nursing home where Dylan's grandfather had been since his stroke. His gaze dropped to her barely rounded belly, and he leaned forward and kissed her cheek. "I haven't seen you since y'all announced the pregnancy. I'm happy for you, Belle."

Her smile widened as she leaned back against her husband. "I was happy to see you dancing with Hannah also."

"Yeah, well, that didn't end so good." Both Hunter and Belle glanced down at the number on the napkin in his hand. "One of the servers had asked me to invite her kid brother to play ball with us and gave me her family's number so I could clear it with their parents. She was grinning and giggling, and it looked like I'd asked her out."

Belle's face fell and she reached out to place her hand on his arm. "Oh, Dylan, I'm so sorry. You can explain it. I know Hannah would listen."

Shrugging, he said, "Yeah, well, it's probably for the best."

Hunter wrapped his arm around his wife and offered a hard stare toward Dylan. "What the hell makes you say that?"

Giving a quick shake of his head, he said, "Not everyone is destined for what you two have. Or, for that matter, what Colt and Carrie have."

Belle opened her mouth, but Hunter gave her a little squeeze and she glanced between the two men. Dylan was grateful, not wanting to prolong the conversation. Offering goodbyes, he decided it was time to head home. After congratulating Colt and Carrie, he walked around the house toward his truck.

Something blue moved under a clump of trees to the side and caught his attention. He was surprised to see Hannah approaching her car, obviously leaving early as well. An inner battle ensued and the desire to hustle over to explain the server's reason for giving him her phone number was finally defeated. He might not be the player everyone thought he was—hell, or what he encouraged everyone to think—but that didn't mean that Hannah didn't deserve better than him. *Doesn't matter that we've got the same job... I'm still just a good ol' boy.* Sighing, he forced his feet to remain in place, watching as she drove down the lane and out of sight.

5

"You're wasting your time."

"You threw away what could have been an important career."

"You're not living up to your potential."

Words she had heard many times before moved through her mind in cadence with her footsteps. For Hannah, the early morning run on the sandy coast was marred. The words made it difficult to focus on the soft pink of the sky as the sun began to rise, the call of the gulls and pelicans as they plunged into the water in search of a fish or oyster breakfast, a heron on stilt legs hoping for a crab, or the sound of the gentle waves lapping against the sand.

She hated that her early morning run was plagued with unpleasant thoughts crowding out the beauty surrounding her. But her feet continued their steady pace, years of running having taught her the speed necessary for maximum benefit. As her ponytail swung back and forth in rhythm with her feet, a smile crossed her face as she remembered high school years of running cross-country, cheered on by her parents and older brother. By the time she had graduated from college, she'd run in several marathons. The added weight from packs while in the Army made the training more difficult, but she'd been in much better shape than some of her fellow squad members. Running, not only for exercise but to clear out the cobwebs from her mind, was second nature to her.

Having reached a small group of dunes, she slowed and turned around. Now running northeast, she could see the sun peeking over the trees, casting the sky in pale blues. She could have easily continued south for a few more miles but preferred to run alone, and soon there would be others running on the beach.

It wasn't that Hannah minded other people, but today she preferred solitude. Snorting, she laughed aloud at the word. Solitude. That was only found at home, certainly not her job which kept her surrounded by others.

And, coming full circle, thinking about her job brought back the words she'd tried to forget—*wasting your time, throwing away a career, not living up to your potential.* It was no wonder she hadn't been back to Hope City to visit her family in a while.

Refusing to give more headspace to those tangled thoughts, she slowed once again as she approached the end of her run. Staying on the beach for a few minutes as she completed her stretches, she allowed the breeze blowing off the Bay to whisper over her body. She stood, hands on her hips, and stared out toward the

water, tempted to wade in. A glance at her watch let her
know that pleasure would have to wait for another day.
Perhaps tomorrow I'll cut my run short and take a swim.

Walking over the dune, she spied her vehicle sitting
at the end of a small cul-de-sac. A two-million-dollar
home was perched nearby, but she didn't have to worry
about anyone calling the police to complain about her
vehicle. Nor did she have to worry about anyone
breaking into it. As she walked closer, she clicked her
fob to unlock the doors. The words emblazoned on the
side met her gaze. Easton Police Department. The
county vehicle was definitely a perk to her job.

Climbing inside, she lowered the window instead of
turning on the air conditioner. It was only a five-minute
drive to her house, and like most places on the Eastern
Shore, it wasn't difficult to get from one location to
another.

She turned onto a lane that wove through farmland,
coming to a small bungalow painted pale yellow with
teal shutters. The Florida colors seemed incongruent
with her serious personality, but as soon as the realtor
showed it to her years ago, it was just what she wanted.
A place to relax when she wasn't working. A place to
decorate without worrying about anyone else's tastes. A
place to call home.

There was no garage, but she parked under a tall tree
and walked to the side door leading into the kitchen.
She had painted the kitchen walls a pale peach, setting
off the blue-tiled backsplash that met granite countertops. The cabinets were also pale peach but so light they
were almost a warm cream. Crocks and pottery in

various shades of peach, blue, and yellow held cooking implements, flowers, and fruit.

She had spent a great deal of time adding color and touches of whimsy to each room in the small house. There were only two bedrooms, one full bathroom and one half-bathroom, and the family room that flowed into the eat-in kitchen. It was her refuge.

A glimpse at the clock on the microwave gave proof that her well-ordered life was right on schedule. Enough time to shower, dress, eat breakfast, and make the ten-minute drive to work.

"Meow."

The large orange cat weaved between her legs, and she bent to rub its head. "Hey, Percy." The cat preened, lifting up on its hind legs as her hand reached its tail. She poured some food into his dish and said, "No more for you. The last time I took you to the vet, she said you were getting chubby."

"Meow," came the reply.

"Yeah, well, that's easy for you to say." Hannah grinned while giving one last rub and headed into her bedroom. She focused on getting ready, refusing to be late to work. She thought of her busy life filled with work and the American Legion. Her brow scrunched as she tried to think of the last time she'd had a visitor but knew it had been a while. It was so hard to find time to socialize. The image of Dylan sitting on her porch several years ago hit her. *He looked so natural there. Like he belonged...* Wondering why she was suddenly thinking of him, she rushed through her morning preparations.

Less than an hour later, she drove through Easton,

waving at a few early-morning residents out and about. Easton's rich history included the town being situated near the sites of the first English settlements on the Eastern Shore of Virginia in the early 1600s and a historic green courtyard and brick courthouse buildings from the late 1700s drew visitors to the small town all year around. Still the county epicenter, a modern courthouse and large regional jail provided most of the employment in the area while farmland surrounded Easton.

Quaint shops, restaurants, B&Bs, and a hotel that resembled an old-fashioned inn gave visitors places to spend their money and stay or have a meal. She was proud of her small, picturesque town. Proud of knowing the residents. Proud of working to keep them safe.

Walking into the station, she greeted Pearl and started to walk toward her office.

"LE Leaders meeting later… just before lunch." Pearl laughed, "That was a mouthful! I know you didn't forget, but I wanted to make sure to mention it."

"Thanks." Hannah walked into her office, glancing at the simple nameplate on the door. Hannah Freeman. Easton Chief of Police. It didn't matter that she'd had the title for four years. It always sent a zing of pride straight through her, allowing her to push away the words of doubt that she'd heard so often from her parents.

Knowing that Pearl would make sure the conference room was ready for her early staff meeting as well as the LEL meeting, she settled into her chair behind her desk and clicked through her emails. Easton might be tiny, but because it was a town, there was a mayor and a town council. All of those positions were filled with people that had performed those duties for years. She found them easy to work with, and for the most part, they let her do her job with no interference.

Having dealt with her emails, she left her office and walked down the hall to the conference room, which doubled as a break room for her small staff. It soon filled with her sergeant and three officers for their biweekly meeting. They poured their own coffee, greeted each other amicably, and settled quickly. She was lucky with her staff and knew it, appreciated them, and didn't mind letting them know.

Mason Nottingham, her sergeant, began reading the report of incidents, arrests, and complaints. All of their reporting was logged into the computer and Pearl would print out a concise list for Mason before their staff meetings.

"In the last three days, we've had four speeding violations, six failure to stop violations, two drunk and disorderly with one turning into a domestic complaint that was settled."

Hannah lifted an eyebrow. "Stan and Lavinia, right?" Chuckles from her other officers, Robert Sidlow, William Morrison, and Bobby Rodriguez, met her ears.

Robert, still chuckling, shook his head. He took another sip of coffee and said, "I was on duty. Stan was at The Tavern last night, drank too much, and called his wife to come to pick him up at midnight because he wasn't sure he could walk home. Lavinia came, then the two of them got into it in the parking lot. The Tavern called me, and I got their asses settled down and made sure they got home. Same old, same old for those two. Can't stand each other and can't stand being away from each other. Thank God I got my wife trained early!"

Snorting, Hannah said, "Yeah, I'll tell Sally you said that."

"Don't you dare! We've got an anniversary coming up, and I don't want to be in the doghouse!"

Laughter erupted again from the others and she turned her attention back to Mason. "Anything else?"

"Had a break-in reported. Bobby handled that."

It had been a boon to her department when they were able to hire Bobby Rodriguez as an officer. Bilingual, he'd been integral in helping with the migrant farming community that lived and worked in the area. Making sure their children were in school and the adults not taken advantage of by the farmers, he was slowly earning their trust.

"It occurred in the shacks just off of Marker Drive. While the kids were in school and the parents were in the fields, someone busted down a few of the doors. It looks more like vandalism instead of robbery. I got the Sheriff's Department to check footprints around the door, but there were too many to distinguish."

Hannah nodded slowly. "Do you think it's teens? I mean, I know kids should be in school, but the kind of teens that would break into a place might not be in school."

"Could be."

They finished the reports and she reminded her staff

that she was hosting the monthly LEL meeting that morning. With their assignments and schedule posted, they all left the workroom. She headed back to her office, filing reports and making a few notations.

Her cell phone vibrated and she glanced at the caller ID, seeing it was her mom. Her fingers drummed on her desk near the phone, indecision running through her. For many people, a call from a parent in the middle of the workday would indicate an emergency or crisis. But for Hannah, a call from her mother probably just meant she wanted to chat, never seeming to understand that it might not be convenient. The phone stopped vibrating and she sighed in relief that the decision had been taken away from her only to huff as soon as the ringing began again.

"Mom? Is everything okay?"

"Yes, dear. I was just out shopping and saw the most lovely dress that would look gorgeous on you. I thought about buying it then wondered if you would come up this weekend and we could go shopping together."

Closing her eyes, Hannah dropped her chin to her chest. "Mom, my life doesn't exactly fit with dress shopping. I have several for special occasions, but other than that I'm in uniform when at work and jeans when I'm not." An image of dancing in her blue silk dress in Dylan's arms flashed through her mind.

"I know that's what you say, but if you wore a dress occasionally you might not be single—"

"Oh, wow, Mom, something's just come up and I've gotta go. You take care and I'll talk to you soon."

"Wait! What about this weekend?"

"I can't. I've got a… um… meeting to go to."

She heard her mom's sigh, and as much as her mother irritated her, she felt bad. "We'll talk soon, Mom. I promise to come to visit." That seemed to placate her mother, and she disconnected. Leaning back in her chair, she rubbed her hand over her forehead. She often wondered how her parents had gotten together, being so completely different in personality, tastes, and likes.

Her father, former military, quintessential law enforcement, career FBI, and—quite frankly—hard ass. Her mother, kind and sweet, had never held a job, considered it her calling to be a full-time wife and mother. Hannah respected that decision and sometimes wondered if her father didn't encourage that. He wasn't the type of man who would deny his wife the opportunity to work if she'd wanted, but it was as though he truly wanted to protect and care for her. Protect her from the ugliness that he saw in his job every day and care for her in a way that made her happy. *And neither of them seemed to understand my choices at all.*

Pearl stepped into her doorway, drawing her attention away from her thoughts of her parents and back to her job.

"Got the workroom ready. The others will be here soon."

Smiling at the ever-efficient receptionist, she nodded. "Thanks. I'll be right there." Listening for Pearl's footsteps to disappear down the hall, she pulled out her purse from the bottom drawer of her desk. Flipping open her compact, she checked her makeup and teeth. Swiping on a tiny bit of colored lip balm, she re-evaluated her reflection. Snapping the compact closed, she shook her head in derision, frustrated that she was concerned with her appearance.

The only person she'd met that sent a spark through her was Dylan, and she had to admit that his words, while they danced at Colt's wedding, had stayed in her head. *I'm tired of meaningless. I'm tired of pretending. I'm tired of wishing that you and I could become something more than what we are. I came alone because I had no one else I wanted to be with other than the person I'm dancing with right now.*

After he left her house the day he informed her of Melissa's lies, she wondered if he would push for them to resume a deeper relationship, but when she put the brakes on them, needing to focus on her life and career, he'd never asked her out again.

Standing, she hesitated. She hadn't seen him since Colt's wedding. She felt the heat of blush rise over her cheeks again at the memory of being in his arms while dancing, only to have one of his new conquests interrupt to hand him her phone number right in front of Hannah.

Hearing a noise in the hall, she blew out her breath, plastered a smile on her face, and marched into the workroom. Just like always, professionalism slid into place, masking any other emotion.

6

Dylan rushed through his morning routine, having slept through the alarm. He had spent his day off from work going out on his brother's fishing boat. An activity he liked to do, but yesterday felt compelled considering a few of his brother's crew were sick. All day long on the water, he'd been busy but relaxed. Unfortunately, the boat had mechanical problems near the end of the day, and he'd stayed to help David with repairs. Now, he was functioning on a couple of hours of sleep.

After a quick shower, he reached into his closet. As Chief, it was up to him to determine his department's uniform, and once he observed what Mitch allowed for the Baytown officers, he adopted the same style, khaki pants, and a dark blue polo with the Seaside Police Department logo stitched over the breast pocket. His pants were pressed, but not his shirts. "Fuck!" He'd meant to drop them by the laundry the previous day, but that flew out of his mind after getting the call from David to help on the boat.

Grabbing one from the hamper, he gave it a shake and a sniff test. "Not too bad." Running his hands over the material to stretch out a couple of wrinkles, he determined it would have to do.

Ten minutes later, he turned onto the main street of Seaside. The town had less than four hundred residents, all he knew by name. Having been raised in a home just outside the town limits, he was well familiar with every nook and cranny. The town consisted of one main road that ran past the fishing harbor. Considering that Seaside was one of the few harbors on the Eastern Shore, especially on the ocean side, and fishing was the town's main business, it was not surprising that the area around the harbor stayed busy. The Wharf Restaurant sat on one end of the harbor, boasting lunch and dinner of fresh seafood. During the vacation seasons, it offered Sunday brunch as well.

Several businesses located in old brick buildings nearby contained supplies for professional as well as tourist fishermen. More interested in their wares than the aesthetics of their business, the glass windows were rarely clean and the floors barely swept out. But it didn't matter to the customers as they tramped in and out daily.

Side streets offered a few more eateries, a new Dollar General store, a 7-Eleven with gas pumps, and other businesses. To most, he knew Seaside was a tiny dot on the map. The kind of place that you'd miss if you blinked while driving past. But to him, it was home.

He waved to several townspeople before pulling into the parking lot of the one-story building that housed the police department in the front and town council meeting rooms toward the back. Seaside was so small that the Mayor and Town Council received a small stipend and only worked part-time. The city treasurer and town manager were full time, along with his department, consisting of a police sergeant, three officers, and the receptionist. The receptionist handled the non-emergency calls, while the 9-1-1 system for North Heron County was tied into their dispatch system.

"Hey, Barbara," he called, walking through reception. The building was old, and the reception area was not fancy, although it had been upgraded for security. That was one of the first changes he had made when he took over. It was easy to think that a small town didn't need a secure police station, but he'd seen too many situations get out of control quickly when he was stationed overseas with the military police and wasn't going to take any chances.

Barbara sat on a tall chair behind a long counter that was separated from the public area with shatter-proof glass. At first, she'd balked at the changes but now liked having a bit of privacy as well as security.

"Sorry I'm late," he added.

"Late date last night?" she asked, her smile wide as she looked him up and down. Like so many in Seaside, she'd been there since childhood and held the receptionist job since she'd graduated from high school over thirty years earlier.

"Nah, helping my brother." He was almost to his office when he asked, "Anything I need to know about?"

Shaking her head, she replied, "No. Carl and Tom

have been patrolling the harbor while Lynette has handled anything else."

Carl Winters was his sergeant, and his three officers were Lynette Barber, Joe Montrose, and Tom Binion.

"Has there been anything else?"

"Marjorie Sanders is complaining about the noise the motorcyclists make when they drive through town on their way to The Wharf."

"Then I'm glad Lynette's got that. She'll be able to take care of Marjorie." He walked into his office and sat down. Marjorie Sanders had seemed ancient when he was a child, and now that he was in his thirties, she was still cracking the whip. Pushing almost ninety and deaf as a post, he knew she could barely hear the sound of the motorcycles but was convinced a gang of ruffians was going to take over the town.

His ass had barely hit the seat when Barbara called out, "Disturbance at the Bass Hotel. You gotta take it. Lynette's still with Marjorie. Joe's off today."

Hefting himself from his chair, he jogged out to his vehicle and drove down the street to the hotel. Run by Steve Bass, its name also appealed to the visiting fishermen who hoped to catch Striped Bass in the bay. Pulling into the parking lot, he immediately spied the issue.

A man was standing in between two women on the sidewalk outside one of the rooms with his arms extended and his palms facing out, attempting to keep the women separated. Recognizing the man and one of the women, Dylan sighed. Their screaming and arguing continued, so as he pulled in next to them he blasted the siren, jolting the trio into silence as they snapped their mouths shut and turned wide eyes toward him.

Josiah Gambit was standing on the sidewalk with no shoes or socks. He had his pants on, but his T-shirt was inside out and not tucked in. His hair was a mess, standing on end, and Dylan was certain Josiah's eyes were bloodshot. One of the women was a bottle blonde, her hair an equal mess, and looked as though someone had tried to rip it out by the roots. Smeared lipstick and raccoon eyes gave evidence that she had gone to bed without taking her makeup off first. She was also barefoot, dressed in a robe haphazardly tied about her waist. And the other woman was Ellie Gambit, spitting mad but at least dressed.

He climbed from the SUV and stalked over, focusing his glare on the man. "Josiah. You're too damn old to be pulling the same shit." Jerking his gaze toward the smaller woman, he said, "Ellie, I'll say the same thing about you."

"Me?" Ellie yelled. "I'm not the one who's forgetting my marriage vows!"

"No, that's true. But causing a scene and assaulting someone else when Josiah does the same thing every time he goes off on a bender doesn't make any sense. Either accept that he isn't going to change or dump his ass. Hell, you're the one who's working, and if I had to guess, the house is in your name."

Ellie snapped her mouth shut, tilting her head as his words seemed to penetrate. Josiah, on the other hand, looked up toward Dylan, his mouth hanging open.

"Chief Hunt, what the hell are you telling my wife?

You're telling her to leave me? What kind of officer of the law are you?"

Legs apart and fists planted on his hips, he replied, "I'm the kind of officer of the law that's sick and tired of seeing this scene repeated month after month... for years." He let his gaze drop to the other woman, not recognizing her.

"Ma'am, I'm assuming you're staying at this hotel. I'm also going to assume that you're traveling through since I don't recognize you. I'm also assuming that you probably met Josiah last night in the bar at The Wharf. Then I'm going to assume that you brought him back to your room. Your suggestion or his? Don't know, don't care. But you now understand that he's married to a woman who can find him when he doesn't come home."

The woman tucked a wayward strand of bleached blonde hair behind her ear and stepped back away from Josiah and Ellie. "Your assumptions are all correct. I didn't know he was married until this... woman showed up this morning, screaming and threatening me."

"Well, we can handle this in two ways. All three of you will go down to the station with me, give your statements, and decide who wants to press charges. If punches were thrown, then I can charge anyone who threw them with assault. Or this thing breaks up right now, and everyone goes their separate ways." He slowly looked at all three, not surprised to see an uncomfortable silence settled over the trio. "Josiah, if I could charge you with just being stupid, I would. But unfortunately, I can't."

Josiah's face fell, the wrinkles in his hound-dog

appearance deepening. "Oh, dang it, Chief Hunt. Hell, even you've been known to party hard."

Bristling, he snapped, "I'm not the one who's married and can't keep it in my pants. I'm also not the one who's cattin' about town, practically right under my wife's nose. And I'm sure as hell not the one who's standing outside a hotel getting into a screaming match with two women. So keep me the fuck out of this situation."

"I know, I know, Chief. I'm sorry. I was out of line."

Before Dylan had a chance to reply, Ellie snapped, "You're always sorry, Josiah, and you're always the one out of line."

"Okay, so what's it gonna be? Down to the station to give statements and face charges or walk away?"

"Well, for me, I plan on grabbing my suitcase and getting out of this podunk town. I must've been crazy for stopping here, but my friend told me The Wharf Restaurant was one of the best on the Eastern Shore."

"Then maybe you should've stuck to what was on the menu!" Ellie snapped at the woman. She glared at Josiah and looked up at Dylan. "Chief, I agree. Josiah has dragged my good reputation as his long-suffering wife through the mud enough. I don't want to go to the station and press charges. But I am going home. Alone!"

With that, the two women whirled in opposite directions. The blonde headed into the hotel room and slammed the door while Ellie stomped to her car, climbed in, and screeched the tires as she backed out of the parking space.

Josiah sighed heavily and shook his head. "Guess I really messed up this time, Chief."

"No, not just *this* time, Josiah. Just because Ellie's gotten tired of this and is kicking your ass out doesn't mean that it's only *this* time that you've messed up."

"What am I going to do? I love her."

"Those are just words, Josiah. Words are worthless if the deeds don't back 'em up. You work when you feel like it, but Ellie works full time. You may love her, but I think you married her because you felt like she'd take care of you. That makes you weak. A weak, pathetic man. And maybe part of Ellie thought that was love. Being able to take care of somebody. You going off, getting drunk, hooking up with some random person is not love. You know it. I know it. And Ellie knows it."

The hotel door opened, and Josiah's shoes and socks were tossed at his feet. The blonde woman, hair now combed, did not even look at the two men as she rolled her small suitcase out to a car, tossed it into the back-seat, and shot out of the parking lot, much like Ellie had.

"Get your shoes and socks on, Josiah. I'll drive you home, and you and Ellie can talk. But I'm telling you, it's time you did some real soul-searching."

They soon pulled up to a small brick house on one of the back streets of Seaside. Josiah climbed from the seat then turned and looked back at Dylan. "Thanks for the ride, Chief, and the talk. I am sorry I made that smart-ass remark about you. You're a good man. I was just being a dick."

Lifting his hand, he waved it dismissively. "Go on in if Ellie will let you in. If not, sit on the other side of the door and think about what you can say and do to fix your marriage."

He sat in the driveway for a moment and watched as the front door opened, Ellie standing with her hands on her hips, glaring up at her wayward husband. She wasn't saying anything, but he could see Josiah's lips moving. After a moment, Ellie stepped back and let her husband in. Having no idea how their conversation would go or why it would be any different than the many they'd had over the years, Dylan shook his head.

Looking at the clock on the dashboard, he radioed to Barbara. "Took care of the disturbance. It's time for me to head to Easton for the LEL meeting. I'll be back in after lunch."

He looked forward to the monthly meetings with the other police chiefs and sheriffs in the surrounding area, now all close friends.

And, of course, there was Hannah. He hadn't seen her since the wedding a couple of weeks ago, and when they were together professionally, she was business. All business. He'd had female friends when in the military and knew they often had to work twice as hard for the respect afforded to a man. And Hannah was in the same position, so he couldn't blame her, but he knew the minute he laid eyes on her, he'd battle the urge to hold her again. *Yeah, that would go over brilliantly!*

Josiah's words came back to him. *Even you've been known to party hard.* His gramp's words slammed into him as well. *Boy, now that you've got a uniform, you think your shit don't stink. But remember where you came from— you're no one from a nowhere town like the rest of us.*

Sighing, he pulled into the Easton Police Department parking lot and leaned over to peer into the rearview mirror. *Seems like everyone has an opinion about who I am.* Checking his reflection, he snorted as he swiped a hand through his hair in anticipation of seeing Hannah. *Hers is the only opinion I care about.*

Pearl had a large pot of strong coffee made, just like everyone liked it. Hannah pulled several mugs down from the cabinet. The meeting attendees would fix their own coffee, but she would have mugs, creamer, and sugar out.

"Good morning, Hannah."

She smiled as Mitch walked into the room. Her father thought she was crazy for turning down a position with the FBI to become Police Chief of a tiny town and rolled his eyes in surprise at Mitch, who actually left a career with the FBI. Even several years later, her father still mentioned it whenever she went home for a visit.

"Good morning," she replied. "How's Tori?"

If anyone ever wondered what Mitch thought about marrying his childhood sweetheart and starting a family, they only had to look at his face. A wide smile curved his lips, and he immediately pulled his phone from his pocket, flipping through several photographs to show her. She admired Mitch. He seemed to be the kind of person who had it all. Support from his family, love of a good woman, a healthy child, and praises sang for the career he'd chosen and the job he did. She would begrudge him his good fortune if he wasn't so damn likable.

"Your son will soon be ready to play ball with the American Legion group if he keeps growing the way he does!"

Mitch chuckled and shook his head. "He's not ready yet, but if he wants to play in a couple of years, I think my parents will be cheering as loud as anybody to see him play."

The clomp of heavy boots sounded in the hallway, and she looked up in time to see Colt, Liam, and Wyatt walk in together.

Colt greeted Hannah, dropping into the seat next to her. She couldn't help but smile at the change in Colt's demeanor now that he was married and had adopted Carrie's son. *The bigger they are, the harder they fall.*

"Carrie's arranging a party for all the preggers."

"I heard. I'll be there," she assured. Carrie was hosting a baby celebration for their many friends who were expecting babies. At last count, Jillian, Belle, Rose, Lia, and Jade were all pregnant. Having little time off, she appreciated that they were having a joint shower. The Auxiliary was helping to host, and with many of the women bringing gently used items as well as new presents, the new moms would be well taken care of.

Liam headed straight to the coffee pot. "Morning, all." Grabbing the biggest mug, he poured his coffee. "Thanks for this, Hannah. I desperately need the caffeine this morning."

"Well, you know Pearl makes it strong," she commented.

"Had some teenage boys decide to go four wheelin' through old man Gunther's pasture. He'd already warned them off, then decided taking potshots at 'em would do the trick. Between him, the boys who had too much to drink, and their parents threatening to sue everybody, I didn't even get home until after midnight."

The others chuckled at the thought of Liam having to chase down an old farmer and some drunk teenagers in a pasture, but Hannah knew they each could well imagine themselves doing the same thing.

He settled at the table with the others and took a healthy sip of the hot, strong brew. "I thought I'd be the last one."

Just then, Pearl's voice carried down the hall. "You look like something the cat dragged in. You must have had a late night!"

Hannah didn't need to look up to see who Pearl was talking to. She hated the image of what a late night for Dylan would entail. Plastering a smile onto her face as Dylan walked in, she greeted him with the others and waited while he grabbed his cup of coffee, apologizing for being late.

"Sorry... spent my day off yesterday on my brother's boat and half the night helping him repair it." His eyes met hers, and she inwardly winced, having assumed the worst.

Sliding into the only available seat, he was directly across from her, and she dropped her gaze to the agenda sheet she'd provided. It didn't help—she could still feel his eyes on her, and her nerves tingled with strange electricity moving throughout her body.

"Le…" She cleared her throat and began again. "Let's get started." Their monthly meetings were informal, something they found worked well to maintain the interdepartmental camaraderie. Their meetings generally started with each giving a quick rundown on any cases, open or closed, that they felt would have a bearing on the other localities.

"Thanks for the tip about the shoplifters in Baytown, Mitch," Colt said. "I warned my people and we caught two of them at one of the little shopping centers in the county."

"I was informed that the construction on the new hotel would start soon," Dylan said. "I know the inns aren't happy, but the Seaside Town Council thinks it will help tourism if we have more places for them to stay. The Wharf is thrilled, although the mayor is talking about getting another restaurant to come."

"More visitors, more fishing, more business for Seaside." Wyatt grinned. "At least that's what Manteague's Mayor is always telling me."

"I know, and I agree," Dylan nodded, scrubbing his hand over his face, finding a few whiskers he had missed when shaving that morning. "I'm just partial to knowing all the people in my town who are coming and going. Visitors bring in business, but they can also bring in trouble."

She looked between the two. "Specific trouble?"

"I can answer that since I was just getting ready to send a memo to you all." Everyone's attention swung back to Liam. "My counterpart in Maryland has kept me apprised of drug gangs using the Eastern Shore as their thruway between Florida and New York, bypassing Washington D.C. and Highway 95. The only way they get caught is if they're speeding and pulled over, but it looks like the word is out that we closely monitor the speed."

"As much as I hate them going through our counties, I hate it even more when they stop here," Colt added. "We don't need their drugs."

"Some are using boats in smaller harbors to transport, also," Liam added. "I know this hits Mitch, Dylan, and Wyatt specifically since you three have harbor towns."

Hannah looked around at the faces of the men at the table, their frustration clearly visible and matching her own.

Alert, Dylan sat up straighter. "Shit. What's their MO?"

"They have someone waiting when the boat comes in," Liam explained. "They've gotten smarter. Instead of just young punks trying to get into the gang performing menial tasks, they send someone who can blend in. Might be someone who's spending a night in a hotel. Out of state car tags that don't necessarily say Florida or New York."

"What about the Coast Guard?" she asked. "Are they able to board?"

"Yeah, but usually small fishing boats get passed by. Not enough manpower to check everything coming and going."

They continued discussing the various needs of their towns and counties, Hannah carefully checking each item off the agenda. Just as they were about to break for lunch, Colt said, "Got one more thing. We've been advertising for a jail medic to work alongside our nurse."

While each of the small towns' police stations contained a few holding cells, the main jail area was housed in Easton. Colt's Sheriff's Department was responsible for the 250-bed facility that served both North Heron and Acawmacke counties as well as taking prisoners from other districts if the room was available. Housing both men and women, it had its own kitchen, laundry, and medical clinic.

"As you know," Colt continued, "our nurse, Margaret Anderson, is getting on in years. With a jail medic assisting her, it would serve the population more efficiently."

"Have you hired someone?" Hannah asked.

"It took a while to find the right candidate, as you can imagine."

She grinned. People generally did not move to the Eastern Shore for job opportunities, especially for a part-time jail medic position.

"Luke Perdue has just been hired. His background checks out. Army medic. Served in Afghanistan. Originally from Hope City, but said he wanted to live somewhere smaller. He started this week, and so far, Margaret says he's settling in well. He's a big guy but quiet. She said she's noticed no problem between him and any of the prisoners."

"Well, good," Dylan said, his smile wide. "Anyone up for lunch at The Diner?"

"I'll never turn down Joe's cooking!" Mitch said.

Hannah nodded before casting a gaze toward Dylan, finding his eyes pinned on her, a lopsided smile playing about his lips. She couldn't help it... her lips curved upward in response.

7

Dylan hustled to get to the door of The Diner before Hannah, pulling it open and waving her in with a flourish of his hand. She sailed past, and just like every time he'd ever been around her, all of his senses were firing.

The delicate vanilla scent of her shampoo and body wash wafted by, a siren's call that was stronger than any expensive perfume. He'd seen her dark hair down, flowing about her shoulders in a silky wave, and now his fingers itched to pull the offending bobby pins from her tightly controlled bun that she always wore when on duty. Tough, strong, he'd watched her expertly take down a much larger man. But now, his eyes followed her every move and knew exactly where the top of her head came if she was standing next to him. Tucked just under his chin, as he remembered.

Hannah was everything he'd ever wanted in a woman and time hadn't changed that feeling. Following behind her into the restaurant, he plastered the well-worn smile on his face, the one everyone expected.

The bell rang as the door swung closed behind them. Joe waved at them from the back and Mavis nodded toward a large table near the center. Dylan settled into the seat across from Hannah, the others filling the chairs around the table. He smiled as Carrie walked over, and Colt immediately stood to kiss his wife.

Carrie turned to greet the others and said, "I'm glad you came in today. I've got a new server that I'm training. Here's Jolene. She used to waitress at Stuart's Pharmacy diner in Baytown but is working here now."

The pretty blonde's gaze held a mixture of awe at the five people in uniforms and badges sitting around the table. He remembered her working at Stuart's Pharmacy as a teenager, and now that she was an adult, it just made him feel old. Shoving that thought down deep, he caught her eyes on him and pretended a great interest in the menu even though he always ordered the same thing.

Jolene giggled, pulling out her pad and pen. "What can I get y'all?" Her question was directed toward everyone at the table, but her eyes stayed pinned on Dylan.

He rattled off his order, then shifted his gaze, seeing Hannah's eye-roll and lips quirk.

"Damn, am I getting old, or are the women just getting too young?" Wyatt grumbled, putting into words exactly what Dylan was just thinking.

Hannah laughed and Wyatt turned his attention to her. "Does the same thing happen to women?"

"What?" she asked, her head cocked to the side.

Curious, Dylan twisted to see what Wyatt was asking.

Wyatt chuckled. "Well, for men, it's okay to appreciate younger women, but then there comes a point where they're just *too* young." As though needing to clarify, he hastened to add, "Not jailbait younger... just too *young*."

She laughed and shook her head. "Well, Colt and Mitch already have their wives, but for the rest of you, here's a little tip about women."

Dylan leaned forward, his attention pinned on her, barely aware that Liam and Wyatt were leaning forward as well.

"While looking at young man-candy is fine for a while, most women prefer someone more mature. There is nothing sexier than a confident man who's happy with his life, his choices, and what he's doing. Add to that a man who's no longer after an easy conquest but is willing to pursue a woman who adds to his life, not just look good in a bikini... well, that's what a woman wants."

"Damn straight, Hannah," Carrie said, coming up behind them. "You got that right!"

Their conversations continued, and he was glad he'd chosen the seat across from Hannah. It made it easy to continue to admire her without being obvious. Carrie and Jolene soon arrived with their plates. As he ate, he stole glances at Hannah as she relaxed, smiled, and chatted. Her words resounded through his mind. *No longer after easy... willing to pursue a woman who adds to his life... well, that's what a woman wants.*

As the meal came to an end and they were all tossing cash onto the table, he tried to figure out a way to exit at the same time as Hannah, but she received a call and said quick goodbyes. Her gaze hit him for a few seconds, and he could swear she was sending him a message, but he wasn't sure what it was.

His eyes followed Hannah as she walked out the door. There was nothing sexy about her uniform, especially with body armor worn underneath. But he couldn't help but stare as he'd always done. Hannah Freeman was gorgeous.

"I have no idea when you're going to get your head out of your ass," Mitch said, shaking his head. "For years I've watched you stare at Hannah when you think she's not looking."

Swinging his head around, he looked at the other men, their lips all quirking upward. "What?"

Mitch stood to leave, still shaking his head. "You'll have to figure that out on your own." Tossing his hand upward in a wave, he followed Hannah out of The Diner. Colt grinned, then stood and moved toward the back of The Diner to say goodbye to Carrie, leaving Dylan with Wyatt and Liam.

"You two got anything to say?"

"Come on, Dylan. She's an amazing woman," Liam said as they walked to the parking lot.

"You think I don't know that? I just don't know that she'd be interested in me."

"Don't know either," Liam joked, a wide grin on his

face as he climbed into his Sheriff's SUV after a final wave goodbye.

Standing outside the diner, he looked over at Wyatt. "I feel like I'm in fuckin' middle school."

"Nah. I think everybody's just tired of seeing you pine for something that you could so easily have."

"I'm not fuckin' pining over anyone!"

Barking out a laugh, Wyatt tossed his hand upward in a wave as well. "Keep telling yourself that, man!"

Before he knew it, he was standing all alone outside The Diner, his fists on his hips as his chin dropped to his chest. Studying his boots for a moment, they offered no answer to his predicament because the truth that he couldn't tell anyone was that he *did* want to be with her. Finally climbing into his SUV, he drove back to the tiny town of Seaside.

By four o'clock, he waved goodbye to Barbara. "I'm wiped. Heading home. Call me if I'm needed."

Ten minutes north of town, he turned between two trees onto the sandy driveway that led to his house. Unlike other places that faced the Atlantic Ocean where waves rolled in and white beaches covered the coastline, the barrier islands that lay to the east created a completely different topography. The coastline was marshy, and the lots of land did not attract expensive prices, keeping most visitors and homeowners on the bay side.

His grandfather had deeded the plot of land to him when he turned eighteen, just as he'd done for his older brother. Dylan didn't doubt that if his grandfather had known he would never follow in his fishermen's footsteps, the old man would've kept the land for himself out of spite.

His phone vibrated in his pocket and he jolted, realizing he'd been sitting in his driveway staring at his house. Recognizing the caller ID, he said, "Hey, Ma."

"Barbara said you left early since you had to work with David yesterday."

Dropping his chin to his chest, he closed his eyes slowly. "Why the hell is my receptionist telling you what hours I keep?"

"Maybe because she's been my best friend for the past fifty-five years! Anyway, she did say you looked tired. Would you like to come by for supper?"

"Thanks for the invite, but I'm gonna take a rain check. Right now, I just need a shower and my bed."

"Are you sure? I've got a roast in the oven."

That enticement was real. His mom's roast beef could rival a meal at the finest restaurant. "Hate to turn you down, but really, I'm wiped."

"Well, how about if I bring leftovers to you tomorrow?"

"That'd be appreciated."

They disconnected and he climbed from his SUV, walking toward his house. Even on the coastal side, he rarely had flooding, but he'd built his house above the ground anyway. Eschewing a modern look, he had gone for an old-style weathered cedar plank house with shutters that could be closed to protect the windows in an oncoming storm. The two-bedroom, open living and kitchen area house was simple in design but eased his soul at the end of the day. A porch ran the full length of the back, part of it screened in. If it was raining, he sat with his morning coffee or evening beer inside the screened area, choosing the open deck when the cooler weather kept the insects at bay.

Showering off the sweat and fatigue, he grabbed a beer and sat on his deck. Herons wandered in the marsh, graceful on their stilt legs, quickly diving for small fish and crabs. Gulls called overhead, and he leaned back in his chair with his feet on the rail and closed his eyes.

The peace of the evening stole over him, but the face that appeared in his mind was that of the dark-haired, beautiful Hannah. Their paths crossed several times a week, and not always just professionally. He saw her at the American Legion meetings and the AL events. He occasionally ran into her at the grocery store. Always polite. Always friendly. And yet, a bit aloof.

"Yoo-hoo, Dylan! Are you around here?"

His feet dropped from the rail to the deck, and he pushed himself out of the chair, seeing his mom walking around the corner of his house toward the steps leading to the deck. Grinning, he caught a whiff of her roast beef. "You just couldn't resist, could you?"

"Well, I haven't seen you all week, and knowing you were tired, I wanted to get this to you. I won't stay long. Plus, your dad will be off the boat soon."

"He helping David today?"

'Yes. I'll be so glad when your brother can get—and keep—a full crew."

He took the plate from her hands and bent to kiss her cheek. Selma Hunt had been a beauty when she caught his dad's eye as a teenager, and the years had been good to her. Her dark blonde hair, now streaked with silver, was cut to just above her shoulders. Her figure was still trim, helped by the long walks she took each day. His father had given Dylan his height and build, but his eyes were his mother's.

He waved to a chair and said, "Stay as long as you can, Ma."

They sat together, both staring out over the water at high tide with the barrier islands in the distance. For several minutes they chatted about the weather, what the ladies at her church were doing, and the newest gossip in town.

She continued sitting, and he finally chuckled. "Ma, I can tell something is on your mind. You might as well just spit it out."

"Hmph," she groused, rolling her eyes. She remained quiet for another moment, then said, "Caroline Jackson has a niece that's going to be moving here from Virginia Beach. She's got a job at Baytown High School, and Caroline thought it would be nice if someone could show her around."

He rolled his head to the side and stared at his mom's profile. "You're kidding, right?"

"Now why would I be kidding?"

"Show her around? Ma, this town consists of about fourteen roads. I hardly think it's going to take anyone very long to find out what's here."

"Don't be obtuse, Dylan. I think Caroline would like her niece to meet someone her age."

"Not interested."

"And why not? You act so laid back, but you don't fool me. You might do some running around, but you've never introduced a woman to us. That tells me you're not serious about anyone."

"I might enjoy the occasional company of women, but as the Police Chief, I'm not going to parade a bunch of women through my house or have them come to dinner at your place. But I also don't want my mom to fix me up with someone."

Her face softened, and she held his gaze for a long moment. "What about Hannah Freeman?"

Startled, he blinked. "What about her?"

"Is Hannah someone that you'd bring around?"

"Sure," he answered easily. "I don't mind any of my friends or colleagues being here."

"That's not what I mean."

He sighed, rolling his head back so that his gaze was pinned to the ocean vista in front of him.

"She seems like a lovely woman, Dylan."

"She is, Ma."

"And you're not interested?"

"I'd have to be deaf, dumb, and blind to not be interested," he admitted. "But trying to date someone in this profession could prove difficult. If something went wrong…" His words drifted away but the meaning was clear.

"Oh, I see. It could be awkward." Lifting her shoulders in a shrug, she added, "Then just start slow… keep it secret… then, when you're sure, you can let people know."

A grin slipped across his face as he shook his head

slowly. His mother had no idea how close she described what he and Hannah had years ago. "Ma, you have a solution for everything, don't you?" He sighed as he looked back over the marsh. "Anyway, she's law-enforcement elite and you know what gramps always said—"

"That old coot! I love my father-in-law, but the way he acted when you came back from the Navy... well, I told him on more than one occasion to keep his opinions to himself!"

Chuckling, he could well imagine his mother standing up to his grumpy grandfather.

Selma shook her head. "Don't take his words on, Dylan. Don't sell yourself short. Hannah has certainly shown the naysayers who didn't think a woman could handle the job, but then, so have you." Throwing her hand up quickly, she said, "I'm done interfering." Standing, she started to walk down his deck steps when she stopped and looked over her shoulder. "For now."

His laughter followed her as she walked toward the front of the house. He headed inside where he enjoyed the roast beef she'd brought. Fatigue was pulling at him, but he grabbed another beer and went back outside to watch as the sky darkened and the moon began to rise in the distance.

Is willing to pursue a woman who adds to his life... that's what a woman wants. He thought about the way Hannah stared at him when she said those words. Maybe the message she was trying to convey was that she was interested in him pursuing her. Maybe, after all this time, he was now the kind of man she was ready for.

8

The small police department building for Easton had a holding cell, but Hannah processed those arrested with the Eastern Shore Jail. Luckily for her, it was practically next door, unlike the other officers over the two-county area who had to travel there with their prisoners.

Parking outside the jail, she opened the back door and assisted the man in handcuffs to his feet. "Come on, Roland. You know the drill."

The man offered a rueful sigh and said, "You know I'll have the money. I just have to move a few things around."

Roland Bertram had been writing bad checks for as many years as she could remember. He always claimed it was just until he could shift his money around, but the reality was he tended to drink his Social Security check away, then write bad checks for the groceries. Most businesses knew to watch out for him, but a new teenage checkout clerk was caught unaware.

Leading him inside the cool interior of the back

entrance where the prisoners were processed, she waved at the guard as they went through. Once she provided the paperwork, he turned and looked over his shoulder at her before being led away.

"You know, Chief Freeman, you may always be coming after me, but you're a good officer... a good woman."

Chuckling, she waved at Roland and said, "I'll call SueEllen and let her know where you are." In a small town, she saved him a phone call to his wife, knowing SueEllen would get the ball rolling to get him out.

He waved in return, and she turned to leave when she spied Margaret Anderson walking in with a young man in tow. Margaret made eye contact and her smile widened.

"Chief Freeman, how nice to see you."

"Margaret. Good to see you, too."

Margaret, wearing green scrubs, turned to the similarly dressed man next to her and asked, "Have you met our new medic? This is Luke Perdue."

He was tall and muscular. His dark hair was trimmed short and his dark eyes met hers as he offered a chin lift. Stepping forward, she extended her hand. "Nice to meet you, Luke. I'm Hannah Freeman, Chief of Police for Easton."

"Nice to meet you, Ma'am."

"I hope you're settling in well."

"Yes, Ma'am, I am."

"I understand that you're from Hope City originally. So am I," she added.

He nodded but offered no other comment.

She turned her attention toward Margaret. "I'm sure it's good for you to have the assistance."

Margaret offered an emphatic nod. "Absolutely! Luke is catching on to everything quickly, and it's making things easier for me and taking some of the stress off my shoulders."

"I'm glad. Well, I've got to get back to the station. Margaret, it was nice to see you, and Luke, it was nice to meet you." With a wave, she walked back down the hall. It was shift-change time, and she grimaced as she saw one of the guards walking down the hall toward her.

"My lucky day! I get to see the gorgeous Chief Freeman!"

Gary Perkins was the kind of man that made her skin crawl. Nothing to complain about but just smarmy enough to make Hannah want to take a shower after she met him. "Perkins," she said, offering no more than a curt nod.

He laughed as though he hadn't just been dismissed and said, "One of these days I'll get you to go out with me."

She continued out the door, mumbling, "When pigs fly." Walking back across the parking lot, she passed the new county courthouse on her way to the police station. Hearing her name called, she looked to the side and saw Ginny McFarlane and Grant Wilder coming down the front steps. Grant, like Ginny, was one of the officers in Baytown. "Hey. Got court today?"

Both nodded as they reached the bottom of the steps and the trio stood for several minutes, chatting.

"Sorry to run, but Jillian's got a doctor's appointment," Grant said, dropping his sunglasses over his eyes.

"Hope everything is okay."

His wide grin answered her concern, but he replied, "She and baby are perfect. Just a checkup." Waving goodbye, he called back, "See you at the AL game on Saturday."

The American Legion based out of Baytown was very active. The monthly meetings drew a large crowd of men and women who had served in the Armed Forces. The Auxiliary for family members was equally as active. One of the programs they ran was the youth baseball league, providing coaches and teams for young people of all ages, regardless of their family's ability to financially support them. They planned to hold a fundraising game, where the players consisted of the Legionnaires themselves. To keep the teams even, their names would be randomly drawn just before the game.

Standing under a shade tree with Ginny, Hannah asked, "How's your baby?"

Her smile split her face and Ginny gushed, "Gorgeous. Beautiful. Growing." Rolling her eyes, she added, "You should see Brogan. I swear he fretted over getting the nursery complete before she arrived and now has it set up like a princess' castle."

At first, it had been hard for Hannah to imagine the large, tatted, brooding pub owner becoming a father to a little girl. Then, when she'd seen him for the first time cradling his daughter in his arms, her heart melted. And she had to admit her heart pinged just a little for what she hoped would be hers someday. "Are you going to be on one of the teams for the game?"

"Oh, yeah. We both will. But believe me, Brogan's mom, Corrine, will relish the chance to hang with her grandchildren."

Before Ginny had a chance to respond, her eyes shifted over Hannah's shoulder, and she smiled. "Hey, Dylan."

Hannah jerked around, unable to hide the surprise on her face. "Uh... hi, Dylan."

"Hate to rush off, but I've gotta get back to town. Bye, Dylan. See you at the shower, Hannah." Ginny tossed up her hand as she jogged over to her vehicle, leaving Hannah alone on the sidewalk with him.

"What's up?" she asked, her smile genuine.

"Had to meet with the magistrate." He grinned and stepped closer. "I'm glad I ran into you. I wanted to make sure you were playing on Saturday."

"That seems to be what everyone is talking about today," she laughed, "but yeah, I'll be there."

He took another step forward, and she tilted her head back to hold his gaze, surprised he was so close. In the sunlight, his eyes appeared more green than hazel, and she remembered how they darkened when he held her close.

"Earth to Hannah."

Realizing he had spoken, she blushed. "I'm sorry?"

"I said maybe we'll be on the same team." His eyes twinkled and his voice held mirth.

Cocking her head to the side, she narrowed her gaze. "Just what do you have up your sleeve?"

"What makes you think I'm up to something?"

She crossed her arms over her chest, noting the tingle that shot through her at his close proximity. Ever since the wedding when he'd held her in his arms again, it was as though her body had reawakened to the feelings she had tried so long to bury.

His teeth landed on his bottom lip as he held her gaze. "If we're on the same team—and of course, we'll win—then we could have a drink to celebrate."

"And if we're on different teams?" she asked, mesmerized by the slight redness of his lips.

"Well, we could celebrate my team's undoubted win with a drink."

Barking out a laugh, she said, "I'm not sure I see what kind of deal that is. Either way, we go get drinks."

He reached out his forefinger and tapped her nose, winking. "Exactly. And I accept your invitation." He turned and walked off, leaving her staring at his back, wondering what had just happened.

Now, standing alone on the sidewalk, she shook her head before turning in the other direction and making her way back to the station, her mind filled with the notion that her well-ordered life was changing.

Dylan stood outside the Shore Mini-Mart, legs apart and fists on his hips, glaring at the two teenagers in front of him. They were not small, but neither their bodies nor their brains had yet fully grown into manhood. They were sitting on the sidewalk, hands cuffed behind their backs. The chin of one quivered, trying to be brave in the face of being arrested for stealing a six-pack of beer. The other one was starting to expose a crack in his defiance.

"I want to know what made you get up this morning and suddenly have the shit-for-brains idea to shoplift a fuckin' six-pack of beer?" Receiving no answer, he pressed the one he thought might speak up. "Bill?"

Shoulders hefted in front of him, Bill shook his head. "I don't know, Chief Hunt," he said, his voice shaky. He glanced to the side at his friend and said, "We thought we could get away with it."

"And why was that?"

"You know Old Man Jefferson. He can hardly hear and can hardly see."

"Oh, so instead of two upstanding young men in the community deciding to help out an older man whose retirement years are spent having to run the store because he's got no other livelihood, you decided to take advantage of him. Now, what the hell does that tell me about what kind of boys you are?" Seeing Todd's glare shoot up toward him, he continued, "Yeah, *boys*. Because you sure as hell aren't men yet. Not the kind of men I want to know. Not the kind of men I want in my town."

"I'm sorry, Chief Hunt." Bill twisted his head around and wiped his nose on his shoulder. "It was stupid. It was wrong, and it was stupid."

"That's the smartest thing I've heard you say, Bill."

Before Dylan had a chance to say more, Todd erupted, "This whole place is stupid."

Dylan didn't speak but crossed his arms over his chest and waited, his stare heavy on the young man.

"What the hell are we supposed to do? Born and raised in a little podunk town. My dad's a shopkeeper selling tackle and bait to a bunch of fishermen. My granddad started the store. They think that's what I'll do when I graduate." He huffed, his frustration evident on his face. "Hell, there's nothing else to do in this town."

A bark of laughter erupted from Dylan, drawing stares from the two boys. Figuring they wondered if he'd lost his mind, he explained. "Y'all know I was born and raised here. You think I didn't have the same thoughts? I can tell you for sure that fishing was not in my blood. But I sure as hell didn't go around trying to rob stores! I figured out what I could do, what I was interested in, and worked to get there."

"You were in the Navy. That's what I heard," Bill said, wiping his nose again.

"Yeah, I was. I wanted to get off the Eastern Shore. I wanted to see more of the world. I wanted to find what else was out there for me to do."

A derisive snort came from Todd. "Must not have been much if you ended up back here."

"For me, I realized that the chance to be close to family while doing something I loved, away from the hustle and bustle of big crowds, out where I can breathe clean air free and easy was all I needed. For you? Maybe leaving and finding something else out there is exactly what you need. But you're not going to be able to do that if you're sitting in jail for being a thief and a dumbass."

Bill's eyes jerked open wide, fear evident. Todd's face carried more emotion—fear, still mixed with defiance. And anger. Anger at what, Dylan wasn't sure. Maybe anger at himself or maybe just anger that he got caught.

Any further talking was interrupted when another police vehicle pulled up in front of the small convenience store. Without having to look, he knew Lynette had arrived to assist.

She climbed out of the SUV and stomped over, her stance appearing much like Dylan's with her hands planted on her hips. "Seriously? *Seriously?*" Her voice rose on the second word.

"What's gonna happen to us?" Bill asked, his gaze shooting between the two officers. "Are we going to jail?"

"You sure as hell aren't going to Disneyland," Lynette bit out, bending forward and hefting Bill to his feet. She shot a glance toward Dylan and he nodded. The boys were sixteen, and Dylan had already indicated they would go to the holding cell and wait until their parents picked them up. She put Bill into the back of her vehicle, and he hauled Todd to the station. The other option was to drive them all the way to the Norfolk Juvenile Detention Center, which he'd done on many occasions when necessary. Where possible, they would release youth to their parents until a court date was set.

The rest of his afternoon was spent with Bill's parents and Todd's father. Bill's parents were upset with their son, terrified of what might happen, and immediately placed him on their own version of house arrest as well as making a stop at the Mini-Mart to apologize to the owner. Dylan handled the paperwork, told them they'd be contacted by court services, and released him to his parents.

Todd's father was also angry, but Dylan didn't get a good feeling about the situation. The man was large, fists like hammers, clenching and unclenching, and Dylan had no doubt imagining the man using those fists later on Todd. Going over the same information with them that he did with Bill's parents, he noticed the man's anger seemed to be directed at Todd getting caught, not so much that he was stealing, to begin with. As he released Todd, he threw out his own condition. "Todd, until your hearing, I want you coming by the station every day to check in with me."

Todd's gaze jumped to his, and something akin to relief seemed to flash through his eyes. His father opened his mouth, and Dylan was sure he was going to complain, but he pushed on, not giving the man a chance to speak.

"You'll be in school every day, and then you'll stop by here after school. Every single day. You'll check in with me and that will give me a chance to check in with you." He swung his gaze to Todd's father and held it.

The man grumbled but finally nodded before following Todd out of the station. Dylan stood in the doorway and watched them leave, hearing someone come up behind him but not wanting to take his eyes off the man until they were out of sight.

"You think he'll hurt him?" Lynette asked.

"I don't know. But if he knows his son is going to come in here every day after school to meet with me, he's gonna have to think twice about taking his fists to him."

"That was a smart move, Chief. A good move."

He turned and looked at her and chuckled. "I do occasionally have a smart idea."

She threw her head back and laughed before pushing on the door and walking out to her vehicle.

Driving home that night, he thought about his encounter with Hannah. He hadn't planned on seeing her, but that had been a fortuitous bonus. Now that he knew she was going to be at the game, he just needed to figure out a way to spend more time with her.

As the evening sun dipped into the west, he sat on his back deck with his bare feet resting on the railing. The breeze was growing cooler; fall was in the air. He tilted his head back, taking another long pull of his beer.

Hannah had never been to his house. It had taken him almost a year to build, doing a lot of the work himself in the evenings and weekends when he wasn't working. For a moment, he wondered how different the house might have been designed if they had stayed together. For a fleeting second, the sharp prick of disappointment twinged.

For a year after they first broke up, every time he saw her, it was a stab straight to his heart. Eventually, the pain had lessened, but the desire to be with her had not. But he'd seen the wisdom of her decision. They both had new, difficult, consuming jobs that needed their attention. And while it galled him at the time to realize, he needed to grow the fuck up.

He thought about the game again, and his offer to get drinks. *She didn't turn me down.* Maybe, just maybe, the time is right. Tipping the bottle up again, the last dregs of the beer slid down his throat. Planting his feet on the wooden deck, he stood, looked out over the dark water, felt the cool breeze on his face, and grinned. "I do occasionally have a smart idea."

9

Hannah could understand why Carrie wanted to host the group baby shower. Colt's house—or rather, Colt and Carrie's house now—was easily able to hold the large gathering of friends. The living room flowed into a wide dining room, which flowed into a massive kitchen. The counter held food, the type that made it easy to go back and continually fill your plate. She only hoped no one noticed how often she'd done that.

The group shower was an interesting concept. With Jillian, Lia, Jade, Rose, and Belle all expecting within the next couple of months, none of them wanted their friends to break the bank trying to host individual showers. Some of the women from the Auxiliary had provided the food, leaving Carrie with little to do but arrange her rooms in a way that made for ease of movement. Tables had been set up along one wall of the living room, gift bags piled high, a random number from one to five attached.

The five women opened the gifts with their designated number, each getting a multitude of items they needed. Occasionally, one of them received a gift that they already had, and fun trading began. Baby clothes, bedding, diapers, carry wraps, teething rings, stuffed animals, and a multitude of other gifts spilled out in piles around each expectant friend. Tori's son and Kate-lyn's son ran around, tossing the ribbons and balloons into the air much to the delight of Ginny's daughter.

Enjoying herself more than she thought she might, Hannah wandered out onto the patio for a breath of fresh air. Carrie had lights strung around the patio and a few of the trees, casting a fairy-like glow over the area. She glanced to one side of the expansive yard, remembering the area set up for dancing at their wedding. Closing her eyes, she could almost hear the music whispering through the trees, the feel of Dylan's hand on her waist pulling her close while holding her other hand tightly between them. She had never thought to be in his arms again after so much time had passed. But she couldn't deny how right it had felt.

Hearing a noise beside her, she looked over her shoulder and spied Ginny, Belle, and Samantha stepping out onto the patio as well. Samantha Collins was the local veterinarian and they had bonded when she'd first brought Percy to her.

"Oh, did you want to be alone?" Belle asked, stopping just outside the door. Her dark hair was pulled back away from her face with a ribbon matching her dress, giving her a Snow White appearance. *Well, a pregnant Snow White.*

Smiling, Hannah shook her head. "No, not at all. It's

just such a lovely evening, I thought I'd get a little air. The only other time I was here was at Colt and Carrie's wedding, and with so many people around it was hard to appreciate their beautiful view."

"I'm taking advantage of others wanting to get their hands on my daughter, giving me a little break." Ginny glanced over toward Belle's protruding belly and said, "You should have a seat. Take a load off while you have a chance."

The four women settled onto the thick, comfortable cushions of the patio furniture.

"You know, I've seen you two together a lot over the years, but I could swear the look on Dylan's face yesterday outside the courthouse made me think that he's got it bad for you," Ginny said.

A denial was so close to slipping from her lips, but with the fairy lights twinkling around and the sound of laughter between good friends coming from inside the house, she felt comfortable with Ginny, Sam, and Belle. "We... well, actually, we dated when we first came to the area." If she thought the other women would react in surprise or shock, she sighed a breath of relief when they simply turned toward her, easy smiles on their faces encouraging her to continue.

"No one knows. I thought with our positions it was best to see where things went first." She cast her gaze back over the dark lawn, the peace of the evening settling like a blanket. "For reasons that I can't go into, the timing just wasn't right. It was a little awkward at first, but we've remained professional colleagues and friendly—if not exactly friends—for the last couple of years."

Belle said, "I know that for me, it's hard being with someone in law enforcement. Hunter has to focus on the job, be responsive and often on-call, and sometimes it's hard for him to let go of things at the end of the day."

Ginny chuckled and looked over at Belle. "I'm a cop, so I get that, but since you're a nurse, I'd say you have a lot of the same problems."

The three laughed as Belle nodded her agreement. "I suppose I should amend my earlier statement. I imagine it's hard being in *any* relationship nowadays."

"Hear, hear," Sam agreed, sweeping her hand through her hair. "Hard to find time... hard to find the right person... hard to... to... oh, just everything."

Hannah looked over, seeing the frustration on Sam's face.

"What about now?"

The question came from the other side, and Hannah shifted her gaze toward Ginny, realizing she was asking about Dylan. She sucked in a deep breath, thinking over her answer. "To be honest, I thought that ship had sailed. I figured that Dylan would serial date until he found someone that he wanted to be with."

"Maybe he has decided," Ginny added. "Maybe he's decided it's always been you."

"He flirts sometimes, but I'm not sure he's serious."

Eyes bright, Sam asked, "What are you going to do if he does ask you out?"

She thought of his offer to get drinks but wasn't ready to share that tidbit. "I don't know. I keep trying to look at this logically, but sometimes I think Dylan defies logic."

Ginny laughed. "Maybe you should give him a taste of his own medicine. Flirt back. Keep him off balance a little bit."

The door from the patio to the kitchen opened, and Jade called out, "Belle, they're starting to help load the gifts into our cars."

As the women got to their feet, Belle offered a hug to Hannah before moving into the house. Sam hurried after her. "I've got to get home to feed my animals."

Ginny and Hannah followed more slowly, walking side-by-side.

"You know, Dylan used to remind me a little bit of Aiden before he settled down with Lia. With him being my brother-in-law, I got to know him pretty well. He liked to have fun. Considered himself a good old boy. Even had a reputation of a Peter Pan. My Brogan was an old soul from the moment I met him." She laughed and shook her head. "I remember Lia being very cautious around Aiden at first, especially since she had a daughter. But the time was right, and Aiden and Lia were perfect for each other."

Hannah shoulder-bumped Ginny and said, "I get the feeling you're trying to tell me something in all this."

"Okay, I'll just come out and say it. Whatever happened that broke you two up must've been over three years ago. A lot can happen in that time, and I can see changes in Dylan. Anyway, I guess I'm just saying that maybe the time is right for the two of you now."

As they stepped through the doorway, Ginny offered

her a hug, whispering in her ear, "And I definitely think a little flirting is perfect!"

As Ginny walked away, Hannah dropped her chin and stared at her feet for a moment, shaking her head. A grin curved her lips at the thought of Dylan taping her nose with his forefinger while winking before saying that he accepted her invitation to drinks.

He's interested... I can tell. But is the timing right? Sucking in a deep breath, she turned to look out the door one last time at the fairy lights twinkling in the trees. A sliver of excitement moved through her and she grinned again. *She wasn't sure of the answer, but she was ready to find out.*

Dylan had planned to arrive at the ballpark early, but a call to check on one of the elderly residents in Seaside caused him to now be searching for a parking place. Thankfully, the older resident had simply slept through hearing his caregiver's call but was fine.

Finally squeezing his truck between two vehicles that barely left enough room between them, he climbed down and hustled past the concession stand and area where food trucks were setting up. Jillian was already under a tent selling coffee and sea glass jewelry from some of the local artists that she normally showcased in her business, Jillian's Coffeeshop and Galleria. The AL Auxiliary had set up tents and were busy selling baked goods. And Lizzie Weston was selling her goat milk lotion and soaps, percentages of proceeds going to the

American Legion to be used for the many projects they offered for the community.

He continued past the stands that were filled with many of the young people that normally he and the other Legionnaires coached as well as their parents. The townspeople also packed the stands. The ballgame was a fundraiser, and children were allowed in free and for adults, it was donation only.

He made his way to the dugout just in time to hear Aiden shouting to the others. A quick look around showed members ranging in age from their twenties to their fifties. Most were men, but several were women from the area that had also served in the military. His gaze immediately cast over the gathering, landing on Hannah's head as she stood next to Ginny.

"Okay, listen up!" Aiden shouted. "Everyone is going to come forward and pull a piece of paper out of this basket. It'll either have a one or two, obviously determining which team you're going to be on. It's totally random and no trading once you've gotten your assignment. Team One will be batting first with Team Two in the field. Once you've got your number, you can go to your area and start warming up."

Dylan made his way through the crowd toward the back of the line, inching forward as they each reached in to grab a piece of paper. Opening his, he spied the number two. He had lost sight of Hannah in the crowd but jogged toward the outfield, seeing half the players included his friends Colt, Zac, Hunter, Scott, Callan, Joseph, and Ginny.

Looking toward the group that was practicing their

batting, he found Hannah, along with Lance, Mitch, Aiden, Jason, Gareth, Grant, and Brogan. He watched as Hannah looked around with her ball cap shading her eyes as she appeared to be searching. When her gaze landed on him, he grinned and tossed his hand up in a wave. Now he just had to make sure his team won so she'd get drinks with him.

The fall day could not be more perfect, with mild temperatures, the sun shining, the scent of grilled hot dogs wafting past, and the sound of laughter and friends greeting each other filling the air. *Fucking perfect.*

Two hours later, the ballgame was coming to a head. The cheering crowds had been delighted as the competition had the teams joking almost more than they were playing baseball. Except for Dylan. He was growling at his teammates, scowling at the umpires, and generally pissed off at everyone. So far, he'd barely seen Hannah and hadn't had a chance to speak to her. The teams were large, and in an attempt to give everyone a chance at bat or in the outfield, their paths had not crossed.

Now, at the bottom of the ninth inning, the score was only separated by one run... his team behind but at-bat. Next up, Colt hit a line drive and made it to first base, where Dylan could see that Hannah was now playing the first baseman. As though the sun beamed down brighter, he realized that he'd be able to get onto first and have a moment to stand there with her. It might only be a moment, but after the disappointment of not speaking to her all morning, he couldn't wait.

The next two batters struck out, but now he was up and with ease managed to get to first base, allowing

Colt to reach second. As soon as he landed on the base, he turned and grinned at her. "Well, fancy seeing you here." Tossing the batter's helmet to the side, he slapped his baseball cap onto his head, shading his eyes so that he could focus on her face.

"Took you long enough," she laughed, her gaze bright as she stared up at him. Inclining her head toward the next batter, she said, "You know, as soon as this batter strikes out, the game is over."

He was so focused on Hannah, he hadn't realized which of his teammates came up behind him. Swinging his head back around, he smirked. "You might not realize this, but Callan is a powerhouse. Besides Mitch, he was one of the best baseball players Baytown High School ever had." Reaching out and tapping the end of her nose again, he added, "You and your team are going down, and then you have to go out for drinks with me!"

She glanced toward the batter's box, watching Callan take a few practice swings before shifting her intense gaze up to him. "I don't suppose you'd want to up the ante on our wager, would you?"

He knew he should be watching to see if Colt was stealing to third but barely watched as Callan swung and hit a foul. He blinked, his brows lowered, not wanting to give up his chance to have a drink with her. "Change it?" Hearing the crowd cheering in the stands, his head swiveled as he tried to keep an eye on Colt and Callan but mostly focused on Hannah.

"How about if your team wins, I'll take you to dinner?"

His chin jerked back, and he stared at her in

surprise. He knew Callan could hit a home run in the end for a dramatic finish, making his team the winner. His grin widened. "I think you're gonna be taking me to dinner."

A smile spread across her face. "My team won't lose."

He barked out a laugh. "Seriously?"

She leaned forward with her eyes pinned directly on him. Her whispered reply sent her sweet breath across his face. "Absolutely."

Her voice low, the sultry word curled around him, drowning out all the sounds from the players and the crowd. He stared, slack-jawed, and with her lips so close was tempted to bend and claim them. Somewhere in the background a crack sounded, and he realized Callan had hit the ball, but he was unprepared. "Shit!" he yelled, whirling, and starting to run toward second. His hesitation made all the difference, and he was easily tagged out. Three outs. Game over. Hannah's team won.

The players and crowd rushed the field, all cheering, including the losing team. He turned around and around but was unable to find Hannah once they were separated. Kicking himself, he couldn't believe the wager he'd made. *I should've said the loser has to take the winner to dinner, no matter which team it was!* As he wandered around the field determined to find her, he had a new plan. *I'll offer her a congratulatory dinner. Surely, she won't turn that down if she was willing to take me to dinner!* Now, he just had to find her.

Finn's Pub was crowded, most of the Legionnaire ballplayers and their spouses and children filling all the tables and booths, keeping the servers hopping as they brought out pitchers of beer, platters of wings and nachos, pub burgers, and house-cut fries.

The laughter and congratulations amongst the friends flowed as freely as the beer and food, although quite a few razzed Dylan mercilessly for being so distracted on first base.

"What the fuck happened to you, man? Why didn't you get halfway to second base before the hit?"

Rolling his eyes toward his teammates, he said, "I lost my concentration."

"Damn, man, we should've put Hannah on first base for the whole game," Mitch said, his grin wide as he wrapped his arm around Tori, bouncing his son in his lap. "She could've distracted all the single players."

Shooting Mitch's scowl, he hated the idea that Hannah would have flirted with anyone but him.

Feeling a clap on the back, he turned to see Scott standing next to him.

"I feel you, man."

Cocking his head to the side, he waited for Scott to explain.

"Hannah. Smart, driven, pretty. And independent. It takes a lot of work to interest her, but the rewards would be worth it. Take it from someone who now has that."

Dylan smiled as Lizzie Weston slipped under Scott's shoulder, allowing him to wrap his arm around her. He knew Lizzie was not an easy conquest and Scott had had to work to get in there.

"I hear you. And you're right, she's worth it." Sometimes it was hard to not let anyone know that he and Hannah had dated, but then again, if they knew he'd had her and lost her, he'd look like a bigger fool than he already did. "By the way, has anybody seen her? I've been pushing my way through this crowd but haven't had a chance to talk to her."

"She got a call out just as soon as the game was over," Brogan said from close by as he pulled more beers from behind the bar. "Not an emergency, but she was on-call, so it fell to her."

"She complained she was missing her pub burger," Ginny said, a slight smile playing about her lips, lifting her brow in a silent message. "Too bad she had to go hungry."

He offered a chin lift in response and turned his attention back to the good food and good friends, although his mind stayed firmly on the beautiful first baseman who'd distracted him with great finesse. *Hell, she was so close I could almost have kissed her.*

Making his way to the corner of the bar, he pulled out his phone and thumbed his way to his contacts, finding hers. Hesitating, he finally typed out a message.

Congratulations on the win. How about renegotiating the wager?

His finger hovered over the button, uncertainty filling him. Finally, dragging in a ragged breath, he hit send. Hearing his name called out, he looked up and maneuvered through the crowd to the other end of the bar where he stood with more of his friends, laughing and shooting the shit.

After a while, he felt his phone vibrate and his heart lurched just as his pub burger was set in front of him. He knew the message could be anyone, but the possibility that it was Hannah responding had his hand shaking as he slipped his phone out of his pocket and glanced at the screen.

A *winner* should *always* be gracious. We can renegotiate.

The air left his lungs in a rush as his lips spread in a wide smile. Throwing back the rest of his beer, he tossed plenty of bills onto the bar and asked the server to bag his burger. Tossing a wave to his friends, he jogged out into the sunshine with their hardy goodbyes ringing in his ears. Climbing into his truck, he cranked the old engine and wondered what his next move should be. *Call her? Text her? Drive by her station?*

Making his decision, he pulled out onto the road

and headed to his destination, the smile still firmly planted on his lips.

Hannah sighed as she stepped out of her shower. Percy meowed, and she glanced at the cat sitting in her bedroom staring up at her.

"I don't know what you're complaining about," she groaned, walking over and rubbing his head. "I missed the celebration in the pub with everyone. And why? Because I had to be on-call and deal with the puking guest at The Easton Inn." She battled the desire to gag again while thinking about what she'd been doing.

The owner of The Inn had called with the complaint that one of its guests was in the lobby, loudly arguing over their bill. By the time she drove there from Baytown, the owner had barricaded himself in the office while the inebriated, belligerent guest was still yelling and knocking displays over. Marching in, she'd been hit with the smell of bourbon on his breath and ordered him to cease. Ready to take him down if necessary, she was surprised when he turned and stared glassy-eyed at her, then promptly bent forward and threw up all over her pants and shoes. Radioing for the ambulance, she hauled him into a chair after cuffing his hands behind him.

The owner had peeked out from the office and wrinkled his nose. "Who's gonna pay for the cleaning? My reception stinks!"

Shooting a glare his way, she'd said, "Based on whatever rules you got, you can probably charge the cleaning bill to the credit card that he has on file here."

The owner's eyes had gleamed as they widened, and ignoring the mess in front of him, he rushed to his computer. Having no doubt he tripled the guest's credit card charge, she'd shaken her head.

"When you're finished with that, would you mind getting me a towel? Make that two towels."

"Sorry, sorry!" He'd run to the back and then returned with an old towel, handing it to her. "Wow, Chief Freeman, he really got you, didn't he?"

Rolling her eyes, she'd nodded. By the time she'd wiped off the guest's face and hands then used the other towel on herself, the rescue squad had parked outside. "Check him out, and then he's being charged with disorderly conduct and public intoxication."

Hearing another noise at the entrance, she turned and saw Bobby hustling in. "Sorry, Chief. There was a minor car accident on the other end of town, and I'm just getting here."

She'd filled him in on what had happened, and he said, "You go on home. I'll take it from here."

"You sure?"

"Yeah, Chief." Leaning forward, he'd whispered, "Honestly, Hannah, you really stink."

Growling, she'd left Bobby in charge and walked back to her vehicle, rolling down all the windows so it could air out.

Now, out of the shower, she dressed in comfortable clothes before moving to the washing machine where she'd stripped out of her clothes earlier. Dumping them in with the detergent, she started the washing cycle.

Disappointment filled her at having to spend her hour after the game the way she had instead of going to the pub to celebrate the victory and enjoy time with friends. Leaning her hip against her kitchen counter, she knew there was one friend she'd been looking forward to spending time with. *I finally flirt, and now I don't even know what he thought about it.* Sighing heavily, she threw open her refrigerator door, staring inside to see what might look appealing, grumpy that it wasn't a huge pub burger with fries.

A knock sounded on her door, and she tossed a package of deli meat back into the refrigerator. Not expecting anyone, she peeked through her security hole. Seeing the side of Dylan's head as he looked toward her porch swing, she jerked her head back. She hurriedly opened the door and cocked her head to the side. "Dylan? Is everything okay?" Just as the words left her mouth, the grilled beef scent emanating from the bag he held in his hands hit her. Her gaze dropped from his lopsided grin to the bag and then back up. Eyes wide, she asked, "Is that what I think it is?"

"I heard you got called away, and Ginny said you missed your pub burger. In all honesty, they were so busy it was taking a long time to get served and this is one that I ordered. But if you're hungry, I'm more than happy to split it with you."

"Is this the renegotiation of our wager?"

Shaking his head slowly from side to side, his eyes never left hers. "Nah. This is just two friends sharing a burger. The renegotiation involves the loser—which is me—buying the winner—which is you—dinner at a nice restaurant."

They stood silent for a moment, their gazes holding, unspoken words, and longing mixed with uncertainty and curiosity moving between them.

He chuckled and jiggled the bag in his hand. "Hannah, you're truly leaving me holding the bag."

Dropping her chin, she laughed. "Bad pun, but you're right. Come on in." She stepped back and allowed him to cross the threshold, aware that this was the first time he'd been inside her home. *The last time, we sat on the porch.* Not having expected company, her gaze shifted around the room quickly, both pleased that she kept it neat and yet wondering what he thought of her decor.

He handed the bag to her, then turned slowly, taking in the space before his eyes came back to her, a twinkle in their depths. "Wow, Hannah. This is amazing."

Suddenly self-conscious, she shrugged. "I know it's not what most people expect from me."

"I think it's perfect."

Once again they stood, an easy silence moving between them. Seeing sincerity on his face, she nodded. "I'll get plates." She led the way into her small kitchen where a two-seater table sat next to a window. As she grabbed the plates and pulled the massive pub burger from the bag, she noted he settled onto one of the two stools at the counter bar nearby. She cut the large hamburger in half, placing the sections on the plates and dividing the fries. Opening her refrigerator, she grabbed two beers and set them on the counter as well.

Walking around the counter, she hesitated, seeing how much room he took. Knowing they would have been sitting farther apart if he'd gone to the table, she nonetheless slid onto the stool next to him, aware that his leg was now pressing against hers.

He reached his hands out, encircling the half burger, and lifted it to his mouth. Turning, he grinned at her, wiggled his eyebrows, and said, "Eat up."

Taking a large bite, she closed her eyes as the grilled beef, fresh lettuce and tomato, cheese, and whatever special condiment the Pub put on their burger hit her taste buds. She hadn't eaten since breakfast this morning, and now, by midafternoon she was starving. Moaning while chewing, she finally swallowed and said, "This is amazing." Not hearing a response from Dylan, she turned to see him staring at her, his eyes not moving as they focused on her lips. Grabbing a napkin, she wiped her mouth, but he simply shook his head, shifted on his stool, and turned back to his meal.

Soon, the plates were empty, and she felt guilty that he had given her half of his lunch. She climbed off the stool and pulled a pie plate from the refrigerator, jerking back the plastic wrap. "Mrs. Harker brought a chocolate pie into the station a couple of days ago. It's really good, but there's no way I can finish it." She left it on the counter and cocked her head to the side, staring at him.

Laughing, he asked, "Was there a question in there somewhere that I'm supposed to answer?"

"Sorry, I guess I was waiting to see if you wanted any. I don't want to force you to eat chocolate pie if you don't want it."

"I've never turned down a piece of chocolate pie in my life and don't plan on starting now." He grabbed their plates and walked over to the sink, rinsing them off as she cut a small piece for her and a huge piece for him. Instead of sitting back down at the counter, they stood with their hips leaned against the counter and their plates held in their hands. Soon, like the burgers and fries, the pie was gone, and the only sound was the scraping of their forks over the almost-empty saucers.

He rinsed those dishes, too, and left them in the sink to dry, while she placed the last piece in a plastic container and handed it to him. "You can take this home with you."

Their fingers touched as he reached out and took the container from her, the old, familiar tingling tracing patterns up her arm. Jerking her gaze up to his face, it appeared he still felt it, too.

"Thanks… uh… thanks… I'll just—"

"Would you like to stay for a little while?" Her mouth had spoken before her brain warned her to hold back. But now that the words were out, she rushed, "I mean, only if you want to—"

"Yeah. Absolutely, yeah." His smile quirked up on one side.

"Good. Um… I can put this away, and you can take it when you leave." As he let go of the container, she set it back into the refrigerator. Closing the door, she turned and realized she had no idea what to do now.

"I like your house," he said. "It seems like... well, you."

Leading him into the living room, she turned at his words, unable to hide her surprise. "Me? I mean, yeah, to me it seems like *me*, but other people don't think so." Shrugging, she amended, "Not that many people have seen it, but the ones that have aren't very impressed."

She sat down on one end of her royal blue sofa, leaning against a green pillow, and watched as he settled on the other end, twisting his body to face her. She shifted slightly, tucking her right leg underneath her, relaxing against the cushions. He was still looking around the room, and she watched as his gaze drifted from the brightly colored pillows to the patterned rug on the wooden floor, to the knickknacks on the shelves and the pictures on her walls.

"Okay, Dylan, I have to ask. Why do you think it looks like me?"

Turning his attention back to her, he smiled. "Because it's your place away from the job."

He made the statement so matter-of-factly that she blinked. And yet, with those few words, he'd hit the nail on the head.

He continued, "You and I know what it's like to have to be completely in charge at work. We know what it's like to make tough decisions based on law and not emotions. We wear a uniform, a badge, and a weapon. We help people, we see suffering, and often society is not looking fondly on us when we're just trying to do our job the best we can. I know it's hard for me some-times, and I see how Lynette has to work in a male-dominated world and know it's the same for you. Actually, harder for you since you're the Chief."

Her head nodded slowly, his words ringing exactly true. She waited to see what else he would say, and in typical Dylan fashion, he didn't make her wait long.

"So, when you get off work, I imagine that you want a place that has color. Feelings. A little fun. Definitely whimsical." He inclined his head toward a shelf that held her collection of colorful glass figurines—jellyfish, starfish, dolphins. Looking back at her, he grinned. "You surround yourself with things that allow you to just be Hannah when you're not on the job."

A smile spread across her face as she allowed her gaze to drift around the room as he had, looking at the small treasures she'd so lovingly placed in her home. When she looked back at him, she found him staring at her and her grin widened. "You're exactly right. You've described my house and decorations and what they mean to me perfectly." Laughing, she added, "I feel like I should give you a prize!"

"You already are."

Her breath caught in her throat at the serious tone of his words. Her top teeth captured her bottom lip as she tried to still the pounding of her heart.

"So, tell me about the people who come into your house and don't *get it*."

It seemed Dylan was perfectly capable of easing her nerves and getting her to keep talking, and recognizing what he was doing only made it seem nicer. Rolling her eyes, she replied, "My parents only come a couple of times a year, and each time they're just as critical as the first. They've never been happy with my decision to become a police chief in a little town, so I don't think anything I do with my house would please them."

"That's crazy. I mean, I know you'd indicated how they felt back when we were... um... closer, but I just assumed in time that must've gotten better."

Shaking her head, she said, "Oh, my father still feels like I turned down an FBI career for the boonies. I mean, essentially, he's right, but he doesn't understand that this was the right thing for me. At least my brother does, and that helps."

"If I remember correctly, he was a detective in Hope City?"

"He still is. He comes to see me when he can, and I always make sure to see him the few times I visit up there. He's doing well, likes his partner, likes his work. And he understands that this is the life I've chosen for me and is happy that I found satisfaction."

"And what about the other people who see your house?"

Percy had jumped up onto the sofa between them, and she allowed her fingers to drift through his fur as he kneaded her leg with his paws. Shrugging again, she said, "I don't really have people who come by. I have friends, but it's just that I make them slowly. Plus, there's not a lot of time. Honestly, if it wasn't for the other people in law enforcement and the women in the AL, I'd never socialize. I enjoy company, but I guess I'm just not the *'come and have coffee at my house'* kind of person. That makes me sound standoffish, doesn't it?"

Dylan shook his head, his brow lowered. "No, not at

all. I mean, that goes back to what I was saying about our jobs earlier. It's hard to do the job we have and be Chief. There are so many demands piled on top of us that when we have time off, sometimes we just need to be alone."

Once again, Dylan managed to put into words exactly how she felt. Realizing they'd been talking about her, she wanted to know more about him. They had remained friendly over the years without being true friends. And now, she was allowing herself to give in to curiosity. "What about you? I know you talk about helping your family on the fishing boats. I also know you used to talk about building your house."

He rested his arm along the back cushions of the sofa, his fingertips closing around her shoulder. Nodding, he grinned. "My house is fabulous. It took me a long time to build it because I did most of the work myself and only contracted out what I couldn't do. Granted, I had some friends and my brother who helped, but most of it was me. My design, my building."

Leaning slightly forward, she enthused, "That sounds amazing. I can't imagine you having the time to do your job and build a house." He laughed and it hit her how much she loved the sound reverberating in her home.

"That's why it took a long time. I lived in my tiny-ass cottage on the land while building my house."

"You must've been thrilled when you finally moved in."

"As soon as I got the walls, roof, and windows, I

went ahead and moved my bed into the house. I only went back to the cottage for the bathroom and shower!"

Her laughter joined his. "So, kind of roughing it and kind of not."

"Absolutely."

A gentle peace settled between them, the silence was comfortable, not stilted. For a moment she wondered if she could have had this for the last several years if she had only allowed herself. Uncertain of the answer, she discovered she liked him in her house and hoped he would be there more.

"Well, I really should go," he said.

She jumped up and retrieved the plastic container of pie from the refrigerator. Standing at the door, she handed it to him and once more felt the tingle through their touch.

He leaned forward, and for a second, she thought he was going to kiss her. And she knew beyond a shadow of a doubt she would let him. Instead, his lips landed on the top of her head. As he leaned back, she looked into his face, and for a moment thought she saw insecurity. Before she had a chance to ponder that further, he smiled.

"Hannah, I don't know if you're interested, but I really would like to take you to dinner—"

"Yes!"

His chin jerked back as he blinked, but his smile widened. "Yes?"

"Yes. I'd love to have dinner with you."

"Tomorrow is Sunday. Are you working or on-call?"

"No. I'm completely free."

"Well, all right. Consider yourself officially un-free."

Laughter slipped out, and she nodded. "I guess that just leaves two questions. What time and what should I wear?"

His smile slipped, and he said, "Let me figure it out, and I'll text you." He reached out and squeezed her hand as he kissed the top of her head again. Turning, he jogged toward his vehicle, climbing inside. With a wave, he executed a three-point turn and headed out of her driveway.

She watched until his taillights disappeared. Going back into her house, she looked down at Percy and grinned. Then, with no one looking on except her cat, she threw her arms into the air and twirled around the living room.

11

The pleasure of having spent the afternoon with Hannah followed Dylan all the way home. But by the time he entered his house, an uneasy panic set in. *Where the hell should I take her for dinner?* He knew plenty of restaurants in the area, but since asking a woman to dinner was something out of his norm, he had no idea what would be appropriate. The Diner was too casual. So was Finn's Pub. The Easton Historic Inn was considered fine dining, but he didn't want to take her to dinner in the town where she worked as police chief.

Fuck! How can something so simple be so difficult?

Deciding to call and ask someone, he mentally sifted through his many friends, trying to discern who would give him the best advice. Colt would be loyal to The Diner since Carrie worked there. Aiden, Brogan, and Gareth were all associated with Finn's Pub. He tried to think of the women that his friends were married to but was sure that Hannah would prefer none of them to know about their dinner plans.

Out of options, he pulled out his phone and dialed Mitch, hoping he wasn't making a mistake. "Look, I need to ask you a question, but I need you to keep this under wraps. I'm taking Hannah out to dinner tomorrow and need to know a good place."

Just as he thought he would, Mitch gave him an immediate answer without bullshit. "Forget Baytown. Forget Seaside. Forget Easton. You don't want to take her someplace where you'll run into a bunch of people you know. There's a great seafood restaurant in Manteague that's near the water."

Dropping his chin to his chest, he felt the tension ease. Opening his eyes slowly, he said, "Mitch, you're a lifesaver. I want this dinner to be nice, and I don't want to fuck it up."

"Good luck, man. She's a great woman, and it's about time the two of you got together."

He had no idea why the next words left his mouth, but suddenly, he blurted, "We dated for a couple of months after we first moved here. But something happened, and it got all fucked up. We managed to get to a place where we stayed friends and colleagues, but finally, now, it seems like she's giving me another chance."

"Best thing in the world that could happen is when a good woman opens up her heart and lets you in. Nothing wrong with being older and wiser, Dylan."

Mitch's words hit him and he smiled. Thanking him again, Dylan disconnected and breathed a sigh of relief. He knew the restaurant that Mitch had recommended. It was not elegant dining but definitely a step above the

Seafood Shack. Pulling up his contact list, he sent a message to Hannah.

Pick you up at five. We'll go to Robert's Fish n' Grille in Manteague.

His phone rang almost immediately, and he quickly answered without looking at his caller ID. "Hey!" his voice full of enthusiasm.

"Well, hey to you, too," his brother replied, laughing.

"Shit… sorry, David. Whatcha need?"

"I'm down two men for tomorrow's run—"

"It's my day off—"

"I know that. I called Barbara first. That's why I'm calling."

Grimacing, he shook his head at the idea of his family calling the police receptionist to see what his work schedule was—and that Barbara gave out the information.

"It's just for the morning run. Come on, bro. I'm desperate."

Guilt hit him like it always did. Sighing, he scrubbed his hand over his face. "Okay, fine, sure. But just for the morning."

"Thanks, Dylan," David replied before disconnecting.

Still standing, holding his phone, he felt it vibrate in his hand. Figuring his brother was texting, he glanced down then grinned at the incoming message from Hannah. She'd sent a smiling emoji in response to his dinner announcement, but that was all he needed for his own smile to spread across his face. A perfect plan for a perfect date.

"What the fuck do you mean you want to stay out here for two more hours? The deal was a morning run only!"

His brother owned two commercial fishing boats, but it always seemed like he had trouble keeping his crew. Today, besides David steering the boat, he needed two others to let out the nets and haul them back in.

With an eye on the clock, Dylan said, "I've got to be back at my house by four o'clock."

"What the hell for? It's not like you've got a date. Just go to whatever bar you go to and pick up whoever is there."

Clamping his mouth shut, he wondered if his molars would crack with the pressure as he bit down. He might have deserved that remark from his brother in the past, but it had been a long time since he had picked up a one-night stand at a bar.

David stared at him then chuckled. "You're shitting me. You've actually got a date?" Shaking his head, he added, "Look, I'm not trying to fuck up your evening, but I don't get paid if I don't bring in fish."

He nodded, knowing his brother was right. David had always been cool with him, knowing that Dylan never wanted to go into the family business. His brother had often hushed their grandfather when he was ranting about Dylan abandoning the family.

"Don't worry, we're going to go out to deeper water, and we should get enough that this will be a successful run. I've got two new guys that are starting tomorrow, so I'll be back to a full crew."

"Listen, while we're here, I've got a favor to ask. Can you use a strong teenager to help you in the afternoons after school with the catch once you've gotten back to the harbor?"

"Got someone in mind?"

Nodding, he said, "Yeah. Todd Sears. He got into some trouble, and I've been checking up on him. He's smart but acts out. Dealing with his dad who's a prick, I get why."

"You handin' off trouble to me?" David asked. "I can use the help but need to know what I'm taking on."

"Had a chance to talk to him some, and I think he's got potential. Probably won't stick around after high school, but I'd like to see him have some options."

David chuckled. "You didn't stick around either. But it worked out okay for you, didn't it?" He sucked in a deep breath and nodded. "Yeah, send him around."

"Thanks, bro. And if you have any problems with him, come straight to me."

Several hours later, as the net wound upward and the haul came in, Dylan caught David's excitement at seeing how many fish they'd caught. Grinning, he opened the bottom of the net, letting the fish spill all over the deck. David headed the boat toward the harbor while Dylan and the other crew member, Lorenzo, sorted the fish. The good ones were sent down into the hatch and they tossed the excess over the side.

He had grown warm and taken off the slicker, now wishing he'd kept it on the whole time considering that he was wet, sweaty, and smelled like fish. But as long as he had time to get home and shower, it would be fine.

Suddenly, a grinding of gears was heard and the boat engine sputtered to a stop. Dropping his head back, he stared up into the sky, shaking his head back and forth. *You have got to be fuckin' kidding me!*

David came over, fussing and cussing, not wanting their haul of fish to be held up, and all Dylan could think of was that he was going to be late picking Hannah up for their date.

Since Lorenzo had experience with boat engines, he and David disappeared into the engine room leaving Dylan alone on the deck, separating the fish. Another hour passed and he knew he needed to text Hannah to let her know what was happening and that he was going to be late. Pulling out his phone from his pocket with his slippery fingers, he watched in horror as the phone squirted out of his hand, flew over the rail, and dropped into the Atlantic Ocean. "Fuckin' hell!" he screamed, standing at the rail, his gaze pinned on the water as though his phone would suddenly float to the surface.

David popped his head up from below. "What's the matter?"

"I lost my fuckin' phone! Dropped it in the goddamn water!"

David scowled. "Shit, man, I thought you cut your hand off!"

"Let me borrow your phone so I can at least text Hannah to tell her I'm going to be late."

David climbed up and stomped over the deck, tossing a towel toward Dylan. "Dry your hands first. I don't want my phone to go over the side too."

"You know you're going to have to buy a new phone for me."

"You're getting paid for today. Just use that for a new phone."

Throwing his hands up into the air, he argued, "I need a new fuckin' phone because I'm helping you out!" He looked down at David's phone, then realized he hadn't memorized Hannah's number. It was only by sheer will that he didn't throw David's phone overboard as well.

Suddenly, the engine turned over, chugging noises coming from the engine room. He and David barely breathed for a few seconds as their eyes stayed pinned on the door, then finally, the engine began running in full.

David raised his fists into the air and shouted hallelujah before running back to the bridge. Dylan would've done the same if he wasn't so tired.

It took another hour to get back to the harbor, unload the fish, and pack them on ice. As soon as that was done, David urged, "Go, go! Hopefully, she'll forgive you!"

Flipping his laughing brother off, Dylan jogged to his truck. With no way to contact Hannah, he wasn't sure what to do. Not wanting to keep her waiting for an explanation any longer, he drove straight to her house. Glancing at the clock on the dashboard, he pounded the steering wheel when he saw that it was almost six o'clock. His shirt and pants were wet. His hair was sweaty and plastered against his head. And he smelled disgustingly like fish.

Stopping outside her bungalow, he sat for a moment and debated turning around and driving back home. A movement in front of him caught his eye, and he watched as Hannah stepped out onto her front porch, her fists on her hips. A wraparound dress in emerald green, looking both beautiful and comfortable, showcased her figure. He had no idea what shoes she'd planned on wearing to dinner because now she was barefoot. Her hair had been styled to flow around her shoulders, and as his gaze drifted to her unsmiling face, he swallowed deeply. Now, more than ever, he considered turning around and driving home.

Refusing to take the coward's way out, he climbed down from his truck and walked toward her. The closer he got, the more her nose wrinkled, and her eyes widened.

"Dylan! Where have you been, and why do you smell like that?"

He stopped well short of her porch, not wanting to move any closer, wishing he was not downwind. "I'm so fuckin' sorry, Hannah. I promised my brother that I'd work on his boat this morning, and he turned it into an all-day-long fishing expedition since the morning run yielded such a small amount. Then the fucking engine died and we were stuck out in the ocean. I was the one who had to deal with the fish, and I knew I was going to be late and tried to call you, but my phone slipped out of my hands and went in the water."

For a few seconds, her face held his gaze, showing no emotion. Then suddenly, she threw her head back and laughed, her arms wrapped around her stomach, clenching her middle. "Oh, my God! I totally believe you! First of all, no one could make up a story like that, and second of all, you really do stink!"

Unable to keep a grin from sliding across his face, he said, "I can't believe I fucked up our date. But I don't have a phone, I'm going to have to spend part of tomorrow buying a new one, and there's no way I can get back to my place to shower and then come back here and pick you up to get to Manteague for dinner."

Hannah couldn't remember the last time she'd laughed so hard. And she certainly never expected Dylan to be the cause of her mirth. Seeing him so bedraggled and smelly with regret clearly worn on his face, the irritation that had been building when he was late to pick her up completely fled, leaving only pleasure in knowing he truly wanted to be with her.

She pondered the situation for a moment, then shrugged. "If you want to shower here, you can as long as you don't mind having to wear a ratty old bathrobe. At least you wouldn't have to go home."

He cocked an eyebrow and snorted. "I'm supposed to go to dinner in a ratty old bathrobe?"

"Well, maybe that's appropriate attire at the Fish n' Grille."

The expression on his face could not hide his incredulity, and she burst into laughter again. It was rare that she was able to say something so spontaneous that it took him by surprise. Adopting a laissez-faire expression while crossing her arms over her chest, she tapped her foot. "Well?"

Shaking his head, he said, "I want to take you to dinner tonight more than anything, Hannah, but I can't see myself doing it in a bathrobe." He looked over his shoulder toward his truck and sighed as he turned back to her. "I've got some shorts and a T-shirt in my truck. I can change into those. At least I'd be decent, but it won't exactly fit for the dinner I had planned."

Her top teeth grabbed her bottom lip to keep from grinning. "We're not getting off to a great start on our date, are we?" Her smile slipped out despite her best efforts, and she asked, "How about a change of plans?"

"Wow, are you turning into Miss Spontaneous on me?"

"Seems like I am. Look, you can shower here and change into your clothes, and then we can find something else to do." Another cocked eyebrow had her rushing to explain. "I mean to do for dinner. You know, eat. Food. Eat food!" She reached out and slapped his shoulder as he continued to smirk and wiggle his eyebrows at her suggestions. "Oh, you're impossible." Plopping her fists onto her hips, she added, "Actually, right now, you're just wet and stinky as well as impossible!"

His smile softened as he held her gaze. "I don't want this evening to end, so I'm up for whatever you want to do, Hannah. I'm just glad you're not kicking my ass out."

"I've got some wine, beer, deli meat and cheese, even some fruit. Oh, and I bought a nice loaf of bread from the bakery in Easton. While you shower and change clothes, I'll throw together a picnic. The weather is cool enough we can drive over to the beach." As the words left her mouth, a snake of unease moved through her. What she had just suggested sounded wonderful to her, but to other people, it might seem lame. Forcing her gaze to not leave his face, she watched as his smile spread wider and his eyes lit.

"God, that sounds perfect."

Trying not to let her sigh of relief sound so audible, she met his smile with one of her own. "Okay, go grab your stuff. I'll see if I can find some soap that's less girly scented."

"I don't care what I smell like as long as I don't stink like fish."

She watched as he turned and jogged to his truck, pulling out a small bag. As he walked back to her front porch, his footsteps slowed. Wondering if he'd changed his mind, she asked, "Anything wrong?"

"Just having my clothes in your house is going to stink."

"Go around to the back door which leads straight to the laundry room. You can strip off your clothes and dump them into the washing machine, and I'll stay in the kitchen until you get to the bathroom. As soon as I hear the shower go off, then I can start the washing machine so your clothes can get washed. That will keep the stink to a minimum."

Chuckling, he shook his head again. "You're one seriously amazing woman. It's like there's no situation that you can't figure out the perfect solution for."

Rolling her eyes, she waved dismissively. "Go. I'll meet you around back."

He turned with his bag and started around the house. Closing the front door, she darted down the hall and met him at the back door. Throwing it open, she invited him in and lifted the lid to the washing machine. There was very little room for two people to move around, and the heightened awareness she had of his close body filled the space with electricity. Grabbing a towel that had just come out of the dryer, she handed it to him, trying to keep her voice from sounding breathy. "You can put all your clothes in the washer and then close the lid." She pointed down the hall and said, "The kitchen is through here. The two bedrooms are just off this hall. There's only one full bathroom."

"I can find it, thanks." He lifted his hand as though to place it on her arm then hesitated, wrinkling his nose.

She laughed and shook her head. "I'll be in the kitchen getting things ready. Catch you on the clean side!" She walked out of the laundry room and into the kitchen, making sure to keep her back to where he would be stripping. She tried to keep her mind off what he would look like naked, but it was difficult. His clothes had been so wet it was easy to see the definition of his muscles. Not like it was the first time she had ever seen them. In the last three years, she'd seen him shirtless at ball games or a variety of other times they'd been with friends.

Hurrying into the kitchen, she was grateful when the water of the shower began. Her shoulders slumped in relief only to be quickly replaced by the idea of him being completely naked in her house. Leaning forward, she banged her head on the refrigerator door, hoping to knock some sense into herself. *Jesus, it's not like I never had anyone before... even if it's been a long time.* The truth was, though, even if she'd never had sex with Dylan, he was still unforgettable.

Determined to distract herself from the mental images of him in her shower, she threw open the refrigerator door and began pulling out the food items necessary. Making sandwiches, she wrapped them in plastic and placed them into her wicker picnic basket. The large basket was an impulse buy at one of the Auxiliary yard sales. Rarely going on picnics, it had seemed a ridiculous purchase, and she almost gifted it to someone but chose to keep it. She'd thought what a wonderful basket it would be to take on a picnic someday but was afraid that it might not ever get used. Now, a chance to use it with Dylan made her glad she'd kept it.

Adding plastic containers of cheese and crackers, she also packed several cold beers and a bottle of Moscato wine with two plastic, stemless wine glasses. By then, she heard the water turn off and rushed into the laundry room to dump detergent into the washing machine. Pressing the start button, she was pleased that the smell of fish had not permeated her house.

Back in the kitchen, she finished putting the basket together. Hearing a noise behind her, she turned around and saw Dylan, his wet hair having been swept to the side with his fingers, a tight blue Seaside PD T-shirt and cargo shorts completing his outfit. As her gaze continued downward, she noticed his feet in flip-flops, looking strangely sexy. *How can a man's feet covered in nothing but a few straps of leather look so amazingly sexy?*

He cleared his throat and her gaze jumped back to his face. A blush raged across her cheeks, and she spied the familiar smirk coming from him. Shrugging her shoulders, she grinned. "What can I say? You were always gorgeous, Dylan, and still are."

His eyes widened, and his cheeks heated. "Damn, Hannah. I was just thinking the same thing about you."

Laughing, she inclined her head toward the basket and said, "I think I've got everything in there. Are you ready to head to the beach for our date?"

"You know, I feel like I should apologize for messing everything up, and yet I'm looking forward to just spending time with you however we do it."

Her reply was a smile, not sure any words were necessary. He grabbed the basket as she locked the back door and they walked out the front. She hesitated, looking at his old truck. "Um... is it going to smell like fish—"

"Oh, shit!"

A beleaguered hound dog expression crossed his face and she couldn't help but reach out to place her hand on his arm. "Come on. I think your manhood won't take a hit if you ride in my car."

"How about we use your car and I drive?"

Narrowing her eyes in mock anger, she asked, "You don't like being driven by a woman?"

"I don't mind at all, but I'd like to salvage some of my masculinity on this date."

Throwing her head back in laughter again, she tossed her keys toward him. "I'm all for saving your masculinity, but at least you're not wearing my robe."

Ten minutes later, they drove to the end of a sandy lane and parked near a dune on the Bay.

"This is one of the places I like to come to in the mornings for a run or a swim. Sometimes, I come at night and watch the sunset."

"And are you usually alone?" he asked.

She heard his question but wasn't ready to answer. "Actually, I like to run alone," was her only reply, knowing he wasn't asking about just running. Grateful he let the conversation drop, they walked over the dune and found a perfect spot to picnic.

He had grabbed the basket and the blanket from her hands when they left the car and now spread it out over the sand. Sitting, she tucked her legs to the side and sucked in a deep breath of fresh air before letting it out slowly. When she'd suggested this be their date-night alternative plan, she'd simply thought in terms of not being able to go to the restaurant. But now, her mind was filled with the last time they'd been on a blanket on the beach together over three years ago.

Needing something to do, she opened the basket and began pulling out items, placing them on paper plates. "I didn't know what you might like. Sandwiches, grapes, and apples... oh, I forgot, here's a beer."

Still looking into the basket, she handed the beer to the side, jolting when his fingers moved over hers. Whipping her head around, she found his eyes pinned on her. The same feelings that had always moved

147

through her, the tingling that electrified her body and the pull of magnetism from his gaze, had her breath catching in her throat.

"You can relax, Hannah," he said in a soft voice. "It's just us. No pressure. Just us."

She nodded slowly, offering a little smile. "Sorry, I guess I got a little nervous."

"That's the last thing I want you to be."

She let go of the beer and placed more food items on the blanket between them. Sitting side-by-side with their legs stretched out in front of them, they began to eat and drink. The conversation flowed, comfortable and easy.

"I remember you saying your grandfather had been ill. Is he better?" she asked, munching on an apple slice.

Shaking his head, he replied, "No, not really. He had a stroke about six months ago and was partially paralyzed. Along with dementia, he doesn't really know where he is, but at least he's not in pain anymore."

"I'm so sorry. I know that's hard."

"It's true the old man never cut me any slack, and until his last breath will always consider me to be the family traitor, but I never wished him any ill."

"I'm sure he's probably much prouder of you than you can imagine."

Staring out over the water, he turned and looked toward her. "You think?"

Shrugging, she said, "To be honest, I don't know. I suppose I'd like for you to have that peace."

"Coming from the voice of experience?"

Shaking her head, a rueful chuckle slipped out. "Yeah, I guess it is."

"I kept thinking that one day my grandfather would look at me wearing my uniform with the chief insignia on my shirt and clap me on the back, saying, 'By God, Dylan you did it. You made something of yourself.'" He shook his head quickly and turned toward her, amending, "Not that there's anything wrong with being a fisherman. It was his, my dad's, and my brother's calling. But it would have been nice for my grandfather to have seen that a calling into law enforcement was something to be proud of, also."

"I understand. I keep hoping that eventually my dad will realize that while law enforcement was our shared career goal, we simply had two different tracks to follow."

She was quiet for a moment, still sitting with her legs stretched out in front of her, a wineglass in one hand and her weight resting on her other arm as she leaned back with her palm on the blanket. He was sitting similarly, and their fingertips barely touched. Warmth moved over her. She stared out of the water for a moment before turning her head toward him. "Do you think that parents are destined to have grand plans for their children and then struggle when the children grow up and have different ideas?"

"I don't know. I know my dad would have loved for me to have gone into the family business with my brother, and while he's never come out and said he was proud of me, he also never made me feel like I stabbed him in the back. My mom? She's really cool. She always told me to be whatever I wanted to be."

Laughing, she said, "I don't think I'd want one of my children to go into law enforcement. It's a tough career, not easy for a woman, and I'd be fine if they wanted to write books or paint houses." Snorting, she added, "Of course, they'd probably want to go into law enforcement, and then I'd have to deal with the fear for them."

"You'll make a wonderful mom."

She opened her mouth, then looked at the sincerity staring back at her and snapped her mouth closed. Uncertain what to say, she offered a little smile and turned her attention toward the water. The sun sank lower in the sky, casting brilliant colors of orange and pink streaking through the blue.

"I always loved sunsets," Dylan said. "Even when I was a kid, but especially in the Navy. I could be busy as hell all during the day but would try to take a moment to watch part of the sunset no matter where I was, thinking about it sinking over the Chesapeake Bay."

She shoulder-bumped him and laughed. "Somehow I never thought of you as someone who'd enjoy the simple pleasure of the sunset, but now that I think about it, it fits you."

He twisted slightly, now facing her, and lifted his free hand slowly toward her face, not stopping until it rested against her soft skin. His thumb swept over the apple of her cheek.

Time stood still as though the world had stopped turning. From far away, she heard the gulls cry, but it was as though her entire existence was focused on the feel of his hand cupping her face. His fingertips gripped the back of her head, drawing her ever so slightly toward him. Their gazes never wavered as they grew closer.

When there was the barest distance between their lips, he said, "I want to kiss you. I've wanted to kiss you for a very long time."

Staring into his eyes, she saw memories pass by... the first time they met, their first kiss, the break-up, the ensuing friendship and camaraderie, the longing and desire that was never truly pushed to the background. There were no words to speak, so she closed the distance and kissed him.

The kiss began hesitantly but not uncertain. More like a slow, gentle exploration. Soft and strong. Silk and steel. The delicate mixing tastes of beer and wine, grapes and cheese. His scent filled her senses, a combination of the soap he'd used and his own masculine essence.

The kiss was familiar and yet so new, almost as though every movement was both his asking for permission and celebrating her response. Gone was the cocky, sure-of-himself man. This Dylan, who angled his head to take the kiss deeper, was confident, and yet she felt as though the kiss was full of reverence.

As his lips continued to move over hers and his tongue swept through her mouth, all thoughts left her mind other than the tingle that moved from her lips to her breasts to her core. She wanted this man. She had wanted this man for a long time.

They shifted closer, and he eased her onto her back,

careful to keep her body on top of the blanket and cradle her head with his arm, holding her tight. As her thoughts fled, she was left in a puddle of want and desire.

After an unknown passage of time, he lifted his head from hers. The sound of him dragging a ragged breath deep into his lungs filled her ears, and her eyes opened to see agony crossing his face. She reached up, smoothing her hand over his face, but before she had a chance to ask him what was wrong, he gazed out toward the water and then looked back down at her.

"I want you, Hannah. I've wanted you for so fuckin' long. Ever since I first met you."

It was on the tip of her tongue to give in to the yearnings even though they were lying where anyone could walk by. But he didn't give her that chance.

His smile warmed her deep inside, and he said, "I want to do this right. I never meant for things to get fucked up years ago and I know I hurt you. If I could, I'd shield you from any hurt... even from me."

"I want to do this right, too," she replied, although at the moment she had no idea exactly what she meant by the word *right*.

The sun finished dropping into the horizon over the water, casting shadows about them. He assisted her back to a seated position, kissing her again, only this time much lighter and shorter. Still holding her gaze, he said, "Here's what we're going to do. Pack up the basket, and I'll take you back home. And I'll kiss you goodnight on your porch, and then I'll leave."

She opened her mouth to ask him to stay, but he placed his finger over her lips, stilling her words.

"Not tonight. I don't want to do anything to fuck this up."

"I need to let you know, though," she said, her lips still mumbling against his fingertip. "I want you, too. Even though we called a halt for tonight, I still want you." She watched as the corner of his mouth quirked upward in his familiar smile.

"Okay, tomorrow night, dinner out. Put on the dress you were wearing earlier, and I promise to pick you up on time."

She nodded, and it hit her that she would have agreed to almost any suggestion he made. And that thought didn't bother her at all.

Dylan parked in one of the few available parking spots near the Seaside Harbor. Trucks with empty boat trailers filled the area along with the cars and trucks of the commercial fishermen who were now out on their boats.

He lifted his face toward the sky, the beautiful fall day just cool enough to keep the sun from burning. Shifting his gaze back toward the ocean, he hoped his brother's boats were holding on to their repairs and the fishing was good.

As he walked toward the small building nestled between the harbor and The Wharf Restaurant, his thoughts continually drifted off his job and onto Hannah. Their salvaged impromptu date of a picnic on the beach had turned out to be more than he could have imagined. A chance to reconnect on a personal level, much deeper than the relationship they'd fallen into over the past several years, more reminiscent of what he'd hoped they would become before everything fell apart.

She was beautiful when he first met her, but now there was an added confidence that probably came from several years of being the Police Chief under her belt. No longer having anything to prove, especially to the townspeople that might've thought a woman couldn't handle the job, she'd blossomed. And it was sexier than hell.

Arriving at the door, he jerked his thoughts back to the business at hand. He rapped on the doorframe. "Owen... got a minute?"

"Chief Hunt, good morning. Come on in."

He stepped into the small office and grinned at the man sitting behind the desk. Or at least the wooden table that served as a desk. Papers piled high in stacks that appeared to make no sense, walls covered with old calendars, post-it notes that had long since faded, and shelves that were loaded with more papers and notebooks, the wood having permanently bent under the weight. The man sitting behind the desk was an imposing figure, having been born and raised in Seaside, knowing both the fishing and the restaurant business. Owen Owens.

The first time he'd heard the man's name, he couldn't believe that any parent had decided to give their child a first name that matched the last name. He could only imagine the teasing Owen had taken when he was younger. It probably helped that he was a big man, and perhaps that kept the childhood teasing to a minimum.

Dressed in his usual attire of khaki shorts paired with heavy boots and a thick, cotton shirt, Owen kept a cap on his head to protect his bald pate, having only a little hair on the sides that grew long and stuck out at odd angles from the salty wind.

Owen's family, like Dylan's, had been fishermen from way back, but Owen's grandfather had been the harbormaster, building it up and making improvements. Owen's father became the same but also started a small fish and crab restaurant right next to the harbor, making it easy to obtain fresh seafood. By the time Owen reached adulthood and took over, the restaurant had been enlarged and improved, named The Wharf, and had a reputation that brought in diners from all over the Eastern Shore.

"Take a load off, Chief," Owen insisted.

Nodding his thanks, Dylan settled onto a small chair squeezed into the corner. "Know you're busy, so I'll keep this short." Receiving Owen's chin lift, he launched into his concerns. "With Seaside's harbor reputation, you're doing a great business with lots of boats coming in and out on a daily and weekly basis. I know it's also brought in a lot of new traffic, from recreational fishing to recreational boaters. We've heard from other law enforcement that small harbors are being used by drug runners, and I'm just trying to get a handle on the situation, hopefully before it comes to Seaside or at least to stop it quickly."

Owen's heavy brow lowered, and he leaned forward, placing his beefy forearms onto the top of his desk. "The hell you say." He huffed loudly, turning his gaze toward the doorway and shook his head. "My grand-pappy would roll over in his grave if he even thought something like that was happening."

Dylan remembered Owen's grandfather as being a man even larger than Owen, if that was possible. His lips curved slightly, knowing full well that if the older man were still alive, he'd be cussing a blue streak. "I know. It's hard to imagine something like that touching our little Nowheresville town. I just don't want drug runners to get a strong toehold by using our harbor."

"I've got a feeling you're going to ask me if I've seen anything suspicious. 'Course, if I had, I'd have already come to you. But then, I haven't been looking for anything suspicious. You're right, we got a lot of new people coming and going from here. Visitors from all over, some out of state, coming here to launch their boats. Take a look at the parking lot and you'll see Pennsylvania, New York, New Jersey, North Carolina, Maryland tags are all prevalent, but there's also a helluva lot more. Can you give me a hint at what I ought to be looking for?"

"It would be nice to think that it would just be people traveling under the cover of darkness that would stand out, but from what I've been told, it can be as simple as someone coming in on a boat during the light of day, meeting up with somebody in the parking lot—"

"Well, damn, Chief, that can be just about anyone."

Dylan dragged his hand through his hair, pushing it off to the side. "I know, and it sucks. What I wanted to ask is what kind of security cameras do you have around here? I know you've got some on the restaurant, what about the harbor?"

"Well, you know we had some trouble a couple of years back, so I did have a couple of security cameras put in. I've got one that's directed onto the back area of the restaurant, wanting to make sure no one's trying to slip in at night. I've also got one that's up on the corner of the restaurant, but it aims down toward the boating gas pumps to make sure no one's messing with those either."

Nodding, Dylan pondered the angles of the cameras, wondering how best they could capture more of the harbor. "I know those are your private cameras, Owen, and we both know there's no damn money in the town's budget for more. If I can take a look at them and figure out a way that with just an angle change we could make sure that the back of the restaurant and the gas pumps are still in view but also maybe some more of the harbor, would you be amenable to that?"

"Got no problem with that, Chief. Hell, if you can figure out a way to capture more of the harbor with what I've got, that works for both of us. I'll have a better chance of seeing what's going on and you have a chance of catching anybody coming in doing something they shouldn't."

The two men stood, and he reached out to take the large hand extended toward him, shaking it firmly. "I'm obliged, Owen."

"We're in this together, Chief." Owen walked around his desk and clapped Dylan on the back as they stepped back out into the sunshine. They walked to the back of the restaurant and into the cool interior. "Don't know if you've met Manuel Valesquez. He's the restaurant manager and the security equipment is in his office. He's out checking on the deliveries right now, but I'll send him a message that you'll be taking a look at the cameras. He's a good man and will help you out."

Once again expressing gratitude, Dylan watched as Owen turned to walk away and then stopped. Looking over his shoulder, Owen said, "You've been doing this job for several years now, and I don't think I've ever said this to your face, although I've said it plenty of times behind your back. You're doing a damn good job."

It might not have come from his grandfather, but hearing the words come from a man he respected caused his lips to curve upward even more.

It only took a couple of minutes for Manuel to arrive in the office wearing a Wharf Restaurant polo and khaki pants. His wide smile was bright against his tanned face, and his handshake was firm.

"Chief Hunt, good to meet you. I got a message from Owen telling me what you'd like to do." He moved to a computer screen and began clicking through the security program, showing Dylan where to find the digital feeds, even going so far as to give him the password. "During business hours, my office isn't locked, so if you or any of your officers need to check things, you certainly can. If it's after hours, I live close by. I'll give you my cell phone number, and I can come by just about any time to let you in. In fact, if Owen wants, he can give you a key to this office as well."

"I appreciate this, Manuel. If you don't mind, I'm

gonna call one of my other officers, and we're gonna work on changing the angle of the cameras just slightly to see if we can get more of the harbor."

"Not a problem, Chief Hunt. I'll be in and out of the office while I'm taking care of things for the restaurant, so make yourself at home."

Calling Barbara, he asked if she could check to see if either of the on-duty officers were available to come to the back of the restaurant to assist.

"Looks like Joe's available," she said. "I'll send him right over."

It only took five minutes for Joe to arrive, and they looked over the security feeds in more detail, noting that the two cameras were directed exactly as Owen had said.

"This one has such a wide angle that if we turn it more toward the harbor, we can get the pump area on one side and still be able to see quite a bit of the comings and goings at the harbor. The one at the back of the restaurant could easily be angled to still watch the delivery door while going over to where the pumps are."

Joe nodded and said, "I'll ask Manuel for a ladder for me to use. I'll get up and move the cameras, and you can radio to let me know if I get them into the right place."

For the next couple of hours, he and Joe continued to study the angles of the cameras and then tweaked them to offer a better view of the whole harbor. They were unable to get the entire view on security feed but satisfied they were better off than they'd been before, they called it quits. While Joe replaced the ladder, he shook Manuel's hand, thanking him for his cooperation.

Walking back to the harbor, Dylan and Joe stopped, their gazes cast over the area, before Joe asked, "Do you think it'll help?"

"I don't know, but we don't have enough eyes to be able to keep track of everything coming and going here, especially since some of the drug handoffs are purported to be done in the middle of the day, practically under everyone's nose."

"Could we get some of our regular fishermen to help keep an eye out?"

Dylan stood on the floating pier, the undulating movement underneath his feet as familiar to him as solid ground. He thought about David and what his brother's reaction would be if he asked him to keep his eyes open for unusual activity. Scrubbing his hand over his face, he shook his head. "I just don't know. They're hard-working, their minds always need to be on the task, and I hate to ask anything from them. On the other hand, our local fishermen are in and out of the harbor, they know who's familiar, at least when it comes to other fishing boats. Recreational boats? I don't know how much they'd notice."

"Would it hurt to ask your brother about it?" Joe hastened to add, "I don't mean to suggest you say or do anything that would be awkward with your own brother. I just thought maybe you could bring it up with him to see what he thought."

Nodding, he agreed. "Yeah, I thought about that. At least I can get an idea from him if he or any of the other local fishermen would be receptive to keeping an eye out."

Joe tossed his hand up in a wave before he left, and right on cue, Dylan saw his brother's boat coming into the harbor. With no other calls pulling at his attention, he stood on the pier and waited. Giving his brother plenty of time to get docked and to take care of his catch, he stayed out of their way. As soon as he had a chance, David jogged over.

"Hey, bro. I figured if this was an emergency, you'd say something."

"Yeah, I just wanted to talk to you about something but didn't want to interrupt your work. We don't have to talk now, we can do it later."

"Do you want to come over for dinner tonight? You know Alice always fixes enough to feed an army."

Losing the battle to hide his grin, he nodded. "'Fraid I've got something going on tonight, but we can easily talk tomorrow."

David looked over his shoulder toward his boat and then said, "I've got a full crew today, and they're fine. If you don't mind me getting a beer, we can move over in the shade and talk right now."

With a chin lift acknowledging his brother's easy request, he waited as David gave the last instructions to his crew, grabbed a beer from the cooler, and walked into the shade at the side of the building. It didn't take long for Dylan to explain the situation concerning drug runners using small harbors. As he talked, he watched David's jaw tighten and his eyes flash.

"This kills me, you know? The last thing I want is for

drugs coming through this area. Hell, I don't want my sons around that shit. But I reckon you're telling me this for a reason."

He pointed to the security cameras that Owen had installed and explained how he'd altered their angles slightly so that he could get a better view of the harbor. "The town's got no money for cameras just for the harbor, and Owen is doing us a huge favor by letting us have access to his private security. We can't get it all, but it helps. My question is this: Do you think any of the local fishermen would be willing to keep their eyes open for unusual activity? I'm not talking about anybody policing anything. I'm not talking about anybody playing cops and robbers or going after anyone suspicious. I'm simply talking about notifying us if they see something that doesn't look right to them. But I need you to be honest with me, David—"

"Hell, yeah, Dylan!" David jerked his hand out toward the harbor in the water beyond. "This is our backyard. This is our playground and our workplace. This is our livelihood. And anyone that lives in this area and works here wants to do anything they can to keep that shit out."

Feeling a weight lift off his chest, he grinned. Clapping David on the back, he said, "Okay, here's what we're going to do. I'm going to talk to Sheriff Hudson and a few of the others. I'm going to come up with what we think would be the right way to go about this within the next couple of days, and then we'll get the word out."

"Chief Hunt?"

At the sound, he turned and observed Todd approaching, his eyes wary.

Nodding, he said, "Perfect timing. Todd, I'd like you to meet my brother, David. He runs Hunt Fishing. He's agreed to take you on as a part-time employee after school, here in the harbor."

For a few seconds, he could see the wide-eyed surprise in the teen's expression before doubt settled over his features. True to their agreement, Todd had stopped by the station most afternoons. At first full of suspicion, he'd slouched in a chair, mumbling his responses to Dylan's questions. Dylan still had no idea if Todd's father was abusive or just demanding, but over time, the teen relaxed, and they talked.

"I've only worked in the tackle shop," Todd admitted, jutting out his chin in defiance of his self-doubt.

"Don't have to know anything about commercial fishing," David piped up. "I need someone reliable, someone who's not afraid of hard work, and someone who wants to make money."

At the mention of money, Todd's eyes lit and interest sparked. "What do I have to do?"

"See those men over there?" When Todd turned and looked at David's crew emptying the catch and putting it on ice, David continued. "If you're here after school, that's about when we get in. I can always use an extra pair of hands. After the catch is squared away, we need to hose down the boats and get everything ready to go out the next day. My day starts early, and I don't have time to waste getting everything ready in the mornings."

Dylan stayed quiet. If Todd was going to accept or turned down the offer, it had to be his own decision.

Finally, with a quick nod of his head, Todd agreed. "Yeah, sure. I don't mind hard work and I'd like to make some money." He jerked his gaze quickly over toward Dylan. "Uh... my dad?"

"I'll square this with your dad. The money you make from this job is yours, but make sure you get all your homework done, and do the best you can here as well."

Shrugging, Todd said, "School is easy. I'll have no problem keeping up with that." Lifting his shoulders, he looked at David and stuck out his hand. "I appreciate the offer, Mr. Hunt."

Dylan's chest swelled with pride, and he fought to keep the grin off his face. Accepting Todd's chin lift as he waved goodbye, he watched the young man jog back to his vehicle.

"You used to pick up strays, bro. Looks like that still happens," David laughed, finishing his beer before chucking it into Owen's recycle bin.

Giving in to his smile, he waved as his brother ambled toward his boat. Having run out to buy a new phone that morning, he glanced at the screen, relieved to see there was no message from Hannah calling off their date. Excited to see that his workday had come to an end, he radioed Barbara and then headed home.

14

Her day had been average, for which Hannah was exceedingly grateful. Paperwork, patrols, staff meeting, and a quick check-in with the Mayor. The last item on her list before going home was to drop off paperwork with the magistrate, whose office was in the jail.

Entering, she went through the usual security checks, then down the hall to Marcus Kranski's office. A handsome, dark-skinned man with a ready smile, he grinned as she walked in.

"Hannah, nice to see you. Have you got something for me?"

"I needed to drop these by. It's the updated charges for Jonas Smith who was brought in this morning."

"This is my day to have the chiefs come by," he said, taking the paperwork from her and giving it a cursory glance. "Dylan was here this morning."

She had felt on edge ever since last night when Dylan kissed her. All day long, her body had hummed. At first, she wondered if she had a temperature, praying she wasn't getting sick. But the vibrating electricity that moved throughout her whole body flared every time her thoughts turned to him. Now, hearing his name, she felt the vibrations increase. Pushing those thoughts down, she merely smiled at Marcus, considering her brain had short-circuited and she couldn't think of anything to say. Relieved that he didn't notice her lack of response, his gaze stayed on the paperwork.

Looking up, he nodded. "Everything looks fine here. I'll take care of it."

With a chin lift, she called out, "Thanks," and walked out of his office. Rounding the corner, she ran into Luke. Having not seen him since he first started working, she smiled. "Hello, Luke. We've met, but I'm sure you've met so many people it's hard to keep their names straight."

He nodded, his lips barely quirking in an almost-not-there smile. "Yes, Ma'am. I remember you. It's nice to see you again, Chief Freeman."

He didn't give the impression that he had a desire to continue the conversation, so she simply nodded and wished him well. Walking out of the jail, she glanced at the time and smiled. Her day was over, and she could go home and get ready for her date, hoping nothing untoward was going to interrupt again.

Driving home, she thought about the previous evening. Surprised when Dylan had kissed her, she had to admit the kisses from last night were so much more than what she'd remembered from years before. *Were we so very different back then?* Snorting, she knew the answer. While she was not closed off to love, she certainly guarded her heart more since then.

And Dylan? While he'd earned a reputation as a flirt, she hadn't heard his name associated with any one woman. And he'd certainly shown the residents of Seaside that he was more than capable of leading their police force.

An hour later, she stood in front of her mirror, filled with a sense of déjà vu. Her hair was styled, her makeup light, and the green wrap dress was once again show-casing her figure. She had thought about changing into an outfit Dylan hadn't seen, but he'd requested she wear the dress she was going to wear on their original date.

Glancing at the clock, it was almost time for him to arrive and she hoped the feelings of déjà vu would come to an end. But, knowing that anything could happen in their job, she hated the idea of another evening spent pacing in her living room, wondering if he was going to come.

A knock on the door jolted her out of her musings, and she rushed from her bathroom, through her bedroom, and to the front door. Throwing it open, she smiled at the sight. Standing in front of her, fresh from a shower, wearing navy slacks and a collared shirt with the sleeves rolled over his forearms, Dylan grinned as he pressed a riot-of-colors bouquet into her hands.

Unable to keep from squealing, she buried her nose as she inhaled the flowers' delicate scent. Lifting her eyes to catch his gaze, she smiled. "You didn't have to bring me flowers, but this is so nice. Come on in." She turned and led him inside, going directly to the kitchen to get a vase. Filling it with water, she arranged the stems, thrilled with the simple gift.

Turning, she found him right behind her. His hands encircled her waist as her arms lifted to place her fingers around his neck. And in a movement that seemed so natural, she lifted on her toes as he bent, and their lips met. He kept the kiss short and light. She smiled as he lifted his lips from hers and gently kissed the end of her nose.

"I've been thinking of doing that all day," he said. "In fact, it's the only thing that got me through this day... hoping that I'd be lucky enough to kiss you again."

"I've thought about this all day, too," she confessed. "As I was getting ready, I felt a little foolish putting on the same outfit from last night—"

"No, you look exactly the way I wanted you to look. You were so beautiful when I arrived last night, and I hated to disappoint you. Of course, our evening was salvaged in the end, thanks to you. But I wanted to arrive tonight and see you in the green dress, and in my mind, I could pretend that it was our original date."

She shook her head in emphasis and said, "No, I think it's better that this isn't our original date. Last night was great, Dylan. We relaxed. We laughed. We talked. We shared more about each other. We're not the same people we were when we first met four years ago, and even though we know so much about each other, I think it was nice to just have some alone time to learn more."

His arms had stayed encircled around her, pulling her tighter, and he rested his chin on the top of her head. With her cheek pressed to his chest, she felt his words rumble from deep inside.

"That means more to me than you can know. The truth is, Hannah, I loved last night, too." He took her by the arms and gently pushed her back, kissing her lightly once again.

"Are we still going to Manteague for dinner tonight?"

"Your chariot awaits," he said, waving his hand toward the front door.

She secured her house and followed him outside, seeing a new SUV parked next to her smaller one. "Whose vehicle is this?"

"It's mine. I use the old truck when I'm just running around, but a few months ago, I bought this. I wanted to have something to use when the old junker wasn't right. This is what I would've come in last night if I hadn't just come from the fishing boat." He beeped the locks and assisted her into the passenger side.

As he walked around to the driver's door, she sniffed the new-car scent in appreciation. The drive to Manteague did not take long, and once there, they were ushered to a corner table, a spectacular view out the window before them.

She scanned the horizon and smiled. "I see the water often, but with Easton being landlocked, it's not an everyday occurrence unless I'm out running. Since you work at Seaside, you get this view every day."

"I do love the view, but with the marshes and the barrier islands, it's not like I'm staring out directly onto ocean waves," he admitted. "I love it because it's what I know but also love the beaches on the bay side of the Eastern Shore.

They continued their light conversation after ordering drinks, and once the libations were placed on the table, Dylan lifted his beer and said, "To us. Good food, a beautiful woman, and… well… us."

She laughed and nodded. Lifting her wine glass, she agreed, "To us."

As soon as the plates of seafood were delivered, they dug in, moans of appreciation taking the place of conversation. Finally, leaning back, she sighed. "This is a nice restaurant. I've never been here before."

"I didn't want to go anywhere in Seaside or Easton. For that matter, I didn't want to go anywhere in Baytown."

"Thank you! It is nice to get out of the towns we live and work in."

"Mitch told me about this place."

She fiddled with the stem of her wine glass for a moment, turning that information over in her head. "Did he know why you were asking about a restaurant?" She stared at her glass before lifting her gaze to his.

"Do you mean did he know who I was going to dinner with?"

She sucked in her lips and nodded.

His brow furrowed as he admitted, "Yes. I told him that I was taking you out to dinner. Was that okay?"

"Yeah… yeah. I guess it will seem a little weird at first."

"I don't know why. Our friends have all been trying to get me to ask you out for years."

Eyes wide, her chin jerked back slightly. "You're kidding!"

Shaking his head, he laughed. "Nope. Everybody thinks you're wonderful, and I guess I wasn't good at hiding the fact that I really like you. I believe their comments have been more of the variety of '*When are you going to get your head out of your ass and ask her out?*'"

Closing her eyes, she dropped her chin while shaking her head. "Oh, my God."

"Don't be embarrassed. You're incredibly liked and respected in this whole area. By the other people in law enforcement. By your townspeople. Your friends. Believe me, the pressure is on me not to fuck anything up."

She jerked her head back up and held his gaze, seeing a bit of insecurity sneaking through his eyes. "There's no pressure, Dylan. We are who we are, and that's all we can be. Our friendship is between us, not everyone else on the Shore."

His smile quirked up on one side. "I agree. But I have to ask… are we just friends?"

"Well, considering I don't kiss my friends like I was kissing you earlier, I'd say we were more."

Now it was his turn to throw his head back and laugh. "I've got to tell you, I don't kiss any of my friends like that, either."

Their check came, and he paid for the meal while she slipped off to the ladies' room. Staring into the mirror, she touched up her lip gloss. Holding her gaze in the reflection, she sucked in a deep breath. *You've got this, girl. He's the man you remembered plus the man you've gotten to know. Whatever happens, you're ready.*

On the drive back to her house, the interior of his SUV crackled with electricity. She almost expected to see the white-blue currents bolting between them. When she'd gotten back to the table, he'd escorted her outside, his hand resting on the lower part of her back, his fingertips branding her skin through her clothing. But now he was quiet, his hands gripping the steering wheel. Wondering if she had misread where their date might end up, she stayed silent as well.

Parking in front of her bungalow, he turned toward her and opened his mouth, then snapped it closed, a crinkle forming between his brows.

"Would you like to come in?" she blurted, both hopeful he would and strangely afraid he wouldn't.

The air left his lungs in a rush, and his shoulders relaxed. "Yeah, I'd love that."

Walking past the front porch, shutting down memories of their kiss last night, she led him inside. Kicking off her shoes, she padded into her kitchen on bare feet, grabbing a couple of beers from the refrigerator. When she turned around, she noticed him still standing just inside the door.

"Come on in, and make yourself at home."

As soon as they settled on the sofa, she blurted, "You're acting odd, Dylan. What are you thinking?"

He leaned forward, his forearms resting on his knees, his hands clasped in front of him but his head turned, keeping his gaze on her. "I had a really good time tonight."

Not having any idea where he was going, she simply swallowed and nodded.

"I don't want to make this weird for you," he continued. "I know you've worked hard to earn the respect of everyone in the community."

"You know, when we got together several years ago, I didn't spend a lot of time thinking about how it might affect our jobs until… well, until it ended. But we'd kept everything private for the couple of months that we dated, protecting ourselves from any blowback. In hindsight, that was good."

"Yeah, that was good. While at the time I wanted to shout to everyone that you were going out with me, I know how horrible that would've been the way things ended."

Silence descended, and she finally said, "Dylan, I get the feeling you're trying to tell me something. I really need you to speak plainly because I'm just not comfortable trying to figure out what's on your mind."

"Sorry," he said, his lips quirking upward. "I'll do whatever you want to do, Hannah. I want us to be more than just a casual date. Or, if I haven't made that clear yet, let me make it perfectly clear now. But I also understand the pressures of our jobs. It's kind of like being a public figure." He snorted and shook his head. "A public figure. Jesus, that sounds so pompous, doesn't it?"

She laughed and nodded as well. "I know what you mean, though. If we were in a big city, it would be easier to blend in. Here, if we step out together in either Easton, Seaside, or Baytown, or almost anywhere, people are going to notice."

"I guess that's what I'm getting at. Do you care if they notice?"

Shaking her head, she said, "No, not really."

He sucked in a deep breath and let it out slowly. "The last thing in the world I want to do is bring up the past, especially something unpleasant. But I don't want there to be a specter of doubt in your mind about me."

"So, is this where you confess your sordid secrets?" she asked, attempting to inject levity into the serious conversation.

Rolling his eyes, he nodded and ruefully grinned. "Yeah, I guess it is. Before you and I started dating the last time, I hadn't been as discriminating as I should have. I know I had somewhat of a player reputation, but I promise you, it was exaggerated. I wasn't looking for a relationship in a bar, usually just finding a physical release. And when I met a woman that had the same goal, we might hook up. For a night only. I made it clear and they always verbalized that they were on board. But I'll also say that those hookups were not nearly as often as the reputation I garnered. Did I do anything to refute the reputation? No. Why? I found that the more you try to deny something the more you give people reason to talk."

She nodded her understanding and reached out to place her hand lightly on his arm.

"But I've always been careful and get tested on the job, so I'm clean. And I always wrap it up. I thought I was being responsible. That's why Melissa's declaration threw me. She was never supposed to be more than a one-night encounter. In case you wondered, I haven't heard from her since finding out that the baby wasn't mine. She wasn't from this area, and I've never seen her again. And I promise nothing like that has ever happened before or since. You were completely different. I knew you were someone special... someone I'd like to be with."

"I admit it hurt at the time, Dylan, only because I liked you so much. I felt like you were being taken away from me before we had a chance to build anything. But maybe things happen for a reason. I've had a chance to grow and develop so much in the last few years, personally and professionally. I'm not sure I would've done that fully if I'd been involved with someone."

He leaned back and twisted, now facing her on the sofa. His left arm rested on the back, his fingers now gliding over her shoulder. "I understand what you're saying. When I took the job of Chief, I had no idea what all it entailed, and truthfully, it's taken almost everything that I have had to give to make it work. I also focused on the American Legion, building up relationships and professional camaraderie. Of course, you've been a part of all of that, too."

"I think in some ways we both had something to prove. You were the town boy who came home and got the job that no one else wanted, but you had to prove that you could do it and that you weren't just the same old youthful Dylan."

His fingertips continued to run along her shoulder, the electricity that had slowed during the ride home from the restaurant now firing once again. "You're right. That describes me perfectly. And you?"

"I was the woman with the resumé. Let's face it, when it came to diversity, I think there was pressure for Easton to hire a woman, even though I'm sure some of the people didn't think that was right. Whatever. I can't worry about the reasons why I was hired, I just needed to make sure to do the job the best I could and prove to them that I was the right person." She leaned forward, closing the distance between them. "Honestly, the best thing we could've done for us years ago was to not date. We needed to focus on ourselves as individuals, including our careers."

"And now? What about now for us?"

"Well, we've built our friendship. We've built our professional camaraderie without sex getting in the way."

He chuckled, wiggling his eyebrows. "The sex could've been so much fun."

"Nothing says it can't be now."

She watched as his eyes widened and his breath halted. Grinning, she closed the distance even further and kissed him.

15

The feel of Hannah's lips crashing onto his sent Dylan's senses into overdrive and his cock swelled, pressing painfully against his zipper. To say he was surprised would've been an understatement. To say he was bothered by her assertive move would've been an outright lie.

The date had been perfect. The conversation was easy and fun. The meal was delicious. All with the beautiful woman that he'd been interested in for years, never believing he'd have another chance with her. But on the drive home, insecurity had slammed into him. Now, as she shifted her body closer to his, he was more than ready to offer whatever she was willing to take. With his hands clasping her waist, he lifted her slightly so that she could straddle his lap, her hot core pressing against his aching cock and her breasts pressed against his chest.

He could not deny that when he first met her years ago, it was her looks that drew his attention right off the bat. She was a combination of athletic build and curves. Toned muscles, firm ass, and breasts that filled his hands. Add to that her sleek, dark hair, full lips, and blue eyes, and he was a goner. Thinking of his former self, that had been enough to get his blood raging. Now, it was her brilliance, her soft voice, her caring manner… not to mention that he'd seen her take down a much larger man, something he found incredibly sexy.

She leaned back, and he missed the feel of her lips on his. Seeing her brow lowered, he asked, "What's wrong?"

"You. I'm kissing you for all I'm worth, and it seems like your mind is somewhere else."

"Shit, Hannah. My mind is totally on you, but I swear, I was thinking of how sexy I thought you were when I first met you years ago, but you *now* absolutely knocks my socks off."

She laughed and leaned in closer, sliding her nose against his. "Well, if I'm knocking your socks off, how about we see what other clothes we can knock off?"

With those words, all other thoughts fled his mind, and his arms banded tighter as he took to his feet, easily scooping her up into his arms. He started down the hall, remembering from the previous day that there were two bedrooms. Choosing correctly, he carried her into hers.

She was easy to carry but difficult to maneuver through the small space considering their lips were still locked. Not wanting to knock her head against any furniture or the wall, he lifted his head and quickly glanced around. A queen-sized bed centered the room, splashed with color from a green, blue, and yellow comforter. A dresser was against one wall, a large mirror hanging over it. The nightstand was squeezed into the corner, adorned by a blue lamp. One door was closed, and he assumed it was the closet since the bathroom was in the hall.

He walked until they were close to the bed, then he gently lowered her until her feet touched the floor. Her eyes sparkled, and a smile played about her lips. Hannah was confident, a trait he found incredibly sexy. Her hands immediately went to the tie of her wrap dress, and she soon allowed the green material to pool around her feet.

Now standing in a green satin bra and matching panties, she reached up, her fingers nimbly undoing the buttons on his shirt. His eyes roved over her barely clad body, awed with the gift she presented. He felt a tug and realized his shirt was unbuttoned, and she was attempting to shift it over his shoulders. Jolting, he took over and stripped off his shirt, letting it fall unheeded to the floor to puddle with her dress. Her hands were already on his belt buckle, and he settled his fingers onto her shoulders, gently sliding her bra straps down. His hands skimmed the material covering her breasts, his thumbs circling her nipples before unsnapping the front hook and watching as her breasts were freed from their constraint.

With his zipper now down, his eager cock was tenting the front of his boxers. Her eyes widened as her fingers moved up and down the front, and he battled the desire to toss her onto the bed, rip her panties off, and thrust deeply. *No, this is Hannah. She deserves gentle, not rough.*

She hooked her thumbs into the front of his boxers and eased them over his erection, pushing them down his thighs. Before he knew what was happening, she dropped to her knees and took him into her mouth. His hands automatically went to her head, his fingers moving through her hair as he threw his head back. "Damn, Hannah. God, that feels so good."

He had planned on taking things slow, but with that one action, his good intentions were shot to hell. Her fist encircled the base of his cock, working him while she sucked. It was all he could do to not give in to the urge to unload into her warm, welcoming mouth, and he finally managed to pull back at the last moment.

"First time with you, babe, I want to be inside."

Her hand slowly wiped her lips, exposing a wide smile. "Then I guess we'd better get to it." She sat on the bed and scooted backward, propping her upper body on her elbows.

Grinning, he leaned forward and placed a knee onto the bed next to her legs. Snagging her panties, he dragged them down and tossed them over his shoulder. "Yes, Ma'am, I aim to please." Wanting to make sure she was as ready as he, he placed his hands on her knees and pushed her legs apart gently, exposing her sex, the scent of her arousal filling his nostrils. Everything combined to create a memory so embedded in his heart, he knew he'd remember this moment for the rest of his life... the sight, the sounds, the scent.

He leaned forward, inhaling deeply. With the flat of

his tongue, he licked her folds, the taste of her essence even more tantalizing.

With his tongue thrusting inside, he expertly worked her until she was dragging her short fingernails through his hair and crying out his name. Finally, inserting his finger and tweaking until he found just the spot that made her shake with need, he pulled her taut bud into his mouth, smiling against her sex as her orgasm shattered over her.

As he crawled further over her body, he licked his fingers, watching her eyes dilate as they stayed focused on his every move. He began kissing over her hip bones, over the slight roundness of her tummy, up to her breasts, where he paid equal attention to each nipple.

Sex with other women had always been about a physical release with no emotion tied into the act. He hoped it was pleasurable for his partner, working to make sure that it was. And, if he was honest, he often put the necessary work in because he knew what was expected. But this was Hannah—and nothing like anything he'd ever experienced.

He wanted to lick her skin. He wanted to memorize the feel of her against his face and on his tongue. He wanted to find the spots that made her jerk with a tickle or moan with delight. He didn't want her to just feel satisfied on a physical level, he wanted her happy.

Dragging his body upward, he reluctantly left her breasts and kissed her neck and jaw, finally landing his lips on hers. By now, she was writhing underneath him, her hips pressing upward. He nudged her legs apart with his hips, reaching his hand down to place his cock at her entrance when his fingers landed on ungloved skin. *Fuck! A condom!* He scrambled off the bed and knelt on the floor, fumbling for his wallet. Pulling out a condom, his fingers shook as he ripped open the foil and rolled it on.

Climbing back over her, he could not miss the smile on her face or the light in her eyes. She giggled, and he growled, "Woman, you should never laugh at a man making a fool of himself trying to get a condom on."

That only made her laugh louder, but she sobered quickly as she placed her hands on either side of his face and drew him down for a kiss. "It only makes you more endearing."

As he held her gaze, he also held his cock at her entrance. "Are you sure? 'Cause this is no fuck. Not now. Not with you. Never with you."

Her hands continued to hold his jaws, her light touch skimming over his face. He had never wanted another woman to touch him this way, discouraging intimacy beyond fucking and having a little fun. But Hannah's touch was both a balm to his soul and the spark setting off fireworks.

"I'm sure, Dylan. I'm sure of this. I'm sure of you." As always, her voice was soft, her gaze intense. Suddenly her fingers tightened, her eyes widened, and she smiled while growling, "Now move!"

Laughing, he thrust deeply, loving the look on her face as he plunged inside her warm, tight sex. Her hands slid to his shoulders and then maneuvered down his chest and around his back until her fingers clung as her heels pressed against his ass, urging him on.

His hips pistoned, each movement sending more tingles throughout his body. With his cock dragging along her tight channel, he knew he wouldn't last long. Determined to bring her pleasure before taking his own, he kissed her deeply, thrusting his tongue in rhythm with his cock's movement. He felt her thighs tighten around his waist, and he kissed along her jaw again, now sucking on the pulse point at the base of her neck. Her moans intensified and he shifted his weight slightly so that he could slide one hand to cup her breast, tweaking her nipple.

She shattered around him again, fingertips digging into his back as her heels pressed against his ass. Feeling her come around him was more than he could've imagined. Not just the signal from a woman that let him know it was okay for him to let loose, but the primal knowledge that their meeting had involved his heart as much as his body.

With a roar, his release pulsed out of him, and he continued to thrust until there was nothing left. Shoving his arms around her back, he rolled to the side, letting most of her weight fall on him as his now-spent cock slid from her body. He held her tightly, their bodies pressed so closely that their heartbeats must have joined. He kissed her forehead, then left his lips pressed against her skin. He was uncertain he could move but was very certain he didn't want her to.

Slowly their bodies cooled, and she leaned her head back slightly to stare into his face. He prayed he would not see regret in her eyes. Instead, she beamed her light toward him, branding his skin. Smiling, he met her gaze, hoping it branded her as well.

"I don't want you to leave," she said.

He had always appreciated Hannah's direct honesty, loving that she wasn't coy or playing games. "I don't want to go."

"Then stay."

He shifted their bodies slightly, now fully facing each other, her head resting on his arm. Their legs were tangled, their hips still nestled together. "Are you sure?"

"I don't think I've ever been more sure about anything."

He closed the scant distance between them and kissed her, sweeping his tongue through her mouth. Releasing her lips, he said, "Actually, I'm not sure wild horses could drag me from this bed."

"Lucky for you I don't have any wild horses in the bedroom."

His laughter rumbled through his chest, and he gave her a squeeze.

"I'll fix you breakfast in the morning before you have to go to your house to change for work."

"What would you say if I told you I had a spare uniform in my vehicle?"

Eyebrows raised, she asked, "Ooh, were you hoping to get lucky?"

"I never know when I might need a spare uniform, so I keep it in there. But let's just say I'm thrilled to be able to use my spare for a reason like this."

"Then we get to sleep a little bit later in the morning since you don't have to make a trip back to your house."

He kissed her long and deep again, then shifted her to her back so that he could slide out of the bed. "I gotta take care of the condom," he said and headed into her bathroom. Emerging, he walked straight to the bed and slid under the covers, still naked, pleased to find that she was also. Wrapping her in his arms again, he wondered if sleep would come, already finding her body's weight settling deep into his side. It didn't take long before he followed her into slumber.

16

The sunlight filtered through the blue, gauzy sheers in Hannah's bedroom, casting the room in cool shadows. She didn't have to ponder the reason why she was naked or feel the weight of a leg over hers. She didn't need to wonder why her mattress dipped to the side or the warm body that was pressed closely. All of that was simply a wonderful reminder of what was first and foremost on her mind when she woke. As though her room had been changed with his presence, she was keenly aware of Dylan the moment her eyes fluttered open.

She listened to the sound of his deep breathing, ascertaining he was still asleep. Twisting her head on the pillow, she stared at the man sharing her bed. The man she'd fallen for so quickly. With sleep easing the small lines in his face, he appeared more youthful, reminding her of when they'd first met years before. The careers they had chosen could certainly age someone prematurely, and she had no doubt her own face carried lines that had not been present a few years ago.

They had both grown and changed in the subsequent time. *We might not have lasted even if we'd tried to stay together back then.*

Her mind drifted to the night before. The dinner. The easy conversation. The comfortable silences. Then coming back to her place. She squirmed slightly, squeezing her legs together at the memory of sex with Dylan. Off-the-charts, rocking-her-world, a-night-to-remember sex with Dylan.

Forgetting her thoughts of letting him sleep, her hand lifted and she gently smoothed his hair away from his face. His eyes opened, and it appeared to take no more than a second for him to realize where he was. His lopsided smile greeted her.

"What a sight to wake up to," he said, lifting his hand to smooth over her cheek. "You're a gift I never thought I could have."

"I didn't mean to wake you, but I was lying here and couldn't resist touching you."

"Babe, I hope you never resist touching me whenever you want." They silently appreciated the moment. "So, what were you doing? Just lying there staring at me?"

Laughing, she said, "Yes... um... no. I mean, yes... I was staring at you. Admiring you. But I was also just thinking."

He tapped her nose with the end of his finger. "You wake up and your mind starts racing with things, doesn't it?"

"Guilty. Usually, as soon as my eyes open, I'm either planning my day, pondering something, or worrying over something."

"Which of those three were you doing this morning with me in your bed?"

"I guess I was pondering." Seeing his lifted brow, she hurried to explain. "I was thinking about how different we are than we were four years ago. Maybe we started too quickly after arriving here. We hadn't given ourselves time to settle into our jobs before we became involved."

He shifted slightly in the bed, sliding his arm under her neck to draw her closer. "Are you saying you think this timing is better?"

Nodding slowly, her thumb continued to glide over his face. "Yeah, I do. It's not like we were teenagers beforehand. We'd both worked, been in the military, had law enforcement experience, had life experience. And yet, becoming involved with each other so quickly might have been disastrous in the end, even if there was no other issue."

"I never really thought about it that way, Hannah. To be honest, I missed what I thought we could have been and what I thought I'd never have a chance at getting. Now, all I can think of is how glad I am to have this second chance with you."

His words wrapped around her as warm as his embrace. "I know, and there's no way to look back and see what could have happened. We've also had to set aside personal feelings to work together professionally, and I think maybe that's good. We understand each other better. We understand what's expected of us from the community."

As soon as she said the word *community*, his eyebrows lifted. "That makes me wonder what's going to come next. Do you want us to hide?"

His question surprised her, especially since she hadn't given it much thought, which was odd for her. Nibbling on her bottom lip, she held his gaze and admitted, "I don't really know. I know that I don't want to run out this morning and tell everyone that we're seeing each other. I'd like to have something that's just for us for a while before inviting everyone else in."

"Good God, I never thought about other people knowing about us as inviting them into our lives. That sounds crowded!"

She laughed again and shook her head. "You know what I mean. Once people know we're dating, they somehow get involved. Maybe it's little comments they make. Maybe it's suddenly asking us to go out with them. Maybe it's just other people's expectations. Whatever, it tends to crowd in, and I'm not ready for that. I'd love to have more *us* time."

"When you put it that way, babe, you've got no argument from me. I certainly don't mind shouting from the rooftops that you're giving me this chance, and I've got no problem with our friends knowing, but private time sounds perfect."

Her sensitive skin tingled as his hands glided over her shoulders and down her arm, skimming her waist to pull her tighter. The electricity that always vibrated between them increased and her nipples ached for attention, already shooting a jolt of nerves to her core. He pressed his ready cock against her pelvis and closed the distance between their lips.

In between nibbling kisses, he mumbled, "How about a little more private time before we get ready for work?"

Grinning, her answer was to pull him close and take the kiss deeper.

After another round of vigorous sex, she insisted he take a shower by himself or they'd be late for work. He grumbled, but she prevailed and hurried into the kitchen to fix breakfast. Usually, she ate light in the mornings, having a bagel with cream cheese and yogurt with granola. Now, glad she'd had the foresight to stop by the store the previous day, she scrambled eggs with cheese and quickly cooked bacon to go along with the bagels.

Percy yowled to make his presence known and she placed food in his dish. "You're just grumpy because I kicked you out of the bedroom last night."

Hearing footsteps, she glanced up as Dylan walked into the kitchen, his damp hair finger-combed to the side. Standing, she stared. *Damn, he makes khaki pants and a police polo look sexy.* Now wishing she'd taken a shower with him, she pushed those thoughts away.

He bent to pet Percy and said, "Don't blame you, man. I'd be pissed if I'd been kicked out of her bed, too."

Laughing, she plated their breakfast as her heart

melted a little more. After eating, she jumped into the shower, glad that her morning routine was easy. A quick blow-dry of her hair and it was pulled back into a bun. Donning her uniform, she met him in the living room as she secured her belt and weapon. Their eyes met and she laughed, twirling in a slow circle. "Not terribly sexy, but then you know that."

He grabbed her around the waist and pulled her close, kissing her hard and fast. "I've always known you were gorgeous, uniform or not. And now that I know exactly what that uniform hides... damn, girl, being around you is going to be hard!"

"It's actually going to be harder today since we start with the LEL meeting."

"Yeah, but I can't complain. I get to spend more time with you first thing this morning."

Lifting her hand, she wiggled her finger back and forth in front of him. "Remember what we talked about. No one's going to know anything about us right now."

"Yes, Ma'am. Can't say it'll be easy, but I'll be good."

Walking out, they kissed again before heading to their separate vehicles, both driving to the Acawmacke County Sheriff's Office where Liam was hosting the group meeting.

Dylan had asked to be put on the agenda, and when Liam nodded toward him, he began. "I want to let you all know what I've done at the Seaside Harbor. I talked with Owen since he's the harbormaster and owner of

The Wharf Restaurant, and because I knew he had security cameras up, I decided to see if we could utilize those. I let him know what I was checking on, and he was more than willing to cooperate. He only has two—one directed to the back delivery area of his restaurant and another one that is focused on the gas pumps for the boats. With his permission, I worked with my officers, and we were able to alter the angle of the cameras slightly so that Owen would still have security on what he wanted but we'd have a wider scope for seeing who comes in and out of the harbor."

"That's great," enthused Colt.

Shrugging, Dylan admitted, "It's not perfect. I can't see everywhere, especially on the far side of the harbor. If someone knew that the cameras were there and studied the angle, they could probably figure out where they could come in and we wouldn't be able to see."

"Any chance of getting more security cameras?" Liam asked.

With his forearms planted on the table, he clasped his hands together and shook his head. "I've already checked with the Mayor, but that was a lesson in futility, not that I expected it to be any different. I get it. Tiny town, tiny budget, but it's frustrating.

The others all nodded, having the same problems with their mayors or Board of Supervisors.

"Any possibility for a grant?" Hannah asked.

His gaze snapped over to her, noting the way the fluorescent lights in the ceiling made her eyes appear bluer. Blinking, he quickly said, "I'm up for any way to get more money, but I'll be the first to confess that I know nothing about how to get a grant."

"I've had a little experience," she said. "I don't mind helping at all."

It was on the tip of his tongue to say *I'll take anything you want to give me'*, but at the last second he managed to choke out, "I'd appreciate the help." The meeting continued, but it took all his energy to stay focused on the matters at hand and not on Hannah. He had chosen to sit across from her instead of next to her, thinking it would be better to not smell the delicate scent of her shampoo or be tempted to press his leg next to hers.

Instead, he noticed the shine of her hair, focusing on one tiny strand that had escaped her bun. He noticed the way her body armor fit over her torso, now wondering if it chafed her sensitive breasts. With her directly across from him, he could see her porcelain skin and knew exactly how soft it was. Her eyes held intelligence, but he also knew they could light with passion. Sucking in a deep breath, the scent of her shampoo reached him anyway. *Fuck! I'm never going to keep this hidden!*

"Dylan?"

Startling, he looked toward Mitch. "Sorry, man. My mind was on the... um... grants that Hannah said we might be able to obtain."

Mitch nodded. "I can understand that. Hell, we're all looking for money. I think the grant idea is a good one, but the problem is that will take some time. Is there anything else we can do now?"

"I've also talked to my brother about helping me keep an eye on the Seaside Harbor."

That news was also met with enthusiasm.

"I don't want the news to get out to a lot of people, but I'm going to have David pass along the idea that we want to be cognizant of anything strange that they see. We don't expect them to be policemen and don't expect them to act, but they can radio when they see suspicious behavior."

Clapping him on the shoulder, Mitch said, "I'm going to talk to our harbormaster, also. Once I get his acceptance, I'll hold a meeting with a few of our regular fishermen in Baytown. I'm glad to hear that your brother was receptive."

At Manteague, Wyatt also had a small harbor. "I've been trying to keep an eye on things with myself and my officers, but your ideas are good. I'll go back and talk to our regular fishermen and see what we can do."

"If nothing else, if the drug runners discover that the Eastern Shore takes this seriously, maybe they'll start avoiding us."

Mitch added, "I've got the Coast Guard that can help me at Baytown, and they can do the same for Seaside. Wyatt, you're just out of their district for our station, but the Coast Guard in Chincoteague would be able to assist you."

"Don't forget about the Virginia Marine Police," Colt added. "I've been in touch with Callan and suggested we have a meeting with them to see what they can help with."

As the meeting concluded, the gathering decided to

go to an Italian restaurant near the Sheriff's Office. Once there, Dylan maneuvered to sit next to Hannah, and he watched her lips curve as his leg brushed up against hers underneath the table. The conversation stayed light, talking about friends, and focusing on the latest American Legion activities. When the lunch was over, everyone said goodbye, but Dylan hung back with her. Standing on the sidewalk near the parking lot, to all the world they looked like they always had... two colleagues, two police chiefs, two professionals chatting. Glancing around, his lips quirked as he said, "This is harder than I thought."

"Harder?" Her gaze dropped to his crotch.

"Stop that. This is hard enough... shit, I mean difficult enough without you staring at my cock."

She threw her head back and laughed, and his lips curved into a wider smile. "I'll behave, I promise," she said. "Anyway, we have an example to set."

"How would you like to see my house tonight?" he blurted. "I might even manage to fix you dinner."

Eyes widening, she tilted her head to the side. "You cook? I seem to remember years ago that was not something you tackled."

His fingers itched to reach out and touch her, so he locked his hands on his hips to keep from forgetting and drawing her near. "Well, you're getting to know the new me. Since I couldn't afford to eat out every night, I had to figure out how to fix more than a grilled cheese sandwich."

"Hey, don't knock a good grilled cheese sandwich."

Holding his gaze, she asked, "I take it that dinner will be casual."

"Oh, yeah, it'll be casual. But bring an overnight bag."

"Are you sure? Do you have neighbors that can see us?"

"No neighbors that can see my house or my driveway. And I've never been more sure of anything in my life."

Her top teeth landed on her bottom lip, driving him to distraction. She looked up and asked, "Is it crazy that I want to kiss you right now?"

"Not any crazier than me wishing you would."

She sucked in a deep breath and he tried to ignore the way her chest heaved with the maneuver. Sticking out her hand, she said, "I'll see you later, Chief Hunt."

His fingers wrapped around hers as he gave them a shake, loving the feel of her palm against his. "Good afternoon, Chief Freeman."

At that moment, the hardest thing he did was turn and walk away, going straight to his vehicle without looking over his shoulder to see if she was still standing there. But once in his vehicle, he could see that she was safely pulling out of the parking lot. He looked around and saw people going about their business, no one aware of the undercurrent of emotions that had just zapped all about them on the sidewalk.

He knew that one day they would have to figure out how to go public with their relationship. But right now, his radio blared, and he needed to get back to work.

17

Dylan had just entered the town limits of Seaside when he saw an old SUV stranded on the side of the road. Recognizing it, he chuckled. Turning on his lights, he pulled behind it and climbed out of his police vehicle. "Sam, when are you gonna put this thing out of its misery?"

Samantha, wearing her standard uniform of blue jeans, big rubber work boots, and a t-shirt with the logo **Hoofs and Paws** looked over and grinned. She plopped her hands onto her hips and shook her head. "As long as I can keep it running, it's better than having to fork over money for a new one."

"Have you called for anyone yet?"

A sour look came across her face, and he bit back another chuckle. Pulling out his phone, he pushed a few buttons. "Jason? It's Dylan. Can you send someone with a tow truck? Looks like Sam needs some more help." He listened as Jason replied, then said, "Yeah, that'll be fine."

Sam's arms were now crossed over her chest, a scowl firmly on her face.

"I don't know why you're grumpy. Jason has the best garage in the area."

"I was going to call someone from just up the road," she complained. "Now you've got me being towed all the way back to Baytown."

"Not if the person can fix it here."

"Oh, is Jason sending one of his mechanics?"

"I don't know," he lied. He stayed by the side of the road, keeping her company, not wanting a woman to be stranded by herself even in a small rural area. Thirty minutes later, the rumble of a large truck could be heard rolling down the road. Samantha lifted her hand over her brow, shading her eyes. She huffed loudly, and Dylan lost the battle to hide his grin.

Joseph Hernandez climbed down from the driver's seat and inclined his head toward her. "Samantha," he rumbled in his deep voice. Looking toward Dylan, he offered a chin lift.

Since almost everyone called her Sam, he found it interesting that Joseph used her full name.

Joseph had been in the Navy and was invited to come to Baytown after his service. He settled into Baytown and worked for Jason who owned both the garage and tattoo shop. Joseph worked part-time at both places. Big, quiet, long hair, and tatted. He kept to himself but had always been ready to lend a helping hand. The few times he'd seen Joseph and Sam together, they mixed like oil and water, but there was something funny about the glares she offered to him and the calm way he seemed to ignore her.

"Well, I'll leave y'all to it," Dylan said, climbing back into his vehicle, ignoring the wide-eyed, pleading expression on Sam's face. As he drove into town, he looked into the rearview mirror, watching as the two of them appeared to argue. Joseph stood in one place, his arms crossed over his chest, while Sam's arms waved and danced around as she talked. Just before he turned onto another street, he noticed her forefinger poke Joseph in the chest.

Shaking his head while laughing, he was almost to the station when his radio alerted him to a problem at the harbor. He drove quickly and parked in the large lot. Owen jumped up, hustling from behind his desk as soon as Dylan walked to the open doorway of the office.

"Chief Hunt, got something you need to see."

Without hesitation, he followed Owen down the boardwalk to The Wharf restaurant where they headed straight to Manuel's office. Manuel twisted around, his eyes darting between both men.

"Manuel, show him what you've got."

Stepping behind Manuel, Dylan peered over his shoulder and stared at the computer screen of the security feed. A glance at the time, and he could see that what he was observing occurred shortly after two a.m. A small motorboat appeared in the upper left corner, barely visible as it seemed to glide to a stop. Along the planks of the pier, they observed a figure in dark clothing with a hood pulled over their head obscuring their face, walking rapidly toward the boat. The activity took place just out of camera range. After only a moment, the hooded figure jogged out of sight, his arms in front of him as though he were carrying something.

"Fuckin' hell," Dylan breathed under his breath. While he could not be certain what they had just viewed, all indications were an illegal transaction of some kind, very possibly drugs. "Everything they did was just at the far edge of his camera view." As those words left his mouth, a snake of suspicion slithered through him. *Did someone know? Was someone informed about the camera angles? If so, who knew?* Two obvious solutions were in the room with him... Owen and Manuel. Of course, the day that he'd worked on the cameras, they were in plain sight of anyone on the harbor, but no one else would have known the exact angle that they had captured.

Realizing the men's eyes were on him, he remained quiet, simply giving a curt nod. "I don't suppose there was anything else, was there?"

"No, Chief," Manuel said. "I checked from this time on to see if anyone else came, but the harbor was quiet until about 4 o'clock this morning when the fishermen began to arrive. I didn't have time to look at it this morning when I got to work, so it was later when I even viewed it."

Nodding, he said, "I appreciate you doing this. If you can let me know of anything else you see, that'd be good."

Walking out of the back of the restaurant onto the boardwalk, he looked around. Some of the fishing boats had docked, men and women milling about, busy at work. Todd, standing near David's boat, looked up. Walking over, he offered a chin lift.

"Are you checking up on me, Chief Hunt?"

Shaking his head, he replied, "Nope. Had some business here I needed to attend to."

Todd nodded, turning back to grab another ice tray, but not before his gaze shot toward the back upper corner of the restaurant where one of the cameras was located.

Tossing a wave goodbye, Dylan walked toward his SUV, suspicion now spreading.

Hannah spent the afternoon serving two summonses, finishing several reports, and checking in with her officers. She signed off on several orders handed to her by Pearl, then went through her files to find the last two grants that she had applied for. Making copies of those, she decided to take them home with her so that she could share the information with Dylan. Just the thought of him brought a smile to her face.

"Wow, what's got you looking so happy?" Mason asked.

As her officer walked into her office, her brow lowered. "What do you mean? Aren't I usually happy?"

"Yeah, but you just had a *cat who got into the cream* kind of smile."

She wished Mason had used different words because now all she could think about was Dylan's head between her legs and the word cream. Clearing her throat, she said, "Was there anything you needed, or did you just come in here to harass me about smiling?"

Chuckling, he replied, "I wanted to check with you about the prisoner that we arrested for stealing from the small engine repair shop. I got a notice from Luke that he has a medical condition, and they're doing the paperwork to make sure they've got the right medication. Was there anything else I needed to do?"

"Nope, they'll take care of it. If there's anything we need to sign off on, we will, but once he's at the jail, they'll handle everything."

"Okay, gotcha, Chief." As he walked out, he looked over his shoulder and grinned again. "Keep smiling. It's a good look on you."

"Get outta here!" she called, hearing his laughter as he walked down the hall.

She turned back to her computer and started searching for do-it-yourself security cameras. Uncertain of their quality of the video, she began digging more. Almost an hour later, she determined several options that Dylan could possibly use for the harbor. They might not be perfect but could certainly pinpoint troubled areas. She pulled out her phone and sent him a text.

I found some security cameras that might work. I'll bring the info with me tonight. See you soon.

Glancing at the clock, she called out to Pearl as she walked down the hall. "I'm heading home. See you tomorrow."

Walking across the sidewalk to the parking area near the courthouse, she saw a small group of elderly tourists

being guided around the historic Courthouse courtyard. Their cell phones and cameras were out, taking
pictures. Just as she approached, an older woman
stubbed her toe on one of the cobblestones and fell
forward onto the sidewalk.

Running over, Hannah dropped to her knees next to
the woman, radioing for the rescue squad. The woman
was bleeding profusely from her forehead, and Hannah
spoke softly, calming her as she pressed a cloth against
the injury. The woman's wrist was also swelling, and
Hannah feared it might be broken. "The squad will be
here in just a few minutes," she assured.

Considering the rescue squad and firehouse was
only a few blocks away, the siren was immediately
heard. Stepping back as the EMTs began working on
the woman, she moved to the tour guide and ushered
the others away. Questioning the group, she obtained
information on the woman, then made arrangements
for the tour guide to have someone be available to pick
her up from the hospital in Acawmacke.

Stepping back over to the ambulance, she gave the
woman's information to Karen, the EMT driver.

Karen nodded her thanks. "She'll probably need
stitches and her wrist set. We'll give them this information so the hospital will know who to call."

The ambulance pulled away, the tourist group
dispersed, and Hannah started toward her vehicle again
when she looked up, seeing Dylan hustling toward her.
His gaze roved over her, but instead of a smile, his
brows lowered.

"I assume that's not your blood all over your uniform."

Glancing down, she shook her head. "We just had an accident where an elderly tourist fell. I was on my way to the car when it happened right in front of me." Looking back up at him, she cocked her head to the side. "But what are you doing here?"

"To be honest, I was hoping to have a chance to see you."

Disappointment rushed through her, and she looked around to assure that they were alone. "Oh, are our plans for tonight off?"

"No, they're still on! I just wanted to see you early. When I got your text about the security cameras, I couldn't wait to see what you had to say."

Laughing, she shook her head. "And here I thought you just couldn't wait to see me."

"Don't tempt me, or I'll show you exactly how glad I am to see you right here in front of everyone."

Her smile widened at the sight of his lopsided grin and roving eyes. "I did do some research, but honestly, you can wait until tonight."

He glanced at the blood on her shirt and sighed. "Well, normally, I'd say I'd rather take care of business during business hours and you and me having our alone time, but I know you want to get home and get showered. Of course, you could always do that at my house."

"Now who's tempting who? But I need to go home and feed Percy. Once I get him fed, take a shower, and change clothes, I'll come to your place. And then we can talk about security cameras."

Rolling his eyes, he said, "Just what I always wanted... to finally get you to my house and we have to talk business."

He escorted her over to her SUV, and as she drove away, she watched him wave through her rearview mirror. Grinning, she couldn't wait to get to his house and discuss the security camera business so they could get down to *their* business.

An hour later, taking a quick shower and making sure Percy was fed, she packed an overnight bag. Percy hopped up on her bed and nestled on top of her bag. "Oh, baby, you can't come with me... at least not now. Maybe someday."

Now, excitement coursed through her as she drove along the beach outside of Seaside and turned by an old, dented mailbox with Dylan's number painted on the side. She remembered him saying that he'd built his house in old-fashioned architecture, using a lot of reclaimed wood and materials to give it the appearance that it had been there for many years. Seeing his mailbox, it appeared that he had done the same with it as well. The gravel and crushed oyster shell drive led her to the perfect view.

Sandy dunes and marshy seagrass covered the area and rising in front of her was a weatherworn, cedar plank, two-story beach house. She knew the area was not in a flood zone, and yet he'd built the house off the ground. The front was simple, with a covered porch facing west. As the driveway curved past the side of the house, she could see that there was another long, wide porch on the back.

Uncertain where to park, the decision was taken away from her when Dylan stepped out of his front door and waved. Parking nearby, she climbed from her SUV and bent to grab her bag from the passenger seat. Hearing footsteps crunch over the gravel, she twisted and watched as he approached.

Stalking straight to her, he didn't stop until their bodies were pressed together. He kissed her lightly, one arm banding around her back, and the other hand sliding her bag from her shoulder. Before she had a chance to completely melt into his embrace, he leaned back and grinned.

"Welcome to my home."

Those four simple words speared straight through her. *His home. Built by him on the land from his grandfather.* She could only imagine how proud he was of his legacy on the Eastern Shore. "I'm honored to be here."

He kissed her again before linking his fingers with hers and leading her up the front steps to the porch as she tried to take in all the details.

He said nothing but smiled as he continued to lead her forward through the front door and into the house. Her gaze roved over the area, anxious to see his home. The inside offered an open, airy feel to it. Instead of stepping into a living area, the kitchen was directly to the left. Cabinets were painted a light gray, blending perfectly with the white backsplash tile and granite countertops. The kitchen led to an open eating area and living room that spanned the entire back of the house. A wide expanse of windows looked out over the marshy shore and allowed light to pour in. The floors were more weatherworn planks stretching across the expanse of the rooms.

Directly opposite the kitchen was a staircase leading to the second floor and a large laundry room and half-bathroom combination.

There was so much for her to take in, it was hard to focus on everything all at once, but her gaze snagged on the few pictures on the wall. Dylan's decorating was minimal, but the pictures he'd chosen to frame and hang were of people that meant something to him. One was of a group of sailors on board a ship, arms around each other, wide grins on their faces. Several were of his family, photographs taken at various times during his life.

And one, in particular, caught her eye, her feet taking her closer, curiosity pulling her along. It was at Finn's Pub after one of the American Legion meetings. Most of their friends were present, all talking and smiling. Whoever took the picture had done so without anyone posing. It was a perfect snapshot, but what drew her attention was that she was front and center, her head thrown back in laughter while Dylan sat nearby, his eyes pinned on her.

Swinging her head around, she watched as he approached, her breath becoming more shallow with each step.

"I thought about taking that picture off the wall when I knew you were coming," he said, his voice soft.

Not knowing how to respond, she remained quiet.

"That picture was taken about a year after we broke up. For a long time when I would see you, it hurt because I felt like we should be together. And I remember that night, sitting at the pub, watching you smile, and realizing that if the only way I could have you in my life was just like that... friends, colleagues, fellow Legionnaires, then I'd take it. Because I wanted you in my life, any way I could have you. I can't even remember who took that picture, but it was one that got shared around. After I had it framed and hung up, I wondered if I was crazy to have that constant reminder that you were not mine. But I know what you said the other day is right... we both had things to accomplish before we could really come together. So, as much as the last years sometimes hurt, it makes you being here right now that much sweeter."

Her throat tightened as she listened to his words. He swallowed deeply, and she bit the corner of her bottom lip in an effort to keep the sob from erupting but was unable to hold back the tear now sliding down her cheek. She lifted her hand and cupped his face. Uncertain if her voice would remain steady, she said, "In my whole life, I've never heard those words from anyone." Stepping closer, she lifted her other hand so that she clutched his stubbled jaw. "So, let me assure you that being here, right now with you, is the only place I want to be."

His lips slammed down on hers, his arms banding around her so tightly her entire front was pressed against his. He bent and scooped her up, taking the stairs two at a time until they reached his bedroom. His soft comforter cradled her back as he lay her on the bed, his body looming over hers.

Grinning, she mumbled against his lips, "And I was so looking forward to a full tour of the house."

Barely lifting his face from hers, he met her grin. "You'll get that. But first, we'll have a full tour of each other's bodies."

Since she couldn't think of anything she'd rather have, she pulled him closer.

1 8

Dylan hadn't planned on jumping Hannah the minute she came into his house. Quite the contrary. While he was not a culinary genius, he could grill a mean steak and get a handle on a baked potato. Other than that, he'd bought a bag salad from the grocery store, had plenty of beer and wine, and even managed to reheat an apple pie he'd bought from the local bakery.

He had even expected them to go over the information about the security cameras while fixing dinner. And then, having drinks on the back deck while watching the ever-changing color of the sky during sunset, he would prove to her that he could show tremendous restraint.

But as he watched her stare at the photograph on his wall, stripping away all his pretenses, the words to explain the meaning behind the picture became imperative. Then having her look at him with such understanding and share her feelings toward him cast all thoughts of going slow out of his mind.

He'd taken his time to worship every inch of her body, knowing the dinner could wait. They kissed and whispered, licked and sucked, and tangled together during sex until they both lay sated and smiling on the bed.

Now, having eaten dinner inside the screened porch after the sun had already set, they leaned back in his double Adirondack chair, complete with footrest. He'd bought it on a whim, knowing it would be lonely on his porch until he had someone to share it with. Considering Hannah was always the woman he wanted to cuddle with, he was now thrilled with his purchase. He rested his beer bottle on one of the wide, flat arms, her wine glass on the other.

"I hate to interrupt our perfect night by bringing this up, but I know you had some information about security cameras."

She nodded. "I brought the grant paperwork that I've done before, and it should be fairly straightforward. Unfortunately, as we've already said, these things take time. I looked online and printed out the forms and thought we could work on them together so you can present it to your mayor. He doesn't have to approve, but it would let him know what you're doing."

"At your suggestion, I started looking into security cameras that I could purchase. I have a little bit of expertise because I put them in here." He lifted his hand and pointed to the back corner of his house. "When I had the house built, I installed a couple of small security cameras that were tied into motion sensor lights. The feed goes directly into my phone app. They're not fancy, but it does the job. Occasionally, the light will go on as a deer walks by, but for the most part, that hasn't been a problem."

"Besides the cameras, does Owen have security lights around the harbor and the restaurant?"

"Yeah, but only the ones behind the restaurant illuminate the entire back. The ones around the harbor enable anyone walking around to see where they're going, but they're not very bright."

He pulled out his phone while she sipped her wine. Scrolling through several websites, he leaned over and showed her the screen. "This is one that has infrared light which would help us be able to see in the dark. I'm not going to have a camera that's also motion sensor lights, because I don't want to alert anyone."

"You want to capture them instead of warn them away."

Her voice held no censure, and as someone else in law enforcement, he was sure she understood. "Might make me sound like a bastard, but I'd rather catch them. If they don't come here, they'll just go to another place and get the drugs through here anyway."

"You're right," she said, nodding.

"I've got some money, but some of these are too expensive. I was thinking about getting a couple to put up on the other side of the harbor."

"I can help with the purchase—"

"Hell, no, Hannah. You don't need to do that. The harbor is in my jurisdiction."

"It's got nothing to do with jurisdiction," she huffed. "You're spending your own money to help keep drugs out of our area. If you can do that at Seaside, then you're helping me in Easton."

"Let's see if this does anything first." He checked the store in Acawmacke where he'd purchased the ones for his house and determined they still had a supply.

Hannah leaned over to see and exclaimed, "Let's go there tomorrow!"

Turning to see her wide-eyed enthusiasm, he chuckled. "You always this excited to shop for security items?"

His gaze dropped to her mouth as her top teeth captured her bottom lip and she shook her head slowly.

"I don't mind shopping, but I can get even more excited if you want to take me back to bed."

He sucked in a quick breath. "Are you done with that wine?"

"Yeah," she whispered.

"Thank fuck." Standing, he scooped her up once more. Barely taking time to secure the back door, he carried her upstairs. Again.

Hannah couldn't help but grin as she and Dylan wandered the aisles of the large hardware store. Her mother despaired when dragging her out shopping for clothes, but that endeavor had never excited her. In the military, she had a uniform. As a police officer, she had a uniform. And as Chief, she set the standard for her department's uniform. Even now, on a day off, she was comfortably dressed in jeans, a long-sleeved T-shirt made out of soft cotton, and sneakers.

She and Dylan had compared the security cameras, and after he made his selection was now talking to one of the owners of the store. Wandering around, she moved up and down several aisles to see if there was anything she might need for her bungalow. Instead, she discovered several things she thought Dylan might want.

A noise toward the back of the store caught her attention, and on instinct, she shifted around the end of the aisle to have a better line of sight. A man rushed from what she assumed was the office, a backpack clutched in his hands as he slammed through the back door.

Darting forward, she saw another man on the floor struggling to sit up, bleeding from a wound on his forehead. Calling over her shoulder to Dylan, she shouted, "10-31, 10-47," just before she made it through the back door. The suspect's footsteps sounded to her left, and she turned to see him fleeing along the back of the shopping center.

Calling out, "Stop, police!" she pounded the pavement behind the small shopping center, reaching into her purse to pull out her revolver.

He twisted his head around, his eyes wide, but kept running toward a truck parked at the end. The engine was running, and a driver sat behind the wheel, his eyes equally as wide as he watched their approach.

Her feet ate the ground between them but she hated that she did not have a radio to let Dylan know what was happening. The man in the truck must have decided to cut his losses because he revved the engine and bolted forward only to slow down at the back corner to make his getaway.

Securing her weapon, she closed the gap, and with a flying leap tackled the thief, taking them both to the ground. She landed hard on her elbow, eliciting a grunt that mixed with the one escaping his lungs at the same time.

Rolling so that she was on top, she pulled her weapon out again and bent low. "Told you to stop, dickhead."

From around the corner, she heard a shot fired and her chest depressed as all air rushed from her body. Eyes wide, her heartbeat pounded, threatening to drown out all other sounds. Looking down, she growled, "Stay there." Pulling zip-ties from her bag, she quickly secured his wrists behind his back. Not wanting him to move, she scooted down and did the same with his ankles. "I'll be right back."

She leaped to her feet and started for the corner when she heard a noise. Lifting her weapon, she saw the driver come into sight, his hands above his head. It only took another second for Dylan to appear, his weapon trained on the driver, his gaze darting around until it landed on her.

For what felt like an eternity, their gazes did not waver, emotions swirling between them. Unable to define what she was feeling, all she knew was it was an emotion unfamiliar to her. And if the expression on Dylan's face was anything to go by, he was just as struck.

She prided herself on her professional focus, but

knowing Dylan was in the area and hearing the gunshot, her heart had skipped a beat and all she could think about was making sure he was safe. Now, staring at him, seeing him unharmed, all words halted in her throat as she tried to remember how to breathe.

He slowly reached out and placed his hand on the driver's shoulder, pushing him down to his knees while keeping his eyes on Hannah. His chest heaved and he sucked in a ragged breath before asking, "Got any ties?"

A stupid-sounding giggle almost slipped from her, caught at the last second as she cleared her throat. Still unsure her voice would not shake, she reached inside her purse as she walked forward, pulling out and handing zip ties to him. He cuffed the driver efficiently as the sound of sirens filled the air.

She finally dragged her gaze away as the screeching of tires surrounded them from the Acawmacke Sheriff's department vehicles. Keeping their hands up until they could be identified, they waited side-by-side as several deputies approached, guns raised.

"Easton Police Chief, Hannah Freeman," she called out.

"Seaside Police Chief, Dylan Hunt."

One of the deputies recognized them, and Hannah stepped to one side while Dylan went with several others, each giving their account of what they saw and what happened. She checked to make sure that a rescue squad was seeing to the man injured inside the store.

As they finished their accounts, the Sheriff's SUV pulled up and she watched as Liam climbed down, his gaze sweeping the scene before landing on her and Dylan. Concern knit in his brow and he stalked over.

"Couldn't fuckin' believe what I was hearing over the radio," he said. "You guys okay?"

Chuckling, she replied, "I'm sure you're wondering if we just came to your county to stir up shit."

Liam's face split into a grin as he shook his head slowly. "Hell, you may have just captured a pair that's been hitting some stores around here."

"We were in the hardware store when I heard a noise and got curious. I saw that one," she inclined her head toward the man she had subdued, "running out of the back with a pack in his hands. I followed him and could see that there was a man in the office, bleeding. By the way, when I tackled him, we went down hard. You should probably have the paramedic check him out before you take them to the jail."

"I ran around the front when I saw the driver starting to peel out. I jumped in front of his truck with my weapon raised and prayed he was going to stop," Dylan said.

She whipped her head around, her mouth open, and stared at him. "Are you nuts?"

"Shit, Hannah, for all I knew he had you in that truck. I couldn't see what was going on in the back."

"Well, standing in front of a moving truck hardly makes any sense!"

"Are you seriously trying to tell me how to do my job?" he asked, his head jerking back.

Huffing, she threw out, "He could have run you down."

Dylan stepped closer and lifted his hand to cup her cheek. "And you think I wasn't having a shit fit wondering what was happening to you?"

"Well, hell, y'all, I feel like I'm intruding," Liam said with a grin. "We'll take the guys from here and since my deputies already have your statements, you two can head out. I'm glad you're both okay and happened to be in the right place at the right time." He leaned closer and grinned wider. "And for the record, it's nice to see you two together." He continued to chuckle as he walked toward his deputies.

Hannah sighed. "Shit, I guess keeping our relationship a secret is out of the question now, isn't it?"

"Normally, Liam is closed-mouth, but I have a feeling this news will be too much for him to hang onto. So, yeah, get ready for us to go public."

She winced as she lifted her arm toward him, and the smile dropped off his face as his gaze dropped to her elbow.

"Fuck, Hannah, why didn't you tell me you were injured?"

"I didn't think about it. Adrenaline, I guess."

He grabbed her other hand and led her over to the ambulance. "Hey, I need you to check out Chief Freeman."

Her elbow was already bruising, and she had to bite back a grimace when the paramedic gently manipulated her arm.

"Ma'am—sorry, Chief Freeman—there's a possibility that you could have a fracture. You need to have it xrayed. The good news is that you're only ten minutes away from the hospital. We can take you."

"Oh, no, I'm not going in an ambulance!"

"Since you were injured in an official capacity, it'll make sense to let us take you."

She opened her mouth to protest, but Dylan agreed. "Do it. It's not going to hurt your street cred. I'll follow right behind."

Cocking one brow, she repeated, "Street cred?" A burst of laughter escaped and she shook her head. "You're crazy."

"Crazy for you. Now, get in the ambulance."

On the way to the hospital, she allowed them to wrap her arm for stabilization and then chatted with them for the ten-minute drive. Once there, she was immediately ushered into an ER bay where a doctor checked her out and ordered an x-ray. Dylan hung with her the whole time, joking and laughing, telling her that it was the most interesting date he'd been on. Rolling her eyes, she flipped him off with her good hand just as the doctor came back into the room.

"Children, children," the doctor joked, smiling at them. Looking at the x-rays, he said, "Okay, you don't have a fracture of the elbow, but it's seriously bruised. You probably know the routine... rest, ice, compression, and elevation. And, of course, ibuprofen to help with the pain. I'll have someone come in to wrap it for you again. Normally, this is where I would ask if you need a note for work, but since you're the Chief of Police, I'll let you make your own decisions, as long as they're smart."

Thanking him, they walked out of the hospital. Glaring at Dylan as he assisted her into the passenger side of his SUV, she opened her mouth, but he jumped to speak first.

"Shut it, Hannah. Let me do this for you." He leaned in the open door, placing a soft kiss on her lips. Holding her gaze, he said, "I know you're fine. You and I both know the risks of our jobs. But I really was scared. Let me take you home, fix you something to eat, and let's crawl into bed and not leave for the rest of the day."

His words swirled about and moved deep inside her. She shifted forward so that her lips were a whisper away from his. "I can't think of anything I'd rather do more." Before he had a chance to speak, she kissed him.

19

As the adrenaline wore off, Dylan drove in silence, occasionally glancing toward Hannah sitting in the passenger seat. She was fine, did not appear to be in pain, but with her arm wrapped, the stark reminder of what could have happened slammed into him.

He shook his head trying to dislodge the foolish thoughts pummeling him. They were both in law enforcement. They were both Police Chiefs. Same duties. Same risks. Just like many of his other friends. *Hell, just like my own female officer, Lynette.*

And yet, Hannah was different than all the others. *Because I love her.* He knew that, accepted it, and had no problem admitting it. At least to himself—for now.

As scared as he was when he came around the corner of the building to make sure she was okay, the sight of her standing there with her legs apart, weapon in hand, and prisoner subdued on the ground, he had to admit it was the sexiest thing he'd ever seen. If his heart hadn't been wildly beating in his chest, two prisoners present, and the sirens blaring their approach, he probably would've stalked straight to her, swept her into his arms, and kissed her senseless.

"Do you want to tell me what on earth you're thinking about over there? You're quiet, and I have no idea what's on your mind," Hannah said.

Jerking his head around to stare at her, he blurted, "I want to kiss you senseless."

She blinked twice, then burst into laughter. "Well okay, cowboy. Go for it."

Looking back toward the road, they were approaching her lane, having decided to stop at her house so she could feed Percy. Gunning the engine, he came to a skidding stop in front of her bungalow. Jumping down, he hurried around the front of the SUV as she opened her door. Sweeping her into his arms, his lips landed on hers. This was no gentle kiss. It blasted past red-hot and went straight into the white-hot zone, singeing both of them. Heads twisted, noses bumped, tongues thrust.

She sucked his tongue into her mouth, and his cock surged so tightly against his zipper, he figured he'd have a permanent tattoo mark running down his dick. Desperation clawed at him, unable to give all he wanted to give and take all he wanted to take while standing in her yard.

He carried her to the front door, and she quickly handed the key to him. He threw open the door, kicked it shut, and glanced down at the large cat already meowing. "You'll get yours as soon as I get mine."

With her laughter ringing out, he made it down the

hall and into her bedroom. He lowered her feet to the floor and wanted to whip her shirt off her, but the sight of her wrapped arm halted his progress, threatening to pour cold water over his heated body.

"No fuckin' way," she said, shaking her finger in front of him. "You're not letting this stop you." She grabbed the bottom of her shirt with his assistance and carefully drew it over her head and down her arm before tossing it to the floor. A quick flip of the snap, and her bra came off as well.

He stared at her naked torso, her perfect breasts with taut nipples beckoning. She was toned and trim, and his gaze snagged on a few bruises along her ribs, but before he could mention them she was already jerking down her pants, dragging her panties along with them.

With his hands under her armpits, he lifted her gently onto the bed and bent to pull off her sneakers. Divesting her of her pants and panties, he tossed them behind him as well.

Her gaze dropped from the pile of clothes on the floor back up to him. "There seems to be an inequitable amount of clothes on the floor, meaning that only mine are there. Don't you think you should do something about that?"

He grinned, mumbling, "Smartass," as he reached behind and jerked his T-shirt over his head. As he dropped it onto the pile of clothing on the floor, she leaned forward and dragged her fingernails over his chest and down his abs. His cock surged again, and he fought to maintain control as he toed off his shoes and shucked his pants and boxers down.

Now, glancing at the huge pile of clothes tangled on the floor together, he asked, "Is that good enough for you?"

She laughed and her gaze dropped to his cock standing at attention. "Oh, hell yeah, cowboy. That's more than good enough for me."

He grabbed her ankles and slowly pulled her ass to the edge of the bed. His hands glided from her feet up to her calves and down her thighs, soothing the skin underneath his fingertips. Every inch of her felt like silk. Her body was the perfect combination of strong and soft.

With her injury, she was unable to prop herself up on her elbows, but he reached over and grabbed a pillow to place under her neck and head so that she could keep her eyes on him.

He dropped to his knees, the scent of her arousal a siren's call. He nuzzled her sex while inhaling deeply. Everything about her spoke to him. Her scent. Her voice. Her laughter. Her smile. Her silky skin. Her eyes. And right now, he was assaulted by all that Hannah was offering to him.

With her legs wide open and her sex bared for him, he dove in like a starving man. Licking and sucking, tasting and tempting, thrusting his tongue. She writhed underneath him, and he continued to soothe his hands over her body as his mouth worked her into a frenzy. As tightly wound as they both were, she shattered quickly and it took all his self-control to not give into his own orgasm while kneeling between her legs. Licking his lips, he crawled forward on the bed after snagging a condom from his jeans. Straddling her thighs, he rolled the condom on, his eyes never leaving hers.

He wanted to give her everything. His body, his protection, his heart. If he could shield her from any disappointment or pain, he would. But right now was not the time to find out how much she was ready to take from him besides his body.

Lining his cock up at her entrance, he leaned forward and kissed her, this time nibbling lightly on her soft lips. Her good arm reached up and clutched his shoulder, her short fingernails digging in slightly, urging him on.

"Please, Dylan, please," she begged, shifting her hips upward.

Grinning, urged on by her encouragement, he plunged balls-deep, and she wrapped her legs around his back, digging her heels into his ass. Their kiss once more flamed hot, and for every thrust, she lifted her hips and met him. Their give and take was a dance as old as time, but with Hannah, he knew he would never take for granted what she was offering.

Leaning his weight into his forearm planted next to her, he palmed her breasts with his free hand, continuing to rain kisses over her mouth and down her jaw, to suckle the quivering flutter of her pulse at the base of her neck. Her body tensed around his, and he wondered how much longer he could last. Kissing his way to her lips again, his tongue swept inside, and he swallowed her cry as her body shattered beneath his.

All rational thoughts fled from his mind, leaving him with no other purpose than to release inside as her inner muscles clenched around him. Light sparked behind his closed eyes as every fiber in his being tightened and his orgasm rushed over him, draining him of every drop as he poured himself inside her. At the last moment, he maintained enough control to shift his weight to her good side, pulling her with him so that she lay on top, their bodies still connected.

Sweat-soaked and panting, he bore her weight easily as they both fought to catch their breath. His cock slowly slipped from her warm, slick sex, and his hands drifted over her back and ass in long, leisurely motions. She lay still for so long, he wondered if she'd drifted asleep. Finally, she lifted her head and smiled, kissed him lightly, then placed her cheek against his thumping chest.

With his nose buried against her silky hair and his arms banded around her, he whispered, "I love you." Her body stiffened slightly in his arms. He winced at the idea that he was rushing and she was not ready to hear such a declaration, no matter how true it was. For a long moment, they lay quiet and still, their bodies slowly cooling and their heartbeats slowing.

Finally, she lifted her head again and held his gaze. Her breath as soft as a whisper over his face, she asked, "You love me?"

"Yeah, I do. You don't have to say it back. You don't have to feel it. You don't have to feel anything other than what's in your heart. It may seem rushed to you, but the reality is that I fell for you years ago. I pushed those feelings away because I didn't think I'd ever be able to act on them. But my feelings for you have never wavered."

He felt as though he stood on a great precipice, and his breath halted in his tight throat, and his heart pounded even harder than when he came. Staring at her face, he swept her tresses away so that he could see her clearly.

Time stood still. Then her lips slowly curved into a gentle smile. She blinked, and he could swear he saw moisture gathering.

"I fell in love with you years ago, Dylan. I knew it was fast. I even knew it might not be the smartest thing to do. But my heart didn't listen to my head, and I fell. When we were forced to part, I knew my heart was broken. I couldn't show that to you. I couldn't show that to anyone. So I buried all those emotions deep, deciding to focus just on me. But now, I think it's truly our time, and I'm ready."

Hearing her words but wanting to make sure he understood her meaning, he licked his dry lips and asked, "You're ready?"

"I'm ready to let you know that I love you, too."

Hannah's eyes jerked open, and she missed the warmth that had surrounded her, instinctively knowing that Dylan was not in bed. Not wanting to move, they'd stayed at her bungalow. They'd had dinner, curled up together on the sofa and talked, then finally went back to bed and made love again. She had fallen asleep with all that was him wrapped around her.

She rolled over and spied him, already dressed, placing a note on the nightstand. "Did you get called in?" That was the only reason she could imagine he was leaving her bed after they'd openly declared their love for each other.

He bent deeply over her and kissed her forehead. "I'm sorry, babe. I didn't mean to wake you. I'm going to run out and get something done, and I'll be back soon."

She sat up, pushing her hair away from her face, trying to make sense of his words. "Run out for what?"

"I want to go ahead and get the security cameras up at the harbor. I don't want to do it during the day where everyone can see me. And if I wait too late, then the fishermen will start coming in before dawn. I know I'm taking a chance that somebody will see me, but I don't want to wait."

She threw the covers back and jumped to her feet. "Give me a minute to put some clothes on, and I'll go with you."

"No, absolutely not," he said, his arms crossing his impressive chest.

She stepped into her jeans and zipped them up. "Why not? If I go, we can get it done much quicker."

"I don't want you out in the middle of the night at the harbor when we don't know what might be going on."

She straightened, indignation steeling her spine. "Dylan," she said, her voice low. "I want you to think very carefully about what you're saying." He started to open his mouth, but her hand snapped up, palm facing him. "I get that you're talking to Hannah, the woman you love. But you cannot possibly forget that I am also Easton's Police Chief, with as much law enforcement experience and seniority as you. To imply that I should not be assisting you is an insult."

They stared without speaking for a moment, then he unfurled his arms, placing his hands on his hips as he dropped his head and stared at his boots. She remained silent, waiting to see what he would say. Finally, he lifted his head and sighed heavily.

"I know. I understand what you're saying. It's just weird, I guess."

Feeling underdressed for the heaviness of their conversation, she bent and snagged her bra off the floor. Sliding it on, she grabbed her T-shirt and pulled it on, wincing slightly. "Okay, that's better. Now, what do you mean it's weird?"

"I've always known you as a police chief. I know you're smart, competent, professional. But you work in Easton, and I work in Seaside, so I don't have to see you daily at times when you might be in danger. And I guess that's good. I can't turn off my desire to shield you from harm, but I know that it's something I have to deal with."

The tension left her shoulders, and she stepped forward, placing her hand on his arm. "When I heard the gunshot and knew that you were out there some-where, I was terrified. So I get it, Dylan. We both have jobs with high risks, and it's probably better that we don't work together each day. But there will be times when we can do things together, and this is one of them. You putting those cameras up helps the security for all of the Eastern Shore. I want to help. I want to be with you."

He nodded toward her arm. "Are you sure you're up to it?"

"It's only a bruise. I'll be fine."

He continued to stare for a moment, then she felt the muscles in his arm relax. Shaking his head slightly, he said, "Okay, Robin, let's go."

Blinking, her head jerked back. "Robin? Why do I have to be the sidekick?"

"Because we're going to be in Seaside. That's *my* jurisdiction, and we're putting up *my* cameras. Therefore, I get to be Batman."

Still grumbling, she slid her feet into her sneakers. "I should at least be Batgirl."

"That seems sexist."

She looked up and blinked, her lips quirking. "Well, how about Batwoman? Equals?"

Throwing his arm around her shoulders, he laughed. "How about just you and me… just us… equals?"

She wrapped her arm around his waist and grinned. "I like that. You and me."

Together, they headed to his SUV in the middle of the night. Thirty minutes later, her soft voice called out, "Not so fast. No, that's not the right angle. A little more to the left."

"Is that better?"

"It doesn't seem to be penetrating deep enough."

"If I shift too much to the left, I'm afraid it's not going to get the needed result."

Knowing if anyone else heard their conversation they'd think that they'd stumbled across a couple having sex on the harbor, she began to laugh. Looking up at Dylan standing on top of the ladder, she met his grin. "You do know what this sounds like, don't you?"

"Batwoman, I guarantee you that I have no problem penetrating deep enough, and I'll always get the right angle."

A new round of laughter erupted, and she jiggled the ladder. "Sorry, sorry!"

Dylan had installed the first camera at the far edge of the harbor with no difficulty. He had downloaded the app to his phone and made sure they synced. She had checked the screen and they were pleased with the view they'd achieved. Now, he was trying to get the middle of the harbor, finding it difficult to manipulate the angle to obtain the perfect view.

"Are you about to finish laughing?"

She looked up and nodded, but his smile gave proof that he was also amused. "I think this is the best we can do with these two. But why don't you take a look at them before we leave?"

She stood back as he scrambled down the ladder. Handing his phone to him, she trotted out onto several of the piers, giving him a chance to check the views. He waved and she jogged back over to him. "Are you happy with what you've got?"

His lips curved in a slow smile and he wrapped his

arms around her, pulling her close. Holding her gaze, he nodded. "Oh, yeah. I'm happy with what I've got."

She rolled her eyes, fighting a grin. "I was talking about the cameras."

"Well, Chief Freeman, the cameras are fine. But for you, babe, I'm more than happy with what I've got."

She wrapped her arm around his waist, and they drove back to her bungalow. Once more, they stripped and crawled underneath the covers. His warmth surrounded her and she soon found peaceful slumber again.

20

"Stop complaining, you big baby." Hannah tried to shush Percy as he yowled his discontent loudly in an attempt to either save his dignity at being stuffed into a carrier or let it be known far and wide how much he hated trips to the vet. Leaning down, she tried to stick her finger out to him, but all she received in return was a hiss and paw swipe. "This is not how I want to spend my lunch break either, you know," she whispered.

Glad when she was ushered into the examination room and away from the curious eyes of those in the vet clinic waiting room, she glared at the recalcitrant feline. "You are so nice at home but turn into a tiger when here." She looked up as the door opened, smiling when Sam walked into the room.

"Hey, Hannah. Percy."

Before Hannah had a chance to speak, Percy offered a long, drawn-out meow, summing up his feelings on the situation.

"I should just make a house call and save you the

discontent," Sam said, efficiently pulling the big cat from his carrier and placing him on the examining table.

"I feel like I should apologize," Hannah confessed, stroking Percy as Sam calmly checked him out.

"Nah, I'm used to this. Cats generally hate to be in carriers, and they always hate the vet. I don't take it personally."

It didn't take long for Percy to obtain a perfect bill of health and Sam readied the inoculations. "So... I saw you and Dylan at The Diner the other day."

Hannah had wondered when the questions would start. She and Dylan had been dating for several weeks, slowly stepping out more in public together while keeping the public displays of affection to a minimum.

"And, if Carrie's information is right, it's not the first time you two have sat closely on the same side of the booth."

Laughing, she shook her head. After all, she was the one who told Dylan that once they went public, it was like inviting everyone into their relationship. "Yes, we have shared a booth. Satisfied?"

Sam's gaze darted up as she continued to stroke Percy. "Hardly! I want details. After all, I have to live my love life vicariously through my friends."

"Well, you wouldn't have to if you'd give Joseph a chance."

Blinking, Sam stuttered. "Jo... Joseph? What on earth are you talking about?"

"Oh, come on... you have to know he's interested."

"You're crazy," Sam replied, looking back down.

Sam's voice held a wistful quality, but Hannah wasn't sure how to interpret that tone. Softly, she said, "What makes you think I'm crazy? I've seen the way he looks at you in the AL meetings." When Sam's gaze jumped up to hers, she continued. "But then maybe you're not interested—"

"We are complete opposites. As closed off as he is, who knows what he's thinking? And God knows I don't have time for his brand of complicated, even if I was interested!"

Now it was Hannah's turn to look confused. "Complicated?"

Sam pressed her lips together as she kept her gaze on Percy, slowly stroking the now-purring cat. "He's quiet... broody. Not rude, but not overly friendly." Shaking her head, she admitted, "I have no idea if he's got baggage or just introverted. But my life doesn't offer any time to help someone sort their shit when I work all day, am on-call most nights, and can barely take care of my own shit. I'm afraid *complicated* just doesn't work for me."

Percy meowed again and as much as she wanted to keep talking to Sam, she knew she needed to get her disgruntled cat home. Offering goodbyes as Sam hustled into the next examining room, she paid and placed his carrier into the backseat of her SUV once again. "Okay, big boy, let's get you home so I can get back to work."

She drove through Easton to get from the vet clinic back to her house, her gaze naturally scanning the area. Suddenly, a car ran a stop sign, causing her to slam on her brakes. Percy's carrier shifted and his yowl met her ears. Pissed, she flipped on her lights and pulled the car over to the side of the road. "Sorry for the delay, Percy, but Momma's got to deal with this guy."

"Ten-fifty-nine at the corner of Barkley and Orchard," she radioed. The license plate scanner quickly sent the number, and she looked to see who the car was registered to. She started to exit her SUV but, glancing down, she noted cat fur on her uniform. Grimacing, she quickly swiped her hand over her shirt.

Approaching the driver's side, she observed only one occupant who had rolled their window down. Her gaze moved through the back window, several cardboard boxes and bags filling the backseat. An object snagged in the corner of her vision, and she slowed her steps. Speaking softly into her radio, she called, "Ten-forty, ten-two."

Maintaining a distance where she could see the man's hands on the steering wheel, she asked for his driver's license and car registration. She accepted them from him, but instead of going back to her vehicle, she stayed where he was in her sight. It only took a moment for another vehicle to appear, and she nodded toward William, one of her officers.

"Sir, I'm gonna need to have you step outside your vehicle, please."

William moved to the other side, glanced through the car, then looked at her over the top, a quick nod indicating he spied the same thing she had.

As the driver alighted, his eyes darting between

them, a nervous smile on his lips, he asked, "Anything wrong, Officer?"

"You ran the stop sign back there, Mr. Jackson," she said, holding his gaze. "Is this your vehicle, Terrence?"

"Oh, I'm sorry," he rushed. "No, it belongs to my cousin."

She escorted him to the side just as another police vehicle arrived, this time bringing in Bobby. By now, William had opened the door and began searching the car. Terrence's eyes widened, and his hands reached forward as though to stop what was happening. Bobby restrained him, moving him back to his SUV while Hannah joined in the search with William.

"Shit, it's like hitting the mother lode," William said, pulling out three guns from the floorboard.

"Go through these boxes while I check the trunk." She moved around to the driver's side and pressed the trunk release before stepping to the back of the car. More boxes and bags were visible and she snapped on a pair of gloves. What was quickly evident was Terrence's trunk contained small bags of what appeared to be cocaine. A quick color test was positive, but she didn't trust that it might not be a false-positive.

She radioed to Pearl. "Ten-thirty-five. Possible drugs found in the vehicle. Call out for a North Heron detective."

The first to arrive was Hunter. She remembered when he landed on the Eastern Shore. Mitch and Colt thought he was a drug dealer, but it turned out he was undercover for the State Police and now worked for Colt. Greeting him, she turned the drugs over to him.

She had jurisdiction in the town of Easton, but with it located in North Heron, the Sheriff's Department had jurisdiction over the whole county. With her meager resources, she was thrilled with the assistance.

By now, Terrence was fast-talking about how it was his cousin's car, the guns weren't his, and he knew nothing about drugs in the trunk. Placing him under arrest, Bobby escorted him to his vehicle, taking him to the county jail. She, William, and Hunter bagged all of the evidence. Calling for a wrecker to take the car to the county's impound lot, she turned to the other officers when a loud yowl sounded from her vehicle.

"What the hell was that?" Hunter asked, twisting around as his head swung toward her SUV.

"Oh, God, I was on the way from the vet with my cat when this car ran a stop sign in front of me."

"Is he okay?"

Laughing, she said, "Yeah, he's fine. He's just letting me know that he's pissed off for staying in his carrier for so long."

William looked over and grinned. "I'll stay for the wrecker and get the paperwork for the impound lot. I know you missed part of your lunch, so why don't you go ahead and take your tiger home."

"I'll do that and then be right back into the office." She offered her hand to Hunter, clasping it in a firm shake. "Thanks for your help."

"Glad to keep this stuff off the streets, whether it was going to stay here on the Eastern Shore or get transported somewhere else." He held her gaze and added, "I know you and Dylan put some cameras up.

Do you think he possibly came in through Seaside Harbor?"

Sighing, she shook her head. "I don't know, but I'll see what I can find out." Tossing her hand up in a wave, she hustled back to her SUV and climbed in, glancing over her shoulder into the carrier. "You do know I have a job, right, Percy? That is how I afford your kitty treats!"

Percy's large eyes simply stared, but he remained silent as though he was judging her. She made it back to her bungalow, and once inside opened the carrier, grinning as Percy crept out, sniffing to make sure he was truly in his home. Her phone rang, and she glanced at the caller ID. "Hey, Dylan. What's up?"

Balancing her phone between her shoulder and ear, she bent to pour food into Percy's dish. As she dumped it into the bowl, her phone slipped out and clattered to the floor. "Dammit!" Snatching it up, she asked, "Are you still there?"

"What the hell are you doing, Hannah?"

"I'm trying to feed my cat and dropped the phone."

"You're at home? I thought you were at work."

"I am at work, but I'm at home." Huffing, she shook her head. "Shit, it's too complicated to explain right now. What's up with you?"

"Barbara heard the chatter over dispatch that you ended up with a car full of drugs."

Not surprised that the news had spread amongst the other law enforcement members in the area, she grinned. "Yeah, I was going to talk to you about that. The guy clammed up and didn't say where he came from or where he got them. He originally said it was his cousin's car and he didn't know anything about the drugs or the weapons."

"Colt take it?"

"Everything was taken in, and Hunter will be the lead detective for North Heron. He'll get drug samples to the lab, of course, do the fingerprint checking. Also, the car is impounded."

"So we don't know where he came from?"

"No, I was going to check with you later to see if anything came through on the security cameras."

"I looked at the last couple of nights, skimming through, and haven't seen anything. But that doesn't mean he didn't come during the day. Once he gets processed into the jail, I'll take his mug shot to see if anyone in the harbor recognizes him."

She appreciated the assistance the area law enforcement provided to each other. Having heard her father complain over the years about jurisdiction problems with the FBI, she was once again certain that she had chosen the right path.

"So, after Percy gets fed, are you heading back out, or are you done for your shift?"

"I'm going back to the station. I need to get my report written, and then I want to go over to the jail once I talk to Hunter again."

His voice softened, and he asked, "Tonight's your place, right?"

As she stood at her sink and looked out the window, she thought about her answer and smiled. She was comfortable with where they were as a couple... seeing each other as often as they could, intertwining their lives, and spending the night in whichever house happened to be the most convenient. But she would be a liar if she said she hadn't thought of what would happen in the future. Turning her head, she glanced around at the colorful interior of her bungalow. She loved every inch of it, having created her own oasis. But it was only a place, one that she could replicate anywhere. It was a great space for a single woman, but not large enough to be a home for a family. One day, she knew she would need to put it on the market to sell or keep it to rent, hoping to call Dylan's home her own.

Not about to give voice to those thoughts at the moment, she simply said, "Yeah, tonight can be here. I'll go for a short, easy run first and will be back before you get here. If neither of us has to work early tomorrow, we can enjoy the sunrise on my back patio."

"I can't argue with the way you think, sweetheart," he said. "I'll start checking around to see if your guy came through Seaside. We'll talk later."

Disconnecting, her feet stayed rooted to the floor as she continued to smile, her heart full. Feeling something swish against her legs, she looked down and saw that Percy had finished his meal and was purring loudly.

"Forgive me now?" Bending, she rubbed his head before jogging back out to her vehicle to return to the police station.

21

Dylan walked along the harbor boardwalk as several of the fishing boats were returning to dock at the end of their day. Scanning the area, he noted Todd had moved toward David's boat, grabbing the lines and helping tie it to the pier. He hadn't asked David about Todd in a while, assuming no news was good news. And if what he was observing was anything to go by, it was definitely good news with the teenager.

He stopped by several of the fishing boats, showed the mug shot, and asked if any of them had seen the man within the last several weeks at the harbor. He received negative replies from all, although most admitted they didn't often pay attention to the faces around them when they were working.

Heading over to David's boat, he greeted Todd and asked, "How are you doing?"

"I'm good, Chief Hunt."

He stepped back and allowed David's crew to unload the day's catch before moving over to his brother. "Take a look at this and tell me if you've seen this man around here recently."

David looked at the photograph of Terrence and shook his head. "I've been trying to pay more attention to the boats in the harbor and around here, Dylan, but I'm usually so focused on what's going on when I'm getting ready to go out and when I come back in, I admit it's hard."

Nodding, he understood how much David's attention needed to be focused on the boat when he was coming and going from the harbor. "I know, bro, and it's all good—"

"I think I've seen him."

Swinging his head to the side, he stared at Todd who was leaning over, looking at the photograph in Dylan's hand. "You've seen this man? Around here?"

Todd leaned closer and his nose scrunched as he stared. When he lifted his head, his eyes darted between Dylan and David before dropping back to the picture. "Yeah, I'm pretty sure I've seen him."

"Do you remember when?"

A nervous expression crossed his face as he pressed his lips together. "I want to help, Chief, but I don't want to fuck anything up."

"You're not going to, Todd. If you tell me when you think you saw him and it doesn't check out, then it doesn't check out. But if it does, then we have a lead."

"It was sometime last week. I don't remember what day, but I remember what caught my attention. He had on a dark sweatshirt hoodie and it was a warm day. I just remembered thinking that he was probably hot with all those clothes on."

"That's good, Todd. Now, did you notice anything else about him?"

"No, I'm sorry. I always get here right after school and usually have to wait a little while before the boat comes in. Sometimes I sit over next to Mr. Owens' office and get some of my homework done. People are always coming and going, and when I'm doing my homework, I tend to just block them out. So, it's probably just dumb luck that I happened to look up. Honest to God, that's all I thought and then I went back to my homework."

"You're doing good. Let me see if I can spark any memories for you. Was he on a boat, with a boat, getting off of a boat, talking to anyone on a boat? Was he by himself or with someone else? Was he carrying anything? Which direction was he walking?"

Seeming to warm to the task, Todd began to nod. "He was by himself and wasn't over where the boats were. He was walking past the gas pumps toward the parking area," he said, waving his arm to indicate the direction. I didn't see anything in his hands, but with the big hoodie on, I guess there could have been something."

Dylan felt a surge of excitement and shook Todd's hand, clapping him on the shoulder at the same time. "This was helpful, Todd. Thank you."

Todd offered an embarrassed grin, then moved back over to the ice chests of fish with David's crew. Offering his brother a wave, Dylan jogged back to his SUV, eager to start looking at the security feed. Since every day last week had been unseasonably warm, he would need to start with Monday. But knowing that the timeframe was after David got out of school but before the boats came in narrowed the field tremendously.

On his way back to the station, he radioed Barbara to call a staff meeting of anyone available. As soon as he arrived, he was grateful to see that everyone was there. Carl was just getting off duty but easily agreed to stay for a meeting. Lynette, Joe, and Tom filled in around the table.

Going over the arrest that Hannah had made in Easton, Dylan explained what Todd had witnessed at the harbor. "I've been looking at the security feeds sporadically but now can specifically go over last week during the afternoons. I confess that having the cameras was a good idea, but no one can man them twenty-four hours a day. Hell, with our duties, we can barely handle watching them with any regularity at all."

"Can we divide the workload?" Lynette asked. "If each one of us took an hour a day, that would be five hours of scanning."

He scrubbed his hand over his face and shook his head. "I have to think about the allocation of our time. I can't justify each of us spending an entire hour a day to comb through video feeds when there might be nothing to find."

"And, of course, there's no extra money in this town to hire this job out to anyone," Joe groused.

The others chuckled, nodding their heads. "Hell, there's no money for any of this," Tom added, waving his hand toward Dylan's laptop. "We've got the technology right in front of us and can't use it all."

"I mostly wanted you to know that I did get some information from Todd and will scan through last week to see if I can find this guy that the Easton police arrested. If I can, then we have a link to someone bringing in drugs through the Seaside Harbor. With that information, I can take it to the Mayor and Town Council to see if we can get more resources."

"And it might identify if he came in by himself or with someone else," Joe added.

Absolutely," Dylan agreed. "We've always had the harbor on our drive-bys each day and night, but we're going to increase that. I want an actual walk through the harbor every day and every evening. Mix it up... different times. Make sure you talk to the fishermen, get them used to looking out for what they might see that's unusual." Dismissing his group, he went back to his office and pulled up the security feeds on his laptop.

For the next hour, he managed to scan the first three days of the previous week from the time that Todd said he got to the harbor until the fishing boats came in. Other than his time in the military and police academy, he'd spent part of every day of his life in Seaside near the harbor. He knew it was a bustling, high-traffic area. But until he sat poring through the video feeds, he had no idea just how much was going on and how many people moved through there daily. Leaning back in his chair, he cracked his neck and glanced at the time. Closing down his computer, he called out his goodbyes and headed home.

That evening after dinner, he and Hannah sat side-by-side on the sofa, their eyes glued to her widescreen TV where he'd connected the security feed from his laptop. It certainly made it easier for his eyes to scan on the large screen and also made it easier for someone else to watch at the same time. Percy curled up on one side of the sofa, content to sleep while they worked.

He glanced to the side at her profile, her bright eyes focused directly on the TV. A grin slipped across his face at the realization that he knew no other woman who'd want to spend an evening together studying his security feed. But, like with everything else, he and Hannah were perfect together.

Hitting pause, he watched as her head swung around, a crease knitting her brow. "I need a break for my eyes," he said. He lifted his hand to cup the back of her head, drawing her forward. He meant for the kiss to be light, a touch, a simple connection. But she melted against him, and he tossed the remote to the coffee table and fell backward onto the sofa, pulling her down with him. Percy yowled his discontent for being woken and jumped down, his tail twitching, ignored by the humans. For several minutes, they made out like two teenagers before finally coming up for air.

"Wow," she breathed. "I like working with you!"

He barked out a laugh, and they sat up together. "Yeah, I needed that break." Clicking the video feedback on, they continued to watch.

Suddenly she startled, sitting up straight. "Which day is this? Last Thursday?"

"Yeah." Leaning forward to see what she was staring at, he recognized one of her officers. "Is that Bobby?"

"Yeah. Let's see, last Thursday was his day off, so that would make sense that he'd be out of uniform doing whatever he needed to do."

"Has he ever mentioned going out on a boat? Or doing some fishing?"

"It's not something that ever came up, but it's certainly not unusual for people in this area."

They continued to watch as Bobby moved up and down several of the piers, a ball cap settled low on his head. He occasionally looked around, but mostly he appeared to peer out into the harbor. Finally, after almost thirty minutes, he turned and headed out of view of the camera in the direction of the parking lot.

"That was weird," Hannah said, her voice quiet. "It would be ludicrous to try to make it more than it was or figure out what he was doing, but I confess, that was just weird."

They continued watching the screen until they both jumped at the same time. "Look, that's him!" Hannah called out. The camera picked up the view of Terrence walking down one of the piers, but unfortunately, the angle kept them from seeing which boat he may have made contact with. Several minutes later, they watched him walking along the main boardwalk just as Todd had indicated. Turning toward Dylan, her eyes were bright. "Finally, our first physical evidence of a connection between the drugs and the harbor at Seaside."

As excited as her voice was, Dylan continued watching, his brow lowering. "What the fuck is he doing?"

After Terrence had passed by the camera, Todd walked down the same pier in the direction where Terrence had come from. Again, unable to see beyond one of the large boats that were in their line of sight, they had no idea who Todd may have talked to or what he was doing. "Fuck, he didn't mention doing anything other than his homework while waiting for David's boat to get in."

"That could just be a coincidence."

Shooting her a hard stare, he said, "And in our line of work, you know as well as I do that coincidences can often have full meanings."

They sat silent for a moment, each to their own thoughts. "You want to keep going?" he asked, finally.

She nodded. "Yeah, let's go ahead and get this done. Once we get the week looked at, then you'll know more about what's going on at the harbor." Leaning in, she blew her soft breath across his cheek and added, "And then we can focus on us."

Throwing his arm around her, he pulled her close, planting a hard, wet kiss on her lips. "With that image front and center in my mind, staring at the TV is going to be almost impossible."

He poured another glass of wine for her and grabbed another beer for himself before settling back on the sofa. They continued watching the security feed of the comings and goings of a small albeit busy harbor. They were almost to the end of the previous night when they both startled once again. This time, it was Luke that caught their eye. The county jail's new medic walked up and down several of the piers after dark the previous evening. In a similar fashion to Terrence and Todd, he disappeared out of sight for several minutes before coming back and heading to the parking lot.

Clicking the remote off, Dylan cursed in frustration. "I swear pier three is the place everyone is going to, but we can't fuckin' see what's at the end. I never noticed that big-ass boat is in the way."

"Maybe we should get another camera. We can mount it in a place that will extend to the end of the piers."

Scrubbing his hand over his face, he nodded. "Yeah, you're probably right. We'll put that on our weekend list of things to do." Turning off the TV, he glanced at her glass of wine. "You almost finished with that?"

Lips curving, she asked, "What's it to you, cowboy?"

"'Cause as soon as you finish that, I'm taking you to bed."

She grabbed her glass, drained it in one large gulp, and plopped it back onto the coffee table. Standing quickly, he scooped her up, exclaiming, "That's my girl."

Her arms wrapped around his neck, and she nuzzled his neck as he stalked toward the bedroom. "Yeah, I am. I'm your girl."

22

Twisting her hair into a sloppy bun, Hannah walked down the hall and into her kitchen. Reaching for the mugs, she flipped the switch on her coffee maker. She and Dylan had slept late, enjoying the fact that they were both on-call for that Saturday, not having to go into their stations. Percy woke them by jumping on the bed, but she didn't mind because as soon as she fed the cat and went back into the bedroom, she was welcomed by a naked Dylan who was more than happy to introduce her to shower sex... the perfect way to start any weekend.

Lifting the carafe, she poured two cups of coffee just as he walked into the kitchen. Her eyes did a quick scan, snagging on his naked chest, bare feet, and jeans that hung low on his hips, the top button left undone. Doctoring his coffee, she shoved it toward him, mumbling, "Damn, you look good."

He rounded the corner and bent, taking her lips in a kiss. "Just thinking the same thing about you, babe." He glanced behind her and asked, "Are you sure you want to make breakfast? I don't mind taking you to The Diner."

Shaking her head, she replied, "No. Going to Joe's means we have to get completely dressed and be around other people, 'cause his place will be packed on a Saturday morning. Right now, I like the idea of you and me and no expectations from anyone else."

He threaded his fingers through her hair, cupping the back of her head. Pulling her forward, he kissed her soundly again. This time, he mumbled, "Damn, your ideas are good."

A knock on the door startled her, unable to imagine who would be coming to visit on a Saturday morning. Glancing at the clock on the oven, she could see it was already ten o'clock, but for a day off, that was still early for visitors, especially since she rarely had any. She walked past Dylan on her way to the front door, noting how he slid in right next to her. She peeked through the security hole, then muttered under her breath, "You've got to be kidding me." Twisting her head around and up, she stared at his eyes, noting his brows cocked in a silent question. "Believe it or not, it's my parents."

For a brief second, she thought about running to her bedroom to change clothes and telling Dylan to put a shirt on. But suddenly, with the idea that her peaceful Saturday morning had just gotten more complicated without warning, she threw open the door and greeted, "Hey, Mom. Dad. Did I miss a call that said y'all were coming to visit?"

She stepped back and waved her arm, inviting them

in. They both smiled their greetings, then their feet stumbled at the sight of a half-naked man standing next to her.

"Oh!" her mom squeaked. "I'm so sorry! We had no idea you had... um... company."

She bit back her snippy comment about how if they'd called first, they would know her plans, instead of focusing on her dad's eagle-eyed gaze pinned on Dylan. "Well, it's not how I planned it, but since you're here, let me introduce you to Dylan. Mom, Dad, this is Dylan Hunt. Dylan, meet my parents, Jacob and Lucy Freeman."

Dylan stepped forward with his hand out, offering a firm shake. "Nice to meet you, Mr. and Mrs. Freeman. If you'll excuse me, I'll go put on a shirt." With a smile, he turned and ambled down the hall.

Trying to ignore the way his ass looked amazing in his jeans, she turned back to her parents. "I was just getting ready to make breakfast. Let me run to the back and make myself more presentable as well." She followed Dylan, leaving her parents rather stunned and wide-eyed. Once in her bedroom, she closed the door and looked at him. "I'm so sorry! I had no idea they were coming. God, this is so embarrassing!"

"Honey, I don't want to embarrass you or anything. Let me grab my shirt, and I'll head on out—"

"You embarrass me? What are you talking about?"

His brow lowered as he cocked his head to the side. "What are *you* talking about?"

Throwing her hands out to the side, she said, "I'm embarrassed about my parents! They didn't let me know they were coming, and they just dropped in. That's so frustrating! You and I had plans… oh, my God, what if we'd been in bed… or the shower?"

He chuckled and stepped closer, putting his hands on her shoulders. "Babe, they're your parents. I know it's been a while since you've been back up to Hope City, so they probably just miss you. Listen, it's fine, I can head back to my place—"

"Oh, hell no! You're in my life, Dylan. I'm not going to have you leave."

He pulled her forward and kissed her forehead. "Are you sure?"

"Absolutely. I want you with me. After all, they might as well meet the man I'm in love with."

He met her grin and said, "Then we better get dressed."

She jerked off her sleep T-shirt, winking as his gaze scored over her naked body. She snapped on her bra and found a clean shirt in her closet, smoothing it over her chest. After pulling on a pair of jeans, she ran a brush through her hair. Turning around, she watched as he buttoned up his jeans and settled the clean T-shirt he'd brought with him over his muscular chest.

He lifted his hands slightly and asked, "Presentable?"

She laughed and nodded. "Well, I liked you half-dressed before, but yes, I suppose this is more presentable for my parents." She turned to walk out of the bedroom when he reached out and captured her hand, bringing her to a halt. She twisted around and looked at him, tilting her head to the side, waiting to see what he was going to say.

"Are you okay? Because you've got to know, I want your parents to like and accept me, but I won't take anyone putting you down."

The simple words wrapped around her heart, and she stepped directly into his space, leaning her head back to hold his gaze. Her lips curved into a smile. "That right there is one of the reasons why I love you."

He pulled her close and took her lips in a quick kiss. "Okay, then let's go have breakfast with the parents."

By the time they made it back into the kitchen, Lucy was already scrambling eggs, toasting bagels, and the scent of sizzling bacon filled the air. Offering her mom a hug, she said, "You didn't have to start."

"Well, we dropped in on you unexpectedly, so the least I can do is fix breakfast. Your dad helped himself to a cup of coffee."

Her bungalow was small, and her kitchen table was only a two-seater. When her parents visited, they usually squished around the table with an added patio chair brought in. With four of them, she was glad the day was nice, and they took their plates onto her back patio where she had four antique metal chairs with soft, colorful cushions.

"Dylan, what business are you in?" Jacob asked.

Hannah sighed, knowing the inquisition was about to begin. Hoping to shoot Dylan an apologetic gaze, he was focused on her dad, a ready smile on his face.

"I'm the Chief of Police at the town of Seaside."

Hannah watched her father blink, knowing that response surprised him.

"Oh, are you Hannah's boss?" her mother asked.

Rolling her eyes, Hannah sighed heavily. "Mom, I'm also Chief of Police. My boss is the mayor of Easton, not the police chief in a completely different locality."

"How big is Seaside?" her dad asked, moving right past his wife's faux pas.

"It has about five-hundred residents. It's in between the size of Baytown and Easton."

"I met the Chief of Baytown. It surprised me that he gave up a career at the FBI to be the Chief of Police of a little town in the middle of nowhere…"

Even though her dad made a statement, she heard the open-ended question dangling at the end. Refusing to let him berate her and Dylan's choices, she said, "I'd think by now you'd be used to the fact that not everyone wants to be associated with the Bureau, Dad. Thank goodness, there are like-minded people that believe in law enforcement for rural areas."

Her dad opened his mouth, then snapped it shut, offering a curt nod. That maneuver surprised her since he usually didn't give up so easily.

"My family is actually in the fishing business, Mr. Freeman. My grandfather started the business, my father continued it, and my brother now runs it. I had a different path, joining the Navy and then going into law enforcement."

Jacob nodded slowly, his attentive gaze moving between Hannah and Dylan. "It sounds like you know exactly what you want."

Dylan looked over and held her gaze and smiled. "Yes, Sir, I do."

From there, the conversation became easy and

pleasant, allowing Hannah to relax. They talked about the Eastern Shore, his family's fishing business, and she gained news about her brother, Alex. By the time they cleaned up from breakfast, her parents expressed interest in seeing more of the area, something they hadn't done in their past visits.

Piling into Dylan's SUV, they drove through Baytown, visited a winery, walked on a historic trail, and as soon as he heard her parents had never spent any time in Easton, stopped at the historic Courthouse area for a tour. As they walked around, Hannah played tour guide as well as greeted town residents that were also out and about on the weekend.

They finally ended up at Seaside where Dylan offered to take them to dinner at The Wharf Restaurant. Sitting next to a window, her mother looked out over the harbor.

"It's so pretty here," she said. "Not at all like I thought it might be... you know, super touristy." She turned and looked at Hannah and Dylan sitting across from her. "As lovely as today has been, I do feel bad because we dropped in. Next time, we'll be sure to check to see what your plans are."

"It's fine, Mom. It's been nice to spend the day with you. It's been a long time since we've done something like this."

Dylan rested his fingers on her shoulder and said, "It was very nice to meet you, and honestly, the only thing we had on our schedule today was to buy another security camera, and we can easily get that done tomorrow." .

"For Hannah's house or yours?" her dad asked, a crease of concern settling between his brows.

"Actually, it's for the harbor out there," Dylan replied, inclining his head toward the harbor and piers.

"You have to buy the cameras?"

"Yes, Sir. There's not enough money in the budget, and while Hannah is helping me write a grant proposal, we need to get something out there. We know it's a point where drug runners are coming in."

Seeing her father's confused expression, Hannah explained, "Dylan bought a couple of cameras a few weeks ago, and we installed them. There's no money for someone to watch them, but if something happens, then we have a little more proof. I arrested someone with drugs in the trunk of their car, and we discovered he may have come in through the harbor. Yesterday we spent part of our evening looking at the feeds. We saw where he came in, but we were unable to get the information on what boat he connected with." Shrugging, she glanced at Dylan and smiled. "We'll get another camera up and hopefully get lucky."

She turned and looked back at her parents, noting her mother's smile, but the expression on her dad's face was unreadable. Uncertain what he was thinking, a snake of unease moved through her, and she prayed he wasn't going to say anything insulting about the limited budgets she or Dylan had to work with. *Especially Dylan. I might be used to it, but Dad had better not go there.*

After dessert, they drove back to Hannah's bungalow to say their goodbyes. As she hugged her mother, she glanced to the side and noticed her father shaking

Dylan's hand, the two having a quiet conversation. Sucking in her lips, she noted that Dylan did not seem angry. Her father walked over to her, and she let go of her mom. Jacob wrapped his arms around her and gave her a short hug and clap on the back.

Thinking that was all, she was surprised when he said, "I know you chose a different path, Hannah, and I've made it no secret that I didn't understand it. But listening to you today with the obvious pride you have in your job and your staff, and meeting Dylan and seeing the lengths that you will go to keep this area safe... well, I now realize how much a place like this needs people like the two of you."

Tears stung her eyes, and she blinked, unable to hold them back. "That means the world to me, Dad."

With more hugs and goodbyes called out as her parents got into their car, Dylan wrapped his arm around her and they waved until the taillights had disappeared.

23

The moonlight cast a shimmery glow over the undulating water in the Seaside harbor. Once more on a ladder propped against a light pole, Dylan worked to secure the infra-red security camera. Glancing down at the beautiful woman steadying the ladder below, he grinned. *Gorgeous, smart, tenacious, accomplished... and mine.*

"You gonna finish up there or keep staring down my shirt?" Hannah quipped.

Snorting, he gave the screwdriver a final twist. "Well, I was admiring the whole package, but now that you mention it, the view of your tits is quite spectacular."

Now it was her time to laugh, shaking her head.

Getting back to the business at hand so that they could go back to her place and get down to their own business, he said, "How's this angle?"

She looked at his phone screen and nodded. "This gives me a view out to the end of the first three piers. The last three piers are picked up by the cameras we already installed." She beamed her smile up toward him. "Looks like we're good."

After scrambling down the ladder, he hauled it next to Owen's office, replacing it on the ground. They were in the shadows of the building and he took the opportunity to grab her around the waist and pull her close. With his back against the wooden wall, he took her weight as she leaned into him, her lips landing on his.

Coming up for air, he mumbled, "Been a long time since I made out in public, babe. Probably not since meeting up with my high school girlfriend under the bleachers."

Grinning, she pinched his stomach, eliciting a grunt. "Guess I'll just have to see if I can replace those memories with some of our own."

Lips meeting again, they kissed for several long minutes, his hand drifting underneath her jacket. Lost in the little sounds she made in the back of her throat, it took a moment for the sound of water lapping louder against the pier to penetrate his mind. Lifting his head, he twisted around, feeling her stiffen in his arms.

"Do you hear that?" she whispered, her eyes pinned out over the harbor as well. A small light bouncing out in the water from a boat could now be seen.

He nodded. "Someone's coming in. They've cut their engine and are drifting in." He kept his hands on her waist as she pushed off him, letting go when he was sure she was steady. Glad they were both armed, they moved to the edge of the building, still hidden deep within the shadows.

He had placed his hands on her shoulders, but the

sound of soft footsteps walking from the parking lot had him reach for his weapon, and he noted she did the same. Catching her gaze, he jerked his head to the side, and she nodded her silent understanding. Leaving her side, he slipped behind Owen's office and moved to the other side to get a better view. The harbor piers were open to the public and not off-limits to anyone after dark... in fact, some of the pleasure boats had owners sleeping on board. But, typically, the middle of the night was quiet and why he chose this time to put the cameras in place.

Obtaining a line of sight in the direction of the parking lot, he spied a lone figure walking along the boardwalk toward Pier Three dressed in jeans, dark jacket, and a dark knit cap pulled low over their head. Turned away from him, Dylan could not identify the man... and by the posture and walk, he was sure it was a man.

Staying within the shadows, he moved with stealth toward the closest boat tied to the first slip on the pier. The man continued to the end where a smaller boat had drifted close to the pier. Wishing he had his radio, he pulled his phone from his pocket, shooting Hannah a text.

Man at end. Boat arrived. In sight.

His phone immediately vibrated and he checked her reply.

Calling for backup.

He watched as the man made it to the end and felt the floating pier move as the boat bumped against the edge. The light pole on the pier cast a little illumination, but he was too far away to see how many people were in the boat or to hear what was being said. He crept closer, still staying within the shadows of the boat in the first slip.

Someone onboard tossed a bundle toward the man who caught it easily. He opened it and glanced inside, then closed the flap.

Dylan hated that he did not have more backup, wanting to capture the boat as well as the man. Unable to communicate with Hannah other than by cellphone, he hesitated then felt his phone vibrate again.

Go for man. I'll go for boat ID.

The man was on the move, hustling back down the pier, coming closer to where Dylan was hiding. Trusting Hannah, he let the man near and then stepped out, weapon drawn, and called out, "Stop. Police."

The boat engine roared to life, and Hannah's footsteps were heard pounding toward the end of the pier. The man's eyes widened as they darted to the side, clutching the bag to his chest. "Don't think about it," Dylan warned. The sound of the boat engine alerted him to its getaway, and he hoped Hannah was able to see it well enough for an identification.

"Get down on the ground," he called out, approaching the man.

The man nodded and started to kneel, then suddenly whirled the bag outward. "Damnit!" Dylan cried, landing on the man as he heard the splash of the bag hitting the water. Pulling the man's arms behind his back, Dylan shifted his weight to get to his zip ties to secure his wrists together.

The sound of running footsteps coming closer caused him to jerk his head around just in time to see Hannah jump into the dark water near where the bag was tossed. *Shit!* While Hannah was close to the pier, he knew from his time in the Navy that it was easy to get turned around and confused while swimming at night.

Leaning down, he said, "Stay put, man. Don't move a fuckin' muscle." More footsteps were coming from the parking lot and he spied Carl approaching. "Hannah's in the water. Watch the suspect," he ordered.

Leaping to his feet, he raced to the edge of the pier, not seeing her. He bent to pull off his boots when her head broke the surface of the water with a splash.

"Hannah!" he called out, dropping to his knees near the edge of the pier and reaching his hand out.

Gasping, she shook her head. "I had my fingertips on it. I can get it." She sucked in a deep breath and dove back under.

His heart pounded as his eyes stayed glued onto the inky, wavy surface, counting the seconds she was submerged. "Fuck it," he breathed, standing to dive in, halting only when she appeared again. Dropping once more to his knees, he reached out as she swam closer.

"Here!" she spluttered, lifting her arm and holding the bag in her hand.

"Jesus," he said, shaking his head. He took the bag, tossed it to the side on the pier, and reached down for her hand.

"Watch my sore elbow," she said, lifting the arm not bruised.

He grabbed her hand, dragging her toward him. Her

weight was slight even with the soaked clothing, and he lifted her easily onto the pier.

She was breathing heavily, and her body shivered. She tried to pull off her jacket but her fingers were shaking. He gently pushed her hands to the side and worked her wet jacket off her body. More approaching footsteps could be heard, and he turned to see Lynette hustling toward them.

"Call for an ambulance."

She radioed the EMTs as she ran back to the parking lot, returning a moment later with a blanket. He wrapped it around Hannah, assisting her to her feet.

"I'm good, I'm good," she insisted. "Just cold." Looking at the pack, she said, "Look inside. I need to know what I jumped into the water for."

Opening the pack, Dylan shined his light down inside, seeing plastic-wrapped packages. Pulling one out, he took his knife and made a slit inside, exposing white powder. "Get some evidence bags, Lynette."

While waiting on her, he glanced up toward Hannah. She stood nearby, shivering and yet with a huge smile on her face. Unable to keep his lips from curving, he said, "You're crazy, you know that, right?"

Shaking her head, she laughed. "Nah... just tenacious."

Lynette came back and assisted him as they bagged the entire pack. He signed off on the evidence and she chuckled. "You don't have to ask, Chief. I'll take it to the lab in Norfolk. If I leave right now, it'll take an hour."

"See if they can get a rush on it," he asked. "At least

have them do a more accurate color test to let me know what we can charge him with."

"Gotcha." She threw out a two-fingered salute and jogged back toward the parking lot.

He and Hannah walked to the harbor's boardwalk where Carl had the suspect now standing, his cap pulled off. Dylan didn't recognize him but kept his eyes on him as he asked his question to Carl. "ID?"

"Maryland driver's license. John Ortega. Twenty-three," Carl said. "He's in the system… priors."

Joe hustled toward them from the parking lot. "His keys fit a vehicle in the lot. Maryland tags. Registered to Paul Velasquez. Hope City address."

Stepping closer, he scanned John. Tall, lean muscles. Dark hair. Dark eyes that held no expression. Completely blank. Not drugs, but someone who knew the risks and would not turn over on anyone above him.

Dylan didn't doubt that when John was processed into the jail, they would discover tattoos that would point to whichever gang he belonged to. Holding his gaze, he said, "This isn't your first rodeo, John, so you know the process. You'll be taken to jail and charged once we get confirmation on the drugs you were carrying. You want to save us some time and tell us what it was?"

John remained silent, his gaze moving beyond Dylan as Hannah approached. A strange flare of possessiveness coursed through Dylan and he flexed his fingers, fighting the urge to put his fist into John's face, warning him to keep his eyes off Hannah. "It's only a matter of time before we find out who you met with."

Jerking his head to the side, Dylan ordered, "Take him in. Book him on suspicion of possession with intent to distribute, to begin with. Make sure to get photographs of any tattoos." Turning toward Joe, he said, "Impound his vehicle."

Hannah stepped closer, her gaze intense on the men walking away. The blanket was still wrapped around her body, and he wanted to get her inside and warm. "Let me get you checked out. Then I'll take you home before heading to the jail."

"Don't you want to know what I saw with the boat?"

Blinking, he cocked his head to the side. "What?"

She laughed and said, "I didn't just rescue the pack, but before that, I got a visual of the boat. Sea Witch. 92-343. There were two people in the boat, and it won't take long to find out who the boat is registered to."

Throwing his arm around her shoulder, he pulled her wet body closer. "Damn, Chief Freeman."

"I'm more than just a pretty face," she laughed.

Bending so that he could whisper into her ear, he said, "Let's get you home, dry, and warm. And then we can fuckin' celebrate."

Standing on her toes, she rested her hand on his chest and whispered in return. "I say we celebrate by fuc—"

Her words were cut off as he kissed her before they walked away from the harbor.

24

Hannah balanced the phone between her shoulder and ear, nodding her thanks to Pearl as another cup of coffee, fixed just the way she liked, was placed on her desk. "I appreciate any insight you can offer," she said.

"Hey, whatever it takes to get my baby sister to call me."

Knowing that the suspect from last night had prior offenses, Dylan would be able to obtain his previous records. But, discovering that he was from Hope City, she wanted to reach out to her brother, Alex, to see if he had any inside information.

"I never dealt with him, but I can tell you he's never stayed in jail very long. Obviously, you can see his records, but he always made bail. He was picked up a couple of times in Miami as a juvenile and has one arrest in Atlanta. He's now got two arrests with us in Hope City. The last time, he was picked up in a sweep with others but only spent six months in jail for that offense."

"Any idea if he's related to a specific gang?"

"He claims allegiance to Mara Salvatrucha. At least, that's what's in the report."

Gang activity was present but not prevalent on the Eastern Shore, but knowing it was on the increase, Hannah stayed advised on the major gangs running up and down the coast, making sure her officers were educated and knew what to look for as well. While it might seem counterintuitive to most people, gang members readily shared their affiliation. To not do so would be an insult to the gang.

"Anything else?" she asked.

"He was always small potatoes, so he was able to fly under the radar. It also doesn't look like any of the detectives had dealings with him."

"Thanks anyway, Alex. At least we've got him in jail for now."

"I can't believe you stumbled onto him while putting up security cameras," Alex laughed.

"Oh, shut up. I'll take an arrest any way I can get it, even if I had to take a flying leap into the water to get the evidence."

Alex barked out another round of laughter. "By the way, I got a call from Mom the other day. She said she liked your new man."

"New man? She called him a new man?" This time she heard Alex snort.

"Yeah, that would indicate you had an old man at some time, right?"

That was one of the things she loved so much about

her brother. Fun conversation. And he was interested in what she did. No judgment.

He continued, "I'll also tell you that Dad mentioned he thought maybe you'd made the right decision with your career."

"He indicated that to me just as they left. You could have knocked me over with a feather!"

"I figured the old man would come around sometime. What you do is important, and you love it. How much more can he possibly want?"

After a few seconds of silence, both spoke in unison. "FBI career!"

He added, "Yeah, I guess we both disappointed Dad with that one." She heard a rueful chuckle from Alex. "It looks like I've got a meeting, so call if you need anything else. And next time, don't wait till it's about a case."

"Love you too, brother."

Disconnecting, she took a grateful sip of her coffee. She and Dylan had only gotten a few hours' sleep before coming into work. She imagined he felt very much like she did as the adrenaline wore off and caffeine was the only thing propping her up. She started to pick up her phone but glanced at the clock and decided to wait until their meeting. It hadn't been a full month since the last LEL meeting, but they'd all agreed, in light of the incident at the Seaside Harbor, a face-to-face sharing of information would be prudent. The meeting would be held in Baytown to make it easier for someone from the Virginia Marine Police to join them.

Bobby walked to her door and knocked. "Got a minute, Chief?"

She looked up and nodded toward the chair in front of her desk.

"Would you have an objection if I asked for two days off in a couple of weeks?"

Cocking her head to the side, she replied, "Of course not. It's helpful for scheduling if you can let me know as soon as possible which days you want, but you're due." She observed him nod, a small smile crossing his face.

"I've been spending a little time on my days off at the Seaside harbor," he said, immediately drawing her attention, having seen him on the security feed. "I know that some of the fishermen have trouble keeping steady crews and a few of the farm workers have indicated that they'd be interested in learning how to commercially fish but had no idea how to approach the boat owners."

"So, you've been scoping things out for them," she said, meeting his smile with one of her own.

"I have several of them that are interested, and I told them that I'd spend a day or so on the pier to make sure they were matched up." He hefted his shoulders in a shrug. "I just want to help them out during the down season for working the farms."

"I think that's great, Bobby. Thank you for letting me know. Get the dates to me and I'll make sure to schedule you for annual leave."

She watched as he disappeared down the hall and some of the tension left her neck. Her phone vibrated, and she glanced down, smiling as she viewed the text.

Pick you up in five.

Within a few minutes into the drive to Baytown, she was stifling a yawn while sitting in Dylan's SUV. He looked over and laughed, and she poked him in the shoulder. "Shut up. You're no more awake than I am."

"I'll have you know I had four cups of coffee so far today," he quipped.

Her eyes snapped open as her jaw dropped. "If I'd had that much coffee, I'd be bouncing off the walls."

He reached across the seat and placed his hand on her leg, giving a little squeeze. "By the way, I had a chance to talk to Todd today."

"Really? What did he say?"

"The day we saw him at the pier was a teacher's workday so the students had it off. He got to the pier early and decided to see if any of the fishing boats with early runs needed help unloading their catch."

Lifting her eyebrow in surprise, she said, "Wow, that was industrious of him… do you believe him?"

"Well, let's just say that he gave me the names of some of the fishermen he talked to. He admitted he preferred working the afternoon there instead of at his dad's store. After he finished, he went back to Owen's to sit and do a little studying for upcoming exams."

"Believe it or not, I had a chance to talk to Bobby. He was out there because he's helping some of the migrant farmers who'd like to stay in the area find employment during the winter months."

"Looks like Bobby and Todd are in the clear. Wonder about Luke."

She wondered the same thing but remained silent.

"So, did you learn anything from your brother?"

"Probably nothing that you didn't already get from the files, but he did say that John had been picked up last time in a sweep, so it wasn't a big undercover bust. There were no detectives that had any notes on him. He did mention the Mara Salvatrucha gang."

"Yeah, I had a look at his tattoos, and it's obvious he's involved with them."

"Did Lynette get back this morning?"

Nodding, he turned onto the road heading toward Baytown. "I should have the analysis report this afternoon, at least the initial one. But she did say the tech went ahead and tested. It was heroin."

"That ought to make a difference with what happens to him here."

"With his priors and the amount that he was carrying, yeah." Turning toward her, he grinned again. "I don't even remember if I said this last night, but thanks for being there. If you hadn't have come along with me, I doubt we would have caught him and certainly wouldn't have had the evidence."

"Hey, it worked out perfectly. Anyway, I wasn't going to let you leave our bed by yourself in the middle of the night. Not when I could go with you."

Pulling into the Baytown Municipal Building's parking lot, he nodded toward one of the trucks. "Looks like Callan is already here. Maybe we can finally start clamping down on what's going on."

They walked into the Baytown police station, greeted by the sight of two women standing in the reception area, their appearance so much alike. Same body shape, same wire-frame glasses, both with tight grey curls. The major difference was one had blue-tinted grey hair and the other one was purple-tinted. Mildred Score and her sister Mable had grown up in Baytown and had their hands in almost everything.

"Mildred. Mable," Dylan greeted as Hannah nodded toward them.

The two women smiled with enthusiasm, Mildred pleased when Dylan asked about her husband. Mr. Score had been a coach at Baytown High School back when Dylan had attended and according to his wife remembered all the boys fondly.

Ushered to the workroom, they were greeted by the other law enforcement leaders as well as Callan Ward and Ryan Coates. An original Baytown boy, Callan had joined the Coast Guard and after several years away was stationed with the unit in Baytown. At the end of his tour, he took a position with the Virginia Marine Police and married another local girl, Sophie. Ryan was his superior, and as Hannah shook his hand she felt the power of his blue-eyed gaze. A little older with a touch of gray at his temples, he exuded raw masculinity and confidence. She dropped her gaze and spied his naked ring finger, wondering why a woman didn't have a claim on him and instinctively felt he'd known tragedy. *God, I am tired!* Giving a little shake of her head to dislodge the random thought, she turned to sit down.

Everyone was on a tight schedule, so Mitch quickly got down to business. The others had already been informed of the arrest the previous evening, and congratulations rang out at the recovery of the evidence.

"The sack contained heroin," Dylan began. "The first initial report showed that it was pure, not cut with anything. I'll find out more from the lab when they send their full report." Inclining his head toward Hannah sitting next to him, he continued. "Hannah was able to get the identification for the boat."

Callan and Ryan shared a look, capturing the attention of the others.

"The boat was reported stolen two days earlier," Ryan stated. "It belongs to a couple who had it parked outside their vacation home."

"The drug runners must have decided to ditch the boat quickly since someone saw them," Callan said. "In their hurry, they didn't do a very good job. It was scuttled on one of the barrier islands, visible to a fisherman out of Manteague. He saw it this morning and called us, thinking someone might be in trouble."

"Damn," Dylan said.

"Well, like I said, they didn't do a good job. I've got a crew that's looking, and we'll at least do fingerprinting to see if anything comes up."

"I'm sure you know John Ortega's prints are in the system. I talked to my brother, a detective in Hope City, this morning, and the only extra thing he was able to tell me was that the most John's ever spent in jail was six months. He's a flight risk, though, so after this meeting, Dylan and I'll go to talk to the magistrate. Hopefully, we can keep that from happening if he can talk to the judge."

"I took a look at his tattoos. It jives with what Hannah's brother said. It looks like he's part Mara Salvatrucha, which is disconcerting considering we already know that Liam's county has a few Crips and Bloods that are starting to come down," Dylan said.

"The last thing I want," Liam added, "is for DMI to get their hands on any of these drugs coming through. I hate for them to have a hold on the Maryland Eastern Shore, but I want them the fuck out of our counties in Virginia."

She knew DMI was a local gang, not violent at this time, but ripe for getting in with a larger, more organized gang.

As they left the building, Dylan pushed open the door and held it for Hannah, his hand reaching toward the small of her back before suddenly jerking away. She glanced to the side and watched as he mouthed 'sorry'. Her lips curving, she gave a small shake of her head.

Once they were inside his SUV, he said, "Damn, Hannah, that's hard. My hand was reaching out for you without me thinking about it. I never want to do anything to embarrass you when we're in uniform."

Now that they were in the privacy of his vehicle, she slid her hand over the console and linked fingers with him. "It's fine, Dylan. We're still figuring this out."

"It's important for you to know that I respect you. Your uniform. Your position."

She squeezed his fingers in acknowledgment. "I know you do. Just as I respect yours." Grinning, she added, "But, of course, when I'm out of uniform…"

"Damn, woman, don't remind me. Then all I want to do is jump you!"

Laughing, they drove back to Easton. Once there, he said, "I'm going to go in and see what Marcus needs. I've already put together a report about his priors."

"That'll be perfect. We can be certain that if he gets out on bail, he'll never show up here for a trial."

25

Hannah and Dylan walked past the courthouse and entered the jail. Making their way through the security checkpoints, they headed straight to the magistrate's office.

Marcus looked up and smiled. "Well, Chief Freeman and Chief Hunt. Two chiefs together at the same time." He looked back down at the file on his desk and chuckled. "But then, it seems like you two had an exciting night."

She laughed and shook her head. "You can say that again." Handing him the information she'd received from Alex, she knew Dylan and the magistrate had several things to discuss. "I'm going to stop by the clinic. I received a message about one of my prisoners being treated for a medical condition. He's an older resident in my town, and Margaret made it sound like he wasn't doing well."

Receiving a chin lift from Dylan, she said her goodbyes to Marcus and walked down the hall. It was a short distance to the clinic, and as she entered, she nodded to the guard just inside and greeted Margaret.

Thomas, the older prisoner sitting on the examining table, was only in his sixties but looked twenty years older. Hard living, hard drinking, and hard smoking had left him with clogged arteries, battered lungs, and ulcers. He lived on the edge of town in a small shack. His wife had died young, and with no children, he worked odd jobs for years to make enough money to live on. Recently, he'd started stealing. She had a feeling he wanted to get caught, deciding that jail with a clean bed, medical care, and three-square meals a day would be better than the way he'd been living. He smiled as their eyes met, always appearing glad to see her.

"Chief Freeman," he rasped. "Am I just lucky today or what?"

"I actually came in to check on you." She smiled as his eyes widened at her statement. "How are you doing?"

"I was feeling mighty poorly earlier, and Miss Margaret said she might have to send me to the hospital. I just don't want all those doctors poking all over me."

She looked toward Margaret, who gave a little shake of her head despite her smile. Turning back to Thomas, she smiled brightly. "Well, I think a trip to the hospital might be just the thing for you."

Noise in the hall caused them to turn their gaze toward the door. Gary showed up with John in tow, a trail of blood running down John's arm. Hannah stepped to the side and said, "Looks like things are about to get busy here so I'll step out—"

"Can you hang on for a moment?" Margaret asked. Turning to Gary, Margaret called out, "Officer Perkins, EMTs are right behind you to take Thomas to the hospital. You and your prisoner are going to need to wait in the hall until I can take care of him."

Luke walked into the clinic, his gaze sweeping around the room before landing on the older man. "Thomas, let me help you." He assisted Thomas from the bed, holding him firmly.

Margaret turned back to Hannah, her face tight as she whispered, "Thomas is in a bad way. I know you've been involved with him for the past few years and wanted you to know."

She reached out and squeezed Margaret's arm. "Thank you so much for telling me. I'll be sure to visit him in the hospital."

Nodding, Margaret turned to follow Luke and Thomas into the hall. "Officer Perkins, I'll be back as soon as I can."

Gary's gaze shifted over Hannah as he leaned against the doorframe, and his smile slithered over his face. "Why, I'll have no problem killing a little bit of time with the pretty Chief."

Shooting him a glare, she moved to the side, allowing Margaret to follow Thomas and Luke out of the room. Gary was standing in the doorway, creating a log-jam of people.

She was trapped in the room with the EMTs settling Thomas onto the gurney just outside the doorway.

Margaret was clucking over him, and her heart squeezed at the thought that Thomas was dying. He looked up at Margaret and said, "Don't be upset. I've got a feeling I'm gonna be seeing my precious wife soon. Been a long life... wasted a lot of years." His voice became low as his body was racked with coughing, and Hannah turned away slightly, her heart hurting as she witnessed the true affection between the old man and the jail nurse that had cared for him off and on over the years.

"Damn fool decided to start his first day here by mouthing off to someone," Gary said, interrupting her thoughts. Noting Gary's attention was on her instead of the prisoner, she glanced toward Luke as he stepped past the guard, walking back into the clinic.

Luke's gaze fell onto John's still-bleeding injury and he said, "Wait here. Margaret will be right back." He walked to the cabinets on the other side of the room and pulled out the suture prep kit from one of the upper locked cabinets. Opening the kit, he laid the items out on the counter that Margaret would need... forceps, scalpel blades, needle holder, and scissors.

"I heard a rumor, Chief Freeman," Gary said, his eyes on her instead of toward John, stepping into the room instead of waiting. "I heard it was you and Chief Hunt caught this one in the middle of the night."

Looking toward John, she noted his dark eyes pinned on her. Just like last night, his expression was blank. Refusing to discuss police matters with the guard, she opened her mouth to snap at him when their attention darted back to the door as Margaret called goodbye to Thomas and the sound of the EMT gurney rolling down the hall met their ears.

In a flash, John rushed past Gary, snatching one of the small scalpels from the table. With a quick slash, he caught Gary on the neck, blood immediately splattering out as Gary went down on his knees. Gary squeaked in surprise before crying out in pain, his hand clapping over his bleeding injury.

Luke whirled around, his arms jerking out to grab John, but he wasn't quick enough. John, still standing behind Gary, grabbed the officer by the back of the shirt and pressed the scalpel against his neck. "All it takes, man, is for me to stick this right here, and he's dead."

Hands up and her palms forward, Hannah moved to get John's attention. "This isn't the way you want this to go, John." Her heart was pounding, but she kept her voice steady.

His lips curved ever so slightly on the corners before falling into a sneer. "Jail isn't holding me."

"Right now, all you've got is possession with intent to sell. You're already racking up other charges the longer we stand here. Let Officer Perkins go and—"

"Shut up, bitch. If it wasn't for you, I wouldn't be here."

Luke remained quiet, his hands up as well, and he didn't move a muscle. She had no idea if he was terrified or simply in complete control. Margaret appeared at the door, crying out as soon as her sharp gaze viewed the scene. Jumping back into the hall, she hit the alarm.

Looking down at Gary, whose eyes were wide as he

clutched his bloody neck, she said, "John, assault is bad enough. Murder means you'll never get out."

His lips curved again as he said, "Oh, I'll get out. And if you step a little closer, this guy is gonna bleed out on the floor right in front of you."

"Ma'am," said Luke.

She wanted to keep her eyes on John, but Luke drew her attention. His face was almost as unreadable as John's, but he offered a minuscule shake of his head.

"Please, please, help me," Gary cried, his voice weak as his hands dropped in front of him.

"If I come over closer, will you let the officer go and allow the medic to get him to safety?" she asked.

"Hell, I've been here a few hours, and I can already tell you this guy's a sniveling shit," John said, inclining his head toward Gary. Shrugging, with the knife still pressed to Gary's neck, he said, "All I need is one hostage. And a pretty little police chief is probably the best thing I could hope for."

Stepping slowly around Gary, she closed the distance between her and John, and he shoved Gary toward Luke. The blade shifted almost instantaneously between Gary and her. Placing his hand on her shoulder, he pushed, ordering, "Sit."

A chair on rollers was nearby, and she sat down. Luke was already bending to grab Gary when John said, "Not yet. Take that gauze and tie the lady up." Luke hesitated, and John added, "Don't fuck with me, man. I've got nothing to lose."

Luke reached out and snatched the roll of gauze off the counter. Unwinding several feet of the white cotton gauze, he stepped over Gary's legs and moved to Hannah. Bending, he wrapped the makeshift rope around one wrist before bringing her other wrist close and began wrapping it as well. He continued tying her wrists together in front of her instead of pulling her arms to the back. Knowing this would make her hands more useful, she was sure John was going to stop him, but he said nothing.

"No fuckin' tricks. Tie her tight."

"I know what I'm doing," Luke growled. "I was in the fuckin' Navy. I know how to tie knots. I'm good at this... I know all kinds of *knots*."

She had no idea why Luke emphasized the word 'knots', but he gave a little tug on her wrists as he stood, then dug his fingers in slightly on her shoulder. Glancing around and up, his face was still blank, but his eyes were sending an obvious message. Praying she was interpreting it right, she hoped that the knots he tied would be something she could escape from.

"Get out," John said, keeping away from Luke but holding the scalpel at Hannah's face.

Bending, Luke grabbed Gary under his armpits and began to drag him toward the door.

"No! Leave the fucker. I don't care if he bleeds out."

Standing, Luke turned and looked at her before shifting his gaze to John. "You can hold me instead of her. We'll walk out of here together."

Snorting, John shook his head. "How stupid do you think I am? The size you are? Fuck no." Grinning, he added, "I've got just the hostage I need. Shut the fuckin' door on your way out."

"This isn't smart. You know that," Luke added, but his eyes jumped back to Hannah as the blade moved closer to her face. With a grimace, Luke backed out of the doorway, pulling the door closed behind him.

The finality of the click of the door joined with the sounds of a multitude of heavy footsteps barely heard over the beating of her heart, and she had no doubt what was happening outside the clinic. The jail would have gone into lockdown, all prisoners back into their cells. Guards with weapons would have been called to strategic points. Colt's North Heron SWAT team would be in place. In fact, the State Police would be showing up as well. And on the other side of the door, just down the hall, was Dylan.

Looking at John, the bloody weapon still in his hand, and Gary's prone body on the floor, she sucked in a quick breath. There was one way this situation might end... in death. Whether or not it would be hers, she had no idea.

2 6

The instant the alarm sounded in the magistrate's office, Dylan took to his feet, his first thought was to get to Hannah. He was not concerned about the jail. It was well-guarded, well-tended, and well-managed. Assuming a fight had possibly broken out in a common area, he knew the guards would soon squelch the problem. But the desire to see Hannah overrode everything else.

"Dammit," Marcus cursed under his breath, looking at his computer screen before standing quickly.

"What is it?"

"We have a system of alarms for various situations. That first sound was a general alarm, letting the guards know that there was a lockdown situation. The message that just came across my computer and phone is letting me know a hostage has been taken."

Hoping that Hannah was safe in the clinic, hearing the word 'hostage' still sliced through him. "I'm going to head down to the clinic and make sure to meet up with Hannah."

Marcus held his gaze and said, "I don't think that's gonna work, Dylan. The area of concern *is* the clinic."

Dylan rushed into the hall, his gaze noting guards with weapons moving silently, taking up strategic positions. A few minutes later, Colt and Under Sheriff Frazier were stalking toward him, Margaret at their side talking rapidly.

"After I handed the paperwork to the EMTs for Thomas, I turned to go back into the clinic. The prisoner that came in with Gary was behind him and must have slashed him in the neck considering the amount of blood that was coming out. Luke was slightly to the side and Hannah was in there as well."

Hearing that Hannah was inside the clinic with an armed prisoner felt like a gunshot to the gut. Colt's gaze moved from Margaret over to Dylan then back again.

"Could you tell what kind of weapon he had?" Colt asked, looking over Frazier's shoulder at the tablet in his hand.

Margaret continued, "No, I couldn't see anything. I know he came in with an injury to his hand, and perhaps Luke was getting ready for sutures—"

"Those materials shouldn't be within reach of a prisoner!" the Under Sheriff proclaimed as he pulled up the security live stream from the clinic camera.

"I told Gary to wait outside until I could get back to the clinic. He wasn't supposed to have brought the prisoner in!"

"What happens next?" Dylan cut in, his words directed to Colt.

Colt held Dylan's gaze and replied "We wait. We gotta do this right and we gotta do this smart." He clamped his hand on Dylan's shoulder and squeezed. "We're gonna get her out of there."

Colt and Frazier looked back at the tablet. Dylan was torn between wanting to look to see that Hannah was safe and terrified of what he'd see.

Another man approached, a military cadence in his stride, and Dylan noted the silver hair cut high and tight, ramrod-straight back, and sharp eyes. Colt caught Dylan's eyes and added, "This is what happens next."

Wondering who the newcomer was, Colt stepped forward and greeted him. "Martin, have you been briefed?"

With a curt nod, the man acknowledged and said, "I got the preliminary as I drove over. A prisoner in the clinic has injured a guard and taken hostages. I understand one of them is a local police chief."

Colt turned to the others. "This is Martin Toombs. He worked for the FBI as a hostage negotiator and retired to the Eastern Shore. Both North Heron and Acawmacke counties keep him on retainer. I called him immediately, and he happened to be near here."

"Who else do we have?" Martin asked, his words clipped.

Frazier said, "The prisoner is John Ortega—"

"Fuckin' hell," Dylan cursed, his knees nearly buckling at that news. "Christ, he just got here less than twenty-four hours ago. What the fuck happened?"

Martin's eyes jerked toward him, and he cocked his head slightly. "You have information?"

"Chief Hunt of Seaside." He identified himself, hearing the shakiness of his voice but unable to steady it. "My office arrested him in the middle of the night for transporting drugs from the Seaside Harbor. He was caught in the act."

Frazier added, "One of my guards reported seeing John and another man talking in the yard, and the next thing the guards knew, John was bleeding on the arm."

Before they had a chance to speak more, movement at the clinic door caught everyone's attention. Noting the activity on the security camera, they left Margaret behind and moved closer. Luke was bent, backing out of the clinic door as though dragging something heavy. Then, suddenly, he stopped and stood, speaking to those inside the clinic. Dylan watched as the medic's face hardened before he leaned forward and closed the door. Watching the security video at the same time, they could see it was the guard's body that Luke had been attempting to drag.

Luke turned and approached the huddle in charge. "He won't let me get Gary out of there."

"What the hell happened?" Frazier asked.

Luke grimaced. "Goddamn Gary Perkins is what happened. He was supposed to wait in the hall, monitoring the prisoner. I was getting the suture kit ready for Margaret when she got back in. Gary was also supposed to keep his fuckin' eyes on the prisoner, away from everyone, but he was too busy blocking Chief Freeman's exit and trying to get her attention." Wiping the sweat off his brow, Luke continued, "He... the prisoner must've had this planned, although he couldn't have known exactly how it was going to go down. Gary played right into his hand."

"What does he want?" Frazier asked.

"All he said was he wanted out, and Hannah was going to be his way to make that happen."

Dylan's blood ran cold as he turned to Martin. "Tell them that I'll go in as his hostage. Switch me out with Hannah."

Martin's narrow-eyed gaze bored straight through Dylan, but he ignored it, not caring what the other man thought about him.

"Is there something I should know?" Martin asked. "Something I'm missing?"

Dylan turned toward the older man and held his gaze. "Chief Freeman—Hannah—is my girlfriend."

Before Martin had a chance to respond, Luke turned to Dylan and shook his head. "I tried that. I don't think he'll go for it." The men stared at Luke as he shrugged. "I'm sorry, Chief Hunt... John figures he's got a small female in there that he can control. He's not going to trade her for one of us." Luke nodded toward the screen in Frazier's hand and added, "He's made one mistake. He had me tie Hannah's wrists together, but they're tied in front, not in back. Also, I was in the Navy... the knot I tied her with looks difficult, but she'll be able to get out of it. I wasn't able to tell her that, but I tried to get her to understand what I'd done."

"The biggest mistake he's made is underestimating Hannah," Colt said, his words clipped.

As Dylan struggled to think of Hannah trapped with John, he barely heard Colt's words.

"Okay, let's get this started," Martin said, reaching out and taking the phone that was provided, making sure he was on speaker. Dylan blinked, refocused, and listened as the phone rang three times before it was picked up.

"Hello? This is Chief Hannah Freeman."

At the sound of her voice, Dylan fought to keep his knees from buckling. He closed his eyes for a few seconds, wanting to remember every word she'd ever said to him.

"Chief Freeman, this is Martin Toombs. I'm a hostage negotiator."

"Call me Hannah, please."

"Okay, Hannah. Can you tell me if we are on speaker?"

Dylan's eyes flew open as he looked at Martin. The man who'd appeared so businesslike and gruff was speaking in a tone that was soft and comforting. The kind of voice he imagined a benevolent grandfather would use. His breath drew into his lungs a little easier with the feeling that Martin's professionalism would help.

"Yes, John can hear you as well," Hannah said.

"Okay, that's good, Hannah. Does he want to talk now, or does John want you to keep talking to me?"

That question brought about muffled words in the background and with an eye on the tablet screen, Dylan watched as Hannah twisted around to speak to John.

Turning back, she said. "Right now, he just wants me to talk to you."

"No problem. You and I can talk, and I know John can hear me. Is there anyone else in the clinic with you, Hannah?"

"It's just me and John and Officer Perkins... he's injured... he and John."

"How badly, Hannah?"

Martin constantly used Hannah's name in a calm voice, and Dylan recognized the negotiator's attempt to humanize the situation, wanting John to see his prisoner as a real person.

"John has a cut on his arm. It doesn't look bad, but I'm sure he needs stitches. Gary has a cut on his neck and is bleeding quite a bit."

"John? With you being injured, I'd like to get help in there for you. We could have the medic come back in and take care of your injury and see to Gary."

Muffled voices were heard again. "He says he doesn't want anyone else to come in."

"Okay. John, we need to talk about how this is going to go down. Things have gotten out of control, and we need to come to a resolution."

"The only resolution I want is to get out of here. I want a car and safe passage out of this fuckin' jail," John bit out.

"I hear what you're saying John, but you know that's not going to happen."

"It is if I got this policewoman with me. She'll be with me to ensure I get out of here."

"John, again, that's not going to happen, so let's figure out a different way to get some help for you."

Dylan glared at Martin, furious that he was backing John into a corner. Opening his mouth to protest, he clamped it shut when a large hand landed on his shoulder. Looking around at Colt shaking his head, he transferred his glare to his friend.

Colt leaned in and whispered, "Let him do his job. He's a master negotiator and knows what he's doing. It's important that John trust him, and you can't earn trust by obvious lying. Martin isn't going to promise things that John knows can't happen."

Determined to stay close, Dylan kept his eye on the screen, not willing to lose one second of seeing and hearing Hannah. He tried to lock his knees to keep his legs from shaking, but the quivers inside his body would not be stilled.

"Okay, John, let's talk about Gary. We want to mitigate the circumstances as much as possible, but that's going to be very difficult if a guard bleeds to death right in front of you and you haven't shown any mercy."

"You think I give a fuck about him? I was hoping just to be able to get in here with the female nurse. This guy made it easy."

"Yes, I can see that. But right now, Gary's not in charge of you, and you've got nothing to fear from him unless you let him die on the floor. If you do that, you've lost all bargaining chips."

John began to pace, his agitation rising. Hannah, still seated with her hands tied in front of her, twisted her chair around and looked upward. "John," she began softly, "you'll still have me. Let's get Gary out of here, and you still have some bargaining power. That will make it so much better for you."

"I'm not letting anyone come in here to get him!"

"I'm sure Mr. Toombs will help us figure this out." Hannah turned back to the phone. "Mr. Toombs? Were you able to hear that?"

"Please, call me Martin, and yes, I could hear that. Let's come up with a plan, John. We can have someone stay out in the hall, and Hannah can push him through the door just enough so that someone can get their hands on them. That would be a perfect way to get Gary the help he needs and lets us get a little closer to resolving the issue."

Resolving the issue? Hearing Martin so calmly refer to Hannah being held against her will sent shakes throughout Dylan's body. His mind told him it was going the way it needed to, but his heart was beating out of his chest. It took all of his willpower to keep from rushing into the room, even without a weapon, and tearing John apart. One way or the other, if anyone was going to get close to Hannah, it was going to be him.

27

Hannah stared at John, her gaze assessing. She remembered from his driver's license that he was twenty-three years old and yet had to admit he looked older. A dark scruff already covered his hard jaw. He was athletic, and while not overly large, she could see that he worked out. His face was interesting, with a slightly off-center nose, probably from previous breaks, and a scar that cut through his left eyebrow.

His short-sleeved shirt gave evidence to the mish-mash of tattoos covering his arms and hands. They appeared to be signs and symbols with no apparent connection of the markings and probably done at different times.

She thought back to the little bit of information she'd gathered from Alex and had no problem imagining that John was either born into the gang lifestyle or his early years had made the gang seem like family. And since he was high enough in the organization to be a transporter, she knew he was clean, and that meant he was smart. Smart enough to know what he needed to do to get what he wanted.

Turning her assessment inward, the initial adrenaline of her situation was wearing off, and she expected a shaky weakness to follow soon. Calling upon all her training and reserves, she remained calm and focused on steadying her breathing as well as her heartbeat.

"You don't use." The words slipped from her lips easily, and as soon as they were out, she wondered what his response would be.

He stopped pacing, his gaze now boring straight into her. "No. Users are weak." Snorting, he shook his head. "What I do, I do for money. I do for respect. I do for my brothers."

She nodded slowly. "I get that." Seeing his sneer, she explained. "The brotherhood, I mean. We all want to belong somewhere."

"Is that why you put on a fuckin' ugly uniform every day? For the *brothers in blue?*"

Refusing to give in to his needling, she nodded. "Pretty much, yeah. Like I said, everyone wants to belong somewhere."

He held her gaze for a long time and then turned to stare off into space. "I'm trusted. Out there. Last night was a fuck up that should never have happened." He glanced back down at her and shook his head slowly, his lips curving down. "Couldn't fuckin' believe it when you jumped into the water. The pack was weighted. Never thought you had a chance gettin' to it."

He was no longer showing heightened anxiety, and

uncertain if she should try to keep him talking or leave all the negotiations to Martin, she watched as John leaned against the counter.

Deciding to keep him talking, she said, "John, when we leave here, you can't take Gary with us. So if he's going to be left here anyway, then it would make sense for us to go ahead and let him get help."

He stopped pacing and looked at her, indecision working behind his eyes as sweat dotted his brow.

She looked down at the unconscious guard, a pool of blood covering the floor. Pressing forward, she continued. "I'm tied up, and you can be right with me. We could just open the door, and I can kneel on the floor near Gary and push him out just enough so that someone else can get in."

"It sounds like Hannah has a good plan," Martin interjected. "John, do you think we can do that?"

"I don't want any funny shit happening," John bit out.

Hannah nodded her agreement. *He's giving in a little bit.* "I just want to get Gary out of here." John didn't disagree, and not wanting to lose momentum, she pushed. "Martin? I think John agrees. Can you let us know how this will happen?"

She could hear the phone connection clicking and knew they'd taken her off speaker while they were deciding what they wanted to do.

"John, I think you and Hannah already have an excellent plan," Martin said, coming back on.

Hannah had to admit she was impressed with Martin's negotiating skills. His voice was calm, he

307

continually called them by name, and now made it sound like the idea to get Gary to safety was part of John's idea. Not wanting to seem overeager, she settled her expression as she waited to see what Martin would say and how John would react.

"Hannah is too small to be able to push Gary all the way into the hall—"

"I'm not letting her go out!" John shouted.

"I understand, John," Martin said. "But she can open the door and push Gary enough that someone nearby will be able to grab his shoulders and pull him the rest of the way out."

After a moment of quiet thinking, he declared, "I'll be right next to her. My blade will be right next to her neck. I didn't strike that shithead guard to kill him, but I'm good with a blade. And if anything happens that I don't like, she's dead."

"We understand. You're going to stay close to Hannah. Now, John, I want you to stay calm. Several things are going to be happening all at once and we want you calm because we don't want anything untoward to happen to anybody, and that includes you. We want everyone coming out of this alive and well."

As she eased off her chair and knelt onto the floor, she glanced at the gauze wrappings around her wrist and the knot Luke had tied. Shifting on her knees toward the unconscious Gary, she said, "John, I want to check on him." She reached out and placed her fingertips on his pulse, glad that it was steady, albeit weak. "Okay, I'm going to maneuver him close to the door. Then I'll reach up to the knob and open it. I'll push

Gary along on the floor, sliding until enough of him is in the hall that someone can pull him the rest of the way out."

She never looked toward the camera in the corner of the ceiling, knowing they were being watched, but instead, spoke loudly. "Martin? I'm on the floor near Gary. He's still bleeding some but not as much. His eyes are closed, but he has a pulse."

"That's good, Hannah. When you open the door, start pushing him out, and I'll have one person nearby to grab him."

"Only one!" John ordered.

"Agreed," Martin said. "Only one."

Now that John was once again nearby with the blade close to her throat, Hannah swallowed deeply, focusing on the task at hand and the task that needed to be accomplished. John wasn't going to offer any assistance with his entire focus on the blade at her neck, so she heaved Gary's heavy body close to the door, leaving a red trail along the tiled floor. It was difficult with her hands bound together and her knees sliding in Gary's blood. When she finally managed to push the top of his head to the door, she stopped. She wiped her bloody hands on her pants in a misguided effort to get them clean and glanced up toward John.

He appeared twitchy again, but she carefully studied his position, wanting to know exactly where he was each second. Lifting her bound hands up, she turned the doorknob, feeling sweat trickle from underneath her arm and run down her side.

"Slowly. Do it slowly."

Obeying the order that came directly from the side of her, she inched the door open. Still on her hands and knees, she peered through the opening, uncertain what she would see. The hard tile floor gave little comfort but made it easier to slide the heavy burden of the unconscious body toward the doorway.

"Stop right there."

Continuing to obey the order from behind, feeling the blade still against her neck, she managed to maneuver Gary's head out slightly. There was no movement in the hallway. It was as though the world had gone completely still, her heartbeat the only sound and her chest heaving the only movement. She looked down at Gary's face, his eyes blinking open in confusion, reminding her that time was of the essence. "I've got to move him out enough so they can get to him." Not waiting on a reply, she moved to Gary's shoulders and continued to push his prone body forward several more inches until the head was now in the hall.

With the knife now held against her lower back near her kidneys, she was still in danger. Keeping her hands out of John's sight, she twisted her wrists and grabbed the end of the gauze knot, giving it a tug. The knot gave way, and still pushing Gary's body on the floor, she wiggled her wrists enough to keep the gauze in sight while allowing her hands to have free movement.

The door opened further, and from the other side, hands moved forward, hooking under Gary's armpits. His body slid further into the hall. Still on her hands and knees, Hannah lifted her gaze as a face appeared. Eyes bored into hers, so familiar. Lips that had so often been slightly turned upward in a smirk now pinched tight with anger. She wanted to lift her hand to cup his cheek in case she never got the opportunity to do so again. But the shifting stance of the man behind her stilled her hand. Instead, she hoped her eyes conveyed the depth of her love.

Another pair of hands appeared from the other side, and Gary was now completely dragged into the hallway. Hannah swallowed deeply, both in relief and in fear. She refused to look away from Dylan, not knowing if she would ever see his face again. Forcing her gaze to drop to her hands, she could tell when he realized they were no longer bound tightly.

As he held her eyes again, she stared as his mouth opened slightly and he mouthed, "You and me." Knowing they had to work together, her lips curved ever so slightly.

With her hands still pressed together as though her wrists were bound, she scooted backward on her hands and knees.

"Close the door," John ordered, moving away from her slightly as he stepped back into the room.

Shifting to a squat, she reached upward with both hands as though to reach for the doorknob, then whirled, her arms separating as the knot fell loose. She slammed her forearm against his. Unheeding the pain that radiated up her arm, she flipped to her back, sliding in the blood, and kicked out, catching him in the groin. He howled and dropped to his knees onto the floor next to her. She punched out again, knocking him backward.

Dylan launched into the room, flying over her body,

tackling John. The men wrestled, but Dylan quickly landed on top as Hannah scrambled to her knees and yelled, "Clear!"

Suddenly the room was filled with guards, their weapons pointing at the men on the bloody floor. Hannah reached down to grab Dylan just as two of the guards rolled John over and cuffed him. Dylan stood, and ignoring the fact they were both in uniform, she rushed into his arms. He grabbed her shoulders and pushed her back slightly, his gaze scanning up and down.

"I'm okay. It's not my blood."

John was hauled upright, surrounded by guards. Colt walked in with the man whose voice she recognized as he greeted her.

"Martin?"

The barrel-chested man with the military haircut that screamed FBI smiled. "It's good to meet you, Hannah. You did very well. You're a credit to the uniform, Chief Freeman."

"It's nice to meet you, too. I know you know what you're doing, sir, but I have to say that your voice calmed him down." Chuckling, she added, "It also calmed me down."

Colt looked at her and said, "Jesus, Hannah, you look like you've been in a slaughterhouse."

She glanced down, seeing blood smeared all over her shirt, pants, hands, and arms. "It's all Gary's blood. I don't know how badly he was hurt, but he bled a lot."

"They're taking him to the hospital. EMTs have

already reported that he is awake and responding, so he should be okay."

Frazier moved into the room and greeted her. "I'm going to need a full report from you, Chief Freeman. There will be an inquiry, and I need to know exactly what happened."

Nodding she said, "I understand. I'm perfectly prepared to give it now, but I feel as though I need to clean up first. I only live ten minutes away. If you give me about forty-five minutes, I can be back here, and we can do the report then."

"Are you sure? It can wait till tomorrow."

"I'd rather do it today."

He turned to Dylan and added, "Chief Hunt. Since you were in the room, I'll need a report from you as well. Luke and Margaret are preparing theirs now."

Dylan clung to her, and she had no complaints. Intense situations heighten awareness, and she wanted to be with him as much as he did her. They drove together to her bungalow, quickly showered together, and changed into clean clothes. True to her word, they were back at the jail within forty-five minutes. They separated, each going to a different room as they wrote their statements.

Dylan's was short, but it took Hannah longer. She knew her words would be corroborated with the phone log and security camera but wanted to make sure she was accurate. One of the questions asked about the mental state of the prisoner. She hesitated, thinking back to her conversation with John, and could not help but think of the future he now had. Sucking in a deep breath through her nose, she let it out slowly, then finished the report.

Exiting the room, she scanned the hall for Dylan, finding him near the doors, deep in conversation with Luke. As she approached, both men swung their gazes toward her. Uncertain if she was interrupting, she walked straight to Dylan, easily accepting his arm around her shoulder. Looking up, she offered a smile.

"I was asking Luke about the Seaside Harbor pier… seeing him on the video," Dylan said.

Luke nodded. "Owen advertised for a night watchman, and I was over there talking to him and checking out the area. I thought it might be a good part-time job for me." He shrugged, adding, "At least until my job here can become a full-time position."

"Thank you for your help in there," she said, reaching her hand out to his arm.

"Just glad you understood about the knots."

Grinning, she said, "Me too!"

As she and Dylan walked out of the jail and settled into his SUV, they sat silent, neither moving. He kept his eyes straight ahead and said, "I was scared. Never been that scared."

Another moment of silence passed before she spoke. "As soon as I saw you in the hall, I knew we'd be fine. You'd shield me, and I'd shield you."

He let out a rueful chuckle as he turned toward her, his eyes boring straight into hers. "You and me, right? Shielding each other?"

Her lips curved. "Yeah… you and me."

He finally started the vehicle and backed out of the

parking spot. Her phone was blowing up with messages from their friends. She sent out a mass text that simply said she was fine, then turned her phone off. Dylan felt the same, and they drove back to her bungalow in silence, their hands linked as well as their hearts.

Dylan found sleep did not come easily that night. He and Hannah ate little, talked even less, but made love with whispered words, caresses, kisses. And when he finally rocked her body with his, her legs wrapped around his back, their combined releases shook him to the core. Hannah assured him that she was fine, but he feared that she would be plagued with nightmares.

Snuggled under the covers, arms around each other and legs tangled, she cupped his jaw. "All I need is you, Dylan. As long as I have you, I'm shielded from nightmares."

She fell asleep in his arms, but he lay awake for hours, thinking of how much he wanted her in his life forever… and how quickly life could change. As the moonlight sifted through the blinds casting a light glow over them, he finally fell asleep.

It seemed as though he had just shut his eyes when a banging on the front door roused them awake. Sitting up at the same time, they blinked their bleary eyes. She grumbled, pushing her hair out of her face. He glanced at the clock by her bed and saw that it was after 8 o'clock. The banging continued, so he shoved the covers back and pulled on a pair of sweatpants as she jerked a long sleep shirt over her head. Still belting her robe, she followed after him as they headed to the front door.

Not wanting her to answer the door without knowing who was there, he peeked out, jerked his head backward, then leaned forward and peaked out again. Feeling a poke in his side, he looked down as Hannah asked, "Who's there?"

"You're not gonna believe it, babe. But get ready." He threw open the door and they both peered onto Hannah's stoop. Standing in front of them were his parents and hers.

"Hannah! You were on the news, and I couldn't get hold of you on the phone! We called and called and called!" Her mother moved past everyone and threw her arms around Hannah, pulling her tight.

She looked over her mother's shoulder toward Dylan and asked, "On the news?"

Dylan's mother walked in next and hugged her son. "It was all over the Virginia Beach newspaper and news shows this morning. There was even a picture of the two of you coming out of the jail!"

Hannah's father moved in next, clapped Dylan on the back, and said, "It sounds like you two were heroes." Then he turned to Hannah and embraced her as well. "I'm proud of you." He swallowed deeply and added,

"But I'm glad I didn't know what was happening yesterday. I'm not sure I could've handled knowing my daughter was a hostage."

She wrapped her arms around her dad and whispered, "I'm fine. Honestly, Dad, I'm fine."

Dylan's father pushed his way into the crowded room, grinning at his son. "I tried to tell your mother that you were fine, especially since the picture on the news showed the two of you walking together. But you know your mother... she had to come to see for herself."

"You need to eat," his mother said, walking into Hannah's small kitchen.

"Mom, this is Hannah's house—" Dylan began.

"Yes, and Hannah needs to eat, too."

Hannah's mom nodded her agreement emphatically. "Stella, let's fix everyone some breakfast."

With the two mothers in the kitchen, breakfast was soon rustled up. Her bungalow could barely hold six adults all trying to eat at the same time, but everyone made themselves at home. Using the living room sofa and chairs plus the floor, plus the coffee table, they all managed to have breakfast at the same time.

Dylan looked over at Hannah sitting on the floor, her eyes bright as she laughed at something his dad said and noted the smile on her parents' faces. He suddenly imagined many times like this... holidays, celebrations, and even impromptu visits. For a brief moment, the wasted time from the past four years assaulted him, but then he sucked in a deep breath and let it out slowly, letting the regrets flow out as well. He caught his mom's eye and watched her eyes twinkle before turning back to laugh at his dad's story as well.

Settling in, he draped his arm over Hannah's shoulder. She turned and graced him with her smile, then fell back against him, tucked into his side. Just where he wanted her to be. And as soon as they were alone again, he planned on making it permanent.

Six Months Later

"Babe! You ready?"

At the sound of Dylan's voice, Hannah smiled as she walked into the kitchen, tucking the last bobby pin into her bun. "Thanks, sweetie."

Both dressed in their uniforms, she stood on her toes and gifted him with a quick kiss on her way to the coffee pot. Their morning routine included her starting the coffee, a shower together, then he made breakfast while she dried her hair.

As she reached for the egg and cheese bagel, her gaze shifted around the room, loving the combination of both of them. She had moved into his house, and her bungalow was now being rented by a teacher at the local high school.

Percy wound his way between their legs, meowing until Dylan placed food into the cat's dish. She smiled seeing the two of them together, Percy now seeking Dylan's lap as often as her own.

He checked his phone. "Got a message from Liam. Topic for our next LEL meeting… he's cracking down on the DMI drug running through his county, but they're still making inroads toward us. It's going to take a concerted effort for us all to keep our counties and towns safe."

She sighed then lifted on her toes to wrap her arms around his neck. "I know it's like Whack-a-Mole, but together, we can do it."

Several minutes later, they headed out to their vehicles. He always stood at her driver's door, kissing her goodbye before climbing into his own.

"Stay safe, babe," he said, sliding his nose past hers, whispering into her ear.

"You and me, sweetheart," she always replied, gaining his smile.

Twenty minutes later, she was walking from the parking lot toward the Easton Police Station when she looked up and spied Luke. He still remained somewhat of a loner and enigma but had settled into the job of jail medic and had started coming to the American Legion meetings. While she would not call them good friends, they had become good acquaintances. "Luke, hello," she called out.

His chin lift was barely perceptible, but his lips curved slightly. "Good morning, Chief Freeman." His gaze shifted from her face to over her shoulder just as she heard a female voice cry out.

"Hannah!"

At the sound of her name being called from behind, she turned to see her pretty renter jogging toward her, waving a check in her hand. The woman came to a stop, her chest heaving as she caught her breath. "I'm so sorry to catch you like this. I forgot to get my rent check to you yesterday, so I wanted to drop it off before I headed to work."

Taking the check, she laughed and said, "Allie, you didn't have to rush. I know you're good for it." The young woman's head turned, and a blush splashed across her cheeks. Hannah was unable to hide her grin as she watched Luke's attention focus solely on Allie.

"Allie, I'd like you to meet Luke, the medic at the jail. Luke, this is Allie. She rents my former house and works as a local teacher."

Luke reached out and shook Allie's hand, and Hannah was certain Allie's blush deepened. Saying her goodbyes, she turned and continued down the sidewalk, determined to not sneak a peek at the two behind her.

As she entered the station, she cast a glance over her shoulder, sad to see that the two were no longer on the sidewalk. *So much for my matchmaking skills. I guess I need to do more than just introduce people.* Turning, she greeted Pearl as she walked through reception. Entering her office, she glanced at the plaque now hanging on the wall. She had received the American Legion Law Enforcement Officer of the Year award from their local chapter. Knowing that Dylan had the same award hanging on the wall in his Chief's office made the honor even greater.

Settling into her chair, her phone vibrated, and she checked the incoming text.

Stay safe, kick ass, fight crime, babe.

Shooting a ***Ditto, sweetie*** text back, she reached for a file when Pearl called out, "Ten-ninety-three. Fire in Sampson's garage."

Hannah jumped to her feet and headed out.

"Chief Hunt!"

Walking along the piers of the Seaside Harbor, Dylan looked toward his brother's boat, seeing Todd throwing his hand up in a wave, smiling. Walking over, he greeted the young man. "How's it going?"

Todd ducked his head and said, "Good, Sir. Real good. I actually had some news I wanted to pass on."

Giving Todd his full attention, he watched as the young man took a deep breath and then let it out slowly.

"Your brother offered me a position on his boat when I graduate, but I had several options I wanted to look at first. I value your opinion, Sir."

Curious, Dylan remained quiet.

"I've been talking to the Navy recruiter. My dad's not real keen on me joining up. I think he figured he'd start charging me rent as soon as I graduated from high school. But I don't want to stay in Seaside and live at home, even with the job David's offering me. I looked at the other branches of service, but I think the Navy is the way I want to go. I know you were in the Navy, so I thought you'd be a good person to check with."

He clapped Todd on the shoulder, his fingers digging in slightly. "I don't blame you for wanting to get out of Seaside. God knows when I was your age, that's all I wanted. And I think that for you, it might be a really good chance for you to see other parts of the country and world."

"And the Navy?"

"I think you could be happy in any of the branches but growing up around the water as you have, some-times it just calls to you. If that's what you're feeling, I think the Navy would be proud to have you."

Todd pulled up to his full height, squared his shoul-ders, looked Dylan in the eyes, and smiled. "Thank you, Sir."

"And just let me add, I'm proud of you, too."

Todd's ears pinkened as he ducked his head, a grin playing about his lips. "That means a lot."

Clapping him on the back again, he watched him walk toward David's boat before he continued his patrol.

That evening, Dylan sat in his double weather-beaten Adirondack chair on his back deck. Hannah walked out, handed him a beer, then bent to touch her lips to his. He lifted his hand to her hip. She started to walk back to the house, but he reached out and snagged her hand.

Pulling her gently back to him, he set his beer down on the planks and patted his lap. "Sit with me, babe."

She set her beer down as well and eased into his lap, one arm wrapped around his neck and the other hand still nestled in his. The sun was setting, casting the sky in a myriad of colors. He reached into his shirt pocket and said, "I kept wondering if there was a right time. A perfect time. But every moment that I'm with you seems like the right time."

She lifted her head and stared at him, confusion creasing her brow. He slid his fingers out of his pocket and held up a perfect engagement ring. She gasped, but he wasn't finished. "I told you the morning that our parents landed on our doorstep that I wanted us to be together. I know that I can't promise that nothing will ever hurt you. But I want to give you this ring to let you know that I will always shield your heart with my love. So, Hannah, I'm asking you to marry me."

As he slid the ring on her finger, he kissed her soundly right in the middle of her acceptance. It was the sweetest kiss he'd ever known.

Don't miss the next Baytown Boys novel!
To Love Someone

Not everyone has a hero's welcome home.

Joseph landed in Baytown when he left the military and had nowhere else to go. Used to being a loner, he

discovered the small coastal town offered friendship...
but love? That wasn't even on his radar.

Until meeting her. The infuriatingly independent
veterinarian. Known to all as Sam, to him she would
always be Samantha.

When danger lurks for her, Joseph privately vows to
protect her. But who will protect his heart when all he
wants is to love someone?

ALSO BY MARYANN JORDAN

Don't miss other Maryann Jordan books!

Lots more Baytown stories to enjoy and more to come!

Baytown Boys (small town, military romantic suspense)

Coming Home

Just One More Chance

Clues of the Heart

Finding Peace

Picking Up the Pieces

Sunset Flames

Waiting for Sunrise

Hear My Heart

Guarding Your Heart

Sweet Rose

Our Time

Count On Me

Shielding You

To Love Someone

For all of Miss Ethel's boys:

Heroes at Heart (Military Romance)

Zander

Rafe

Cael

Jaxon

Jayden

Asher

Zeke

Cas

Lighthouse Security Investigations

Mace

Rank

Walker

Drew

Blake

Tate

Hope City (romantic suspense series co-developed

with Kris Michaels

Brock book 1

Sean book 2

Carter book 3

Brody book 4

Kyle book 5

Ryker book 6

Rory book 7

Killian book 8

Saints Protection & Investigations

(an elite group, assigned to the cases no one else wants…or
can solve)

Serial Love

Healing Love

Revealing Love

Seeing Love

Honor Love

Sacrifice Love

Protecting Love

Remember Love

Discover Love

Surviving Love

Celebrating Love

Follow the exciting spin-off series:

Alvarez Security (military romantic suspense)

Gabe

Tony

Vinny

Jobe

SEALs

Thin Ice (Sleeper SEAL)

SEAL Together (Silver SEAL)

Letters From Home (military romance)

Class of Love

Freedom of Love

Bond of Love

The Love's Series (detectives)

Love's Taming

Love's Tempting

Love's Trusting

The Fairfield Series (small town detectives)

Emma's Home

Laurie's Time

Carol's Image

Fireworks Over Fairfield

Please take the time to leave a review of this book. Feel free to contact me, especially if you enjoyed my book. I love to hear from readers!

Facebook

Email

Website

ABOUT THE AUTHOR

I am an avid reader of romance novels, often joking that I cut my teeth on the historical romances. I have been reading and reviewing for years. In 2013, I finally gave into the characters in my head, screaming for their story to be told. From these musings, my first novel, Emma's Home, The Fairfield Series was born.

I was a high school counselor having worked in education for thirty years. I live in Virginia, having also lived in four states and two foreign countries. I have been married to a wonderfully patient man for thirty-five years. When writing, my dog or one of my four cats can generally be found in the same room if not on my lap.

Please take the time to leave a review of this book. Feel free to contact me, especially if you enjoyed my book. I love to hear from readers!

Facebook
Email
Website

Made in United States
Troutdale, OR
09/05/2023

12653944R00205